CW00968307

Jean-Jacques Lecercle
DELEUZE AND LANGUAGE

Piers Gray, edited by Colin MacCabe and Victoria Rothschild
STALIN ON LINGUISTICS AND OTHER ESSAYS

Geoffrey Ward
STATUTES OF LIBERTY
The New York School of Poets

Moustapha Safouan
JACQUES LACAN AND THE QUESTION OF PSYCHOANALYTIC TRAINING
(*Translated and introduced by Jacqueline Rose*)

Stanley Shostak
THE DEATH OF LIFE
The Legacy of Molecular Biology

Elizabeth Cowie
REPRESENTING THE WOMAN
Cinema and Psychoanalysis

Raymond Tallis
NOT SAUSSURE
A Critique of Post-Saussurean Literary Theory

Laura Mulvey
VISUAL AND OTHER PLEASURES

Ian Hunter
CULTURE AND GOVERNMENT
The Emergence of Literary Education

Denise Riley
'AM I THAT NAME?'
Feminism and the Category of 'Women' in History

Mary Ann Doane
THE DESIRE TO DESIRE
The Woman's Film of the 1940s

Language, Discourse, Society
Series Standing Order ISBN 0–333–71482–2
(*outside North America only*)

You can receive future titles in this series as they are published by placing a standing order. Please contact your bookseller or, in case of difficulty, write to us at the address below with your name and address, the title of the series and the ISBN quoted above.

Customer Services Department, Macmillan Distribution Ltd, Houndmills, Basingstoke, Hampshire RG21 6XS, England

The Writing of Anxiety

Imagining Wartime in Mid-Century British Culture

Lyndsey Stonebridge

University of East Anglia

© Lyndsey Stonebridge 2007

All rights reserved. No reproduction, copy or transmission of this
publication may be made without written permission.

No paragraph of this publication may be reproduced, copied or transmitted
save with written permission or in accordance with the provisions of the
Copyright, Designs and Patents Act 1988, or under the terms of any licence
permitting limited copying issued by the Copyright Licensing Agency,
90 Tottenham Court Road, London W1T 4LP.

Any person who does any unauthorised act in relation to this publication
may be liable to criminal prosecution and civil claims for damages.

The author has asserted her right to be identified
as the author of this work in accordance with the Copyright,
Designs and Patents Act 1988.

First published 2007 by
PALGRAVE MACMILLAN
Houndmills, Basingstoke, Hampshire RG21 6XS and
175 Fifth Avenue, New York, N.Y. 10010
Companies and representatives throughout the world

PALGRAVE MACMILLAN is the global academic imprint of the Palgrave
Macmillan division of St. Martin's Press, LLC and of Palgrave Macmillan Ltd.
Macmillan® is a registered trademark in the United States, United Kingdom
and other countries. Palgrave is a registered trademark in the European
Union and other countries.

ISBN-13: 978–0–230–01327–8 hardback
ISBN-10: 0–230–01327–9 hardback

This book is printed on paper suitable for recycling and made from fully
managed and sustained forest sources. Logging, pulping and manufacturing
processes are expected to conform to the environmental regulations of the
country of origin.

A catalogue record for this book is available from the British Library.

A catalog record for this book is available from the Library of Congress.

10   9   8   7   6   5   4   3   2   1
16   15   14   13   12   11   10   09   08   07

Printed and bound in Great Britain by
Antony Rowe Ltd, Chippenham and Eastbourne

For Shaun, Joe and Mizzy, and in memory of Max

Contents

List of Illustrations

Acknowledgements

I first started thinking about the themes of this book at the Society for the Humanities, Cornell University, 1997–98. I wish to thank my fellow fellows for their pleasurable intellectual companionship, the then Director of the Society, Dominick LaCapra and Suzanne Stewart Steinberg for their subtle history lessons, and Mary Jacobus whose support for this project has been constant. The book was completed with the aid of a grant from the Arts and Humanities Research Centre.

Earlier versions of some chapters have appeared as journal articles. A shorter version of 'Anxiety at a Time of Crisis' (Chapter 1) appeared in *History Workshop Journal*, 45 (Spring 1998); 'Bombs and Roses: the Writing of Anxiety in Henry Green's *Caught*' (Chapter 3) was published in a special issue of *Diacritics*, 28(4) (Winter 1998) on trauma and psychoanalysis; 'Bombs, Birth and Trauma: Henry Moore's and D.W. Winnicott's Pre-History Figments' (Chapter 4) appeared in *Cultural Critique*, 46 (Fall 2000), and 'Human Voices: Hearing them Speak in Wilfred Bion, Muriel Spark and Penelope Fitzgerald' (Chapter 6) was published in *Textual Practice*, 19 (2005). I wish to thank the editors of those publications, particularly Sally Alexander, Karyn Ball and Peter Nicholls for their careful guidance. I am grateful too to the following for kind permission to publish the images in this book: the Art Archive and the Imperial War Museum for Dame Laura Knight, 'The Nuremberg Trial, 1946', The Melanie Klein Trust for the drawing of Melanie Klein by Richard, aged 10, Magnum Photo Agency for David Seymour ('Chim'), *Land Distribution Meeting, Estremadura, Spain, 1936* and *Terezka, a Disturbed Child in an Orphanage, Poland, 1948*, and The Henry Moore Foundation for Henry Moore, *Study for 'Tube Shelter Perspectives: the Liverpool St. Extension', 1941*, *September 3rd 1939*, *Crowd Looking at a Tied-Up Object, 1942*, and *Girl Reading to a Woman Holding a Child, 1946*.

I have been fortunate to find myself working alongside others in the (re)emerging field of studies in mid-century British culture and literature. In particular, I have benefited from the conversation and writing of Maud Ellmann, Joe Kennedy, Marina MacKay, Rod Mengham, Ian Patterson and Neil Reeve. At the University of East Anglia, Clive Scott was brilliant in both tracking down photographs and teaching me how to think about them, and Helen Smith and Jennifer Hodgson helped me put the book together. Thanks too to Cath Sharrock, Laura Scott and Ludmilla Jordanova for being such helpful and interesting interlocutors – and friends. I am tremendously grateful, once again, to Denise Riley for her intellectual support and shrewd editorial judgement. My greatest debt is to my partner, Shaun Hargreaves Heap, who has had to read far too much psychoanalysis than can possibly be good for a theorist of rational choice, and who has done so with such generosity and insight that it is true to say that this would have been a quite different book without him. This is for him, our children, Joe and Mizzy, and in memory of our colleague, Max Sebald.

Introduction: 'Dreading Forward': the Writing of Anxiety at Mid-Century

> Caught up in the turmoil of this wartime, one-sidely informed, without distance from the great transformations that have already occurred or are beginning to, and without a glimmer of the future taking shape, we ourselves are waylaid by the significance of impressions that overwhelm us and by the values of the judgements which we form.
>
> Sigmund Freud, 'Thoughts for the Times on War and Death' (1915)[1]

> 'Whatever else I forget about the war, I hope I may never forget my own dreams, or some of the other dreams I have been told. We have never dreamed like this before; and I suppose we shall never dream like it again.'
>
> From Elizabeth Bowen, Postscript to *The Demon Lover* (1945)[2]

In his famous 1915 essay, 'Thoughts for the Times on War and Death', Freud wrote about how war exposed the madness that lurked at the heart of the West's illusions about what it meant to be civilized. As studies of modernism and trauma have demonstrated, that madness found eloquent and tortured expression in the cultural imagination of the first part of the twentieth century.[3] This book adds to this work by suggesting how the psychopathology of wartime was registered by two second-generations: the generation of psychoanalysts who came after Freud, and whose work thrived in 1940s Britain; and by some of those late modernists who had cut their teeth on the expressive verve of their war-shocked elders, only to find themselves having to re-invent an aesthetic not only for another war, but for the prolongation

1

of a state of war consciousness that was to last for the remainder of the twentieth century – and beyond.[4] This is not, however, simply a book about trauma, but rather has a slightly different starting point which I attempt to describe here, with a perhaps necessary historical awkwardness, as the writing of anxiety.

Anxiety is an affect with a profligate cultural history – there have been many ages of anxiety within the history of modernity, and there are many ways in which the modern history of anxiety could be told: through the history of architecture, for example, through which the anxious spaces of twentieth-century culture find one of their most articulate expressions; or through the history of a philosophy which, from Heidegger through to Beckett, connects our contemporary breathlessness to the anxiety of being in time.[5] The readings of anxiety collected here touch on these larger histories, but their focus is – far too relentlessly no doubt for some tastes – psychoanalytic. It is so, at least in part, because it seems to me that we still have a good deal to learn from thinking about the wartime madness that so troubled Freud when he described how the ego lost its way amid the whirlwind of impressions which was his contemporary wartime. When Melanie Klein and Anna Freud tried to describe what it might mean to be a child in the Second World War fifteen years later, they too were not just talking about the psychic fall-out of war, but about how it is that war settles into the darkest parts of our being, and into our understanding of ourselves as both subjects of war and of a politics – of a 'civilization' – that legitimized war. For writers such as Elizabeth Bowen, Rebecca West, Henry Green, and Rose Macaulay, as for the psychoanalysts who were redefining Freud's legacy amid an imploding Europe that more than justified his bleak imaginings about the future in the early part of the century, it was never in any doubt that war had a psychic charge that was at least as anxiety-provoking as anything that actually might fall from the sky.

Then (as now), anxiety fills the gap between reason and imagination. It is what we feel when we are caught in a situation which, as Bowen put it in the postscript to the American edition of her collection of wartime short stories, *The Demon Lover*, is radically 'out of proportion to our faculties of thinking and knowing'. Commenting on the hauntingly oneiric quality of the stories, Bowen writes:

> The hallucinations in the stories are not a peril; nor are the stories studies of mental peril. The hallucinations are an unconscious, instinctive saving resort on the part of the characters: life, mechanized by the controls of wartime, and emotionally torn and

impoverished by changes, had to complete itself in *some* way [...]
Dreams by night, and the fantasies – these often childishly innocent – with which formerly matter-of-fact people consoled themselves by day were compensations. Apart from them, I do not think
that the *desiccation*, by war, of our day-to-day lives can be enough
stressed. The outsize World War news was stupefying; headlines
and broadcasts came down and down on us in hammerlike chops,
with great impact but, oddly, little reverberation. The simple way
to put it was: 'One cannot take things in'. What was happening
was out of all proportion to our faculties for knowing, thinking and
checking up.[6]

Although the consciousness of Bowen's characters stretch across time
and space with a mind-distorting elasticity, neither they nor her writing
are completely shattered by historical experience. They dream on,
and Bowen writes on, disclosing with a verbal brilliance that captures
the claustrophobia of wartime in the contortions of her syntax, what
happens to the modern psyche when it is confronted by a situation
which is 'out of all proportion to our faculties for knowing, thinking
and checking up'.

In his famous essay on Baudelaire, first published in 1939, Walter
Benjamin described how the 'issueless private character', the dreams,
memories, and hallucinations that make up the troubled subjectivity
of estranged modernist consciousness, did not emerge spontaneously
in the latter half of the nineteenth century but were a response to a
situation in which 'man' was 'increasingly unable to assimilate the data
of the world around him by way of experience'.[7] When data shocks but
fails to reverberate, there is no meaningful place left for consciousness
to go except, as it were, back into itself, in a movement that reconnects
the subject to history precisely by marking its estrangement from it
(Baudelaire, notes Benjamin, intended the intense lyricism of his poetry
to be understood as thoroughly historical).[8] Along with Proust, Valéry
and Baudelaire, one of Benjamin's key reference points in the opening
pages of his study is Freud and, in particular, *Beyond the Pleasure Principle* (1920). Trauma turns us neurotic, Freud notes in this crucial and
complex text, not when it wounds our bodies, but when it fissures our
minds; leaving us shattered and out of time by something we fail to
comprehend. This quality of the 'missed encounter', of not quite being
in an experience which nonetheless manifests itself in your repetitions,
your dreams, your hallucinations and imperfect memories, has generated much work in contemporary trauma theory.[9] Back in 1920 Freud

was still trying to work out what kind of mind could emerge from the overwhelming catastrophe of the First World War. Before we learned to say, with Lacan for example, that the death drive takes us way beyond the self-mastery of any putative ego, there remained, for Freud at least, quite a few ways for the subject, emotionally torn and impoverished by change as she might have been, to react to the history she was failing to comprehend.

This is where anxiety becomes important to Freud. In *Beyond the Pleasure Principle*, trauma is what happens when anxiety fails to do its work. ' "Anxiety" ', writes Freud, unlike fear or fright, 'describes a partic-ular state of expecting the danger or preparing for it, even though it may be an unknown one.' Anxiety tilts us towards the hammerlike blows; as breathlessly paralysed as we might be in the face of a history that seems incomprehensible, anxiety is also the affective register of a form of historical anticipation. 'I do not believe', Freud continues, 'anxiety can produce a traumatic neurosis. There is something about anxiety that protects its subject against fright and so against fright-neuroses.'[10] Anxiety is a 'protection' against trauma; it is a way of staying in relation to history without being consumed by it. (Another reason for thinking about the psychopathology of wartime in terms of anxiety might be that substantially more people are anxious about, rather than actually traumatized by, war – pinched at the nerve ends by its uncer-tainties but not, as Freud describes the real victims of traumatic neur-oses, psychically blasted to pieces.) And while anxiety might work as a prophylactic against trauma, as a sort of psychic defence against history, it is not an emotion that has much truck with a concept of history perceived in terms of linear time. Anxiety dreams, writes Freud, are 'endeavouring to master the stimulus retrospectively, by developing the anxiety whose omission was the cause of the traumatic neuroses'.[11] It is this sort of energetic out-of-time way of responding to trauma in Freud's essay that so attracted Benjamin in the late 1930s. The writing he was drawn to was one that registered the shocks of modern life (and so prevented them from becoming traumatic) *and*, 'if need be', enlisted the work of dreams and memories to recreate the anxious capacity for receiving more shocks.[12] What Benjamin rediscovered in Baudelaire, on the eve both of the Second World War and of his own death, then, was a writing of anxiety of the most exemplary kind for his time. And while the lyrical exuberance with which Baudelaire parried the shocks of modernity may well have been lost to the generations of writers who followed him, the writing of anxiety – a writing which is eloquent on the subject of trauma, but not consumed by its impossibilities – was not.

Thus Virginia Woolf, also writing at the beginning of the war and on the eve of her suicide, reflected upon her 'shock receiving capacity' as a writer in her memoir, 'A Sketch of the Past'. 'I hazard the explanation', Woolf noted in a passage which reads as a good place to start thinking about modernism and trauma, 'that a shock is at once in my case followed by the desire to explain it. I feel that I have had a blow; but it is not as I thought as a child, simply a blow from an enemy [...] it is or will become a revelation of some order.'[13] Parrying the shocks for Woolf creates an opportunity to affirm the mysteriousness of human consciousness. Woolf too was looking back at an earlier version of modernism – not least, of her own. Yet while the manner of her writing testifies to the capacity for memory to more than compensate for the out-of-life experience of trauma, Woolf's repeated insistence on the transcendent power of art also points to an aesthetic under pressure. As much as the memoir beautifully recreates the exquisite living-pains of her famous childhood, the present war is never far from its writing: 'every night the Germans fly over England', 'John came in, looked white about the gills, his pale eyes paler than usual, and said the French have stopped fighting', 'invasion still impends', 'five German raiders passed so close over Monks House that they brushed the tree at the gate'.[14] The closer the war gets to the gate, the more urgent Woolf's memorializing becomes; as if her hallucinations ('the feeling [...] of lying in a grape and seeing through a film of semi-transparent yellow'[15]), might allow something like consciousness to survive in anticipation of an imminent trauma: '[i]f we are beaten then – however we solve that problem, and one solution is apparently suicide [...] – book writing becomes doubtful. But I wish to go on, not settle down in that dismal puddle.'[16] 'Dreading forward' was the phrase Henry Green used at the beginning of the war to describe a similar kind of anticipatory response to the uncertainty of the future. The writing of anxiety in Green's wartime fiction, as I describe in Chapter 3, fleshes out such anxious memorializing with an erotic exuberance which, like Baudelaire's, insists on being read as historical.

The writing of anxiety, then, can be read as describing a kind of historiography of trauma; a writing which treats history not so much as enigmatic or unrepresentable (common tropes in much trauma writing), as a form of imaginative provocation. A provocation is how I think that many writers and artists thought about history in the 1940s: from the shocking power of the first photographs to emerge from the Spanish Civil War in the late 1930s, to the perpetual crises of aerial warfare during the war, to the numbing horror of the Nuremberg war crimes tribunal; the decade was characterized not only by the shocks of history, but by a demand that the imagination should continue to discover ways of being in history – or perhaps ways of *staying* in it. A constant theme of this book is the extent to which for many 'dreading forward', also meant recycling versions of the past, as Rose Macaulay discovered when she tried to create a poetics capable of articulating post-war guilt; or returning to versions of pre-history, as Henry Moore's drawings of the anxious spaces of wartime Britain reveal. 'The past is literally blasted into consciousness with the Blitz in London', noted the poet H.D. in 1944, as she sat down to write her memoir of her analysis with Freud, *Tribute to Freud* (1956).[17] The rubble of the Blitz proved fertile ground for the growth of new primitivisms and for the late flowering of mythic modernism. In this book, however, I am not so concerned with the cultural iconography of such pre-historical turns as with what they imply for an understanding of a question Freud raised back in 1915: if wartime also signifies the emergence of a state of war-consciousness (and war-unconsciousness), how is it possible to maintain a relation to a history whose violence is felt as an extremely poignant type of discontinuity in the very depths of the psyche?

Keeping anxious, Freud had argued in *Beyond the Pleasure Principle*, was a way of ensuring the mind could endure – if only in its dreams and hallucinations. Six years later Freud wove this insight into his final theory of trauma in *Inhibitions, Symptoms and Anxiety* (1926). Although this is not a text that figures much in contemporary trauma theory, as I argue in the first chapter, its premises were crucial for the thinking of the second generation of psychoanalysts who were working in wartime Britain. By the late 1920s Freud is describing trauma, not so much as a kind of breaching or effraction, both metaphors that dominate *Beyond the Pleasure Principle*, but in terms of object-loss. Freud's emphasis now is on how the ego manages an anxiety that, in effect, defines the ways in which we are able to imagine ourselves in the world. The ego, says Freud, is the 'seat' of anxiety. The ego, however, turns out to be a somewhat incommodious piece of furniture; a fragile entity which while shaped by anxiety (without object-loss there can be no ego), is simultaneously always threatened by it. *Inhibitions, Symptoms and Anxiety* raises two key problems for Freud's followers. First, by linking anxiety with the origins of the object, Freud also linked affect to questions about representation and meaning. Second, and in the same move, Freud raises the question of what kind of subject is addressed by anxiety. The issue thus is not only what (and how) does anxiety signal our relationship to trauma (what is it telling us about our place in the world?), but *who* is anxiety talking to – what kind of subject does it address? Does anxiety continually put the ego into question by harassing it from both inside and out? Or does the anxiety 'make' the ego out of the defences of this shattered psyche? Does the helplessness it signals end with self-mastery (existential transcendence through the back door of psychoanalytic theory)?[18]

In 1926 Freud also moves anxiety backwards; away from the nightmares of returning soldiers and back to the inhibitions and phobias of the nursery that had first made its appearance in Freud's case history of the five-year-old Little Hans in 1909, and which had re-emerged in his famous account of his grandson's game with a cotton-reel in *Beyond the Pleasure Principle* itself.[19] It was this emphasis on what can be described as the childhood of anxiety that was to fascinate those child-analysts, such as Melanie Klein, Anna Freud, Donald Winnicott, W.R.D. Fairbairn and Wilfred Bion, who were so boldly to take the war into the nursery in 1940s Britain. This fascination with the most primitive of anxieties is partly what makes their work so illuminating to read alongside some of their late modernist contemporaries. Both disclose an imaginary world in which cartographies of fantasy are also those of war – history happening in the mind; but both also ask how it is possible for the self to establish itself, to find a location, within such a world – the mind happening (or failing to happen) in history.

Where is the ego in all this anxiety? is a question Freud was compelled to ask himself again and again in *Inhibitions, Symptoms and Anxiety*, and one that I have found myself asking repeatedly in these pages. What seems to be so overwhelming about the first atrocity photographs that emerged from the Spanish Civil War (discussed in Chapter 2), for example, seems to have as much to do with their shocking nature as it does with the way our responses to them reveal a kind of psychopolitical helplessness. Similarly, behind the mythic monumentalism of Henry Moore's best-known war art, the subject of Chapter 4, there is an anxiety-provoking doubling of the visual field in a series of drawings which suggests a far more uncomfortable relationship with history than is often associated with his work. The ego slips its moorings amid the anxiety of wartime, I attempt to argue here, but it doesn't necessarily always lose its place. As Anna Freud and Melanie Klein discover in their work with child-evacuees, while anxiety might set a limit on historical agency, it also has an inventiveness that allows the ego to survive in ways which do not so much transcend wartime, as re-work its most violent pathologies into some kind of relationship with the future.

The question of psychic agency emerges frequently in the chapters that follow. For psychoanalysis, as for the writers and artists I discuss here, there is no outside simply attacking an inside, no shelter for psychologism, but an anxious self often hopelessly entangled with the violence it is witness to. Wartime, as Samuel Weber has argued apropos of Freud's 'Thoughts for the Times', newly reveals the extent to which self-determination itself is a form of violence; in its strenuous efforts to re-imagine a place for itself within the whirlwinds of wartime, the ego (as Freud describes it) redoubles the violence it feels to be internal onto the outside world – which is one reason why witnessing the deaths of so many others is not as ego-shattering as it perhaps ought to be.[20] How it might be possible to apprehend the world without either losing oneself in it or reduplicating its violence turned out to be a question that persisted beyond the immediacy of the war. How, for example, asks Rebecca West in her writings on the Nuremberg trials, is it possible to make guilt meaningful when the metaphorics of the war-machine have gobbled up the capacity for agency? What do the self-determinations necessary for democracy mean, asks the psychoanalyst Wilfred Bion, working out of his experience with groups of war-ravaged soldiers, when we find the psychic proximity of other people's voices intolerable?

Post-war, the writing of anxiety in Britain took its own existential turn. What I have tried to do here is to find a way of addressing a moment that comes after modernism but just before the war and its shocking moral aftermath became the 'human condition'. My emotions, Sartre wrote in the late 1930s, signify something for my psychic life: they allow me to perpetuate myself in the imaginary, to apprehend what I can of the world without losing myself in it. The more subtle emotions, he adds, can transcend themselves: my anxiety in the face of horror, thus, can also give me an 'intuition of the absolute'.[21] In the claustrophobic and agoraphobic spaces of wartime Europe, Sartre was not the only one for whom anxiety had come to signal something about the determinations of psychic life. For Sartre those determinations were intended to be lived. In *Existentialism and Humanism*, first published in Britain in 1948 (his short stories had started to appear in John Lehmann's *New Writing* in the early 1940s), Sartre describes the dilemma facing a young man who comes to him, after the death of his only brother, unable to decide whether he should join the resistance or whether, mindful of his mother's loss, he should save himself for her. Sartre's point is that the boy should turn his anxiety into an act of self-determination; that he should find a way of transcending his uncertainty and so rediscover his historical agency.[22] For psychoanalysis we can never transcend anxiety (for Freud, as for Kierkegaard, anxiety is always a form of destiny) and nor, indeed, should we: that way lies mania – the everyday mania, perhaps, of historical self-determination.

But as this book I hope demonstrates, it does not follow that all subjects of wartime are destined to live a life repeating an experience that they overwhelmingly failed to comprehend first time round. Wartime isn't incomprehensible: even at its most traumatic (and even if the history of war could somehow be reduced to the sum of those traumatic effects), it demands new forms of comprehension, new ways of staying, as it were, with a history that is always threatening to undo those who have to live it from within. The writing of anxiety has its own kind of awkward and compromised historical agency; it at least allows us to dream on, as Bowen said, to 'complete' ourselves 'in *some* way'.

* * *

This book is organized in three parts each containing twinned chapters. The first two chapters focus on the 'childhood of anxiety' as it emerges in British intellectual culture in the late 1930s and 1940s. When Sigmund and Anna Freud escaped from Nazi-occupied Austria to London, they were greeted by a flourishing psychoanalytic movement. Chapter 1 describes a moment in the history of psychoanalysis when its theory of anxiety went public – in the work of Mass Observation, for example, and in radio broadcasts and surveys. Against the backdrop of a culture that was beginning to understand the psychological impact of war, Freud's legacy was contested in the fast-growing field of child-psychoanalysis. Reading Freud's final theory of trauma in the light of the war work of his daughter Anna, and of her opponent, Melanie Klein, I trace how the crisis of the war pushed psychoanalysis into new engagements with its own wartime imaginary.

The figure of the child, for psychoanalysis in this period, was not only one of anxiety, but also one which generated anxiety. In Chapter 2, I discuss the emergence of these anxious children in two different but as it turns out related contexts: the relatively new anxiety of historical spectatorship as it was felt, most acutely, by those trying to find a way of looking at photographs of the dead and displaced children of the Spanish Civil War; and in the ways in which the anxious children of psychoanalytic theory were realized in a figure that was to dominate wartime Britain and Europe – that of the evacuated child. Small whirlwinds of something barely present, these war children articulate the disorientation of wartime existence with a poignancy that goes beyond historical pathos.

The vertiginous and claustrophobic spaces of wartime are the concern of the next section which is made up of two close readings of the wartime work of two Henrys: Henry Green and Henry Moore. Green's 1943 novel

Caught is haunted by yet another figure of a small boy abducted, as it were, on several levels: kidnapped in the text's melodramatic plotting; evacuated to an icy-cold countryside in Green's evocative historicism, and about to fall headlong into a mass of vibrant colour as he stares at the toys in a brightly-lit department store in a poetics about the vertigo of imagery which cuts right through the novel. To be 'caught' in anxious historicity in Green's writing is to be caught up in a relationship to the image. Writing in his (somewhat premature) autobiography at the beginning of the war, Green describes himself as actively remembering things to die with. In *Caught*, this kind of remembering turns out to be a form of protest against death or, at the very least, an effort to master trauma through the authoring of images.

The hallucinations that give Green's writing, like Bowen's, its weirdly powerful historical appropriateness find their visual equivalents in much art from the period. Bill Brandt's haunted city-studies of the Blitz for example, puncture historical time by seeming to capture a moment that is frozen just before or just after the falling of a bomb. Lee Miller's surreally elegant photographs of wartime Britain turn the landscape of the Shell Guides into dreams where geese chase giant silver balloons. Famously, John Piper's war-torn landscapes of the British countryside use colour to confer a mythological élan to Britain's war, which is at least as vibrant as that found in the most explosive apocalyptic poetry of the period. It is, however, the claustrophobic spaces of Henry Moore's famous drawings of the underground shelters extemporized in the London tube system that have come to represent the suffering of the civilian population in wartime most emblematically. Chapter 4 returns to these images, and reads them alongside a more unsettling sequence of drawings that Moore was also working on in this period, including, for example, the surreally disturbing 'Crowd Looking at a Tied-Up Object'. More anxiety-provoking than redemptive, Moore's drawings ask us to think about how the most primitive of feelings can tell us something about the difficulty of inhabiting the present. The odd temporality that comes with trying to assemble something like an ego also concerned Winnicott as he trod his way through the buried rubble of his patients' primordial traumas in the same period. These pre-historic turns are not retreats from history, but fitting testaments to the complexity of establishing a relation to a world which it is impossible to see straight.

The inability to fix the world into some kind of visual, historical or, indeed, moral order is compellingly rendered in Laura Knight's 1945 drawing of the Nuremberg Trials. Knight was in the broadcasting box, which gave her a view looking down upon the proceedings (Figure I.1). So

Figure I.1 Dame Laura Knight, *The Nuremberg Trial 1946*

iconographic has Nuremberg become that we can recognize its defendants merely by the back of a head or an off-angle profile: Goering's evasive
and arrogant slouch, Hess's pathetic craziness, the way that Schacht, the
Reichsbank president who was eventually acquitted, physically recoils
from his compatriots; all recognizable signatures for the denouement
of a war that was ending on the ground, but which was only really
beginning to make its effects felt upon the cultural imaginary. Knight

captures the anxiety of keeping the recent past in mind by turning the edges of her picture into a warscape. Behind the defendants, the white helmets and the court officials, a town still burns, while the debris of human and stone are scattered in front of them. But Knight doesn't keep the two histories separate: a naked human arm grasps at the bench of the defence team, as if it is about to pull its own corpse into the courtroom. The recent past intrudes into the interior sending everything out of proportion. Knight's picture refuses to establish visual priorities: indeed, what makes this painting so much of its time is the way it refuses to settle anything.

The last two chapters of this book also deal with the unsettled accounts of the post-war period. Chapter 5 examines Rose Macaulay's and Rebecca West's late modernist attempts to find a place for war guilt in a post-Freudian context. (The 'sense of guilt', Freud noted in *Civilization and its Discontents*, 'is at bottom nothing else but a topographical variety of anxiety'.[23]) Macaulay discovers a newly resonant topography for anxiety in the wilderness of London's bomb-sites. But while the ruins are a fitting correlative for a post-war sense of guilt, Macaulay's writing struggles to make guilt historically or morally meaningful. The difficulty of making guilt guilty enough is also powerfully explored in West's accounts of Nuremberg. Guilt, for West, is horribly ensnared within both a kind of psychoanalytic materialism for which historical agency is always compromised by the workings of desire and identification, and within a historical context – West calls it the 'war-machine' – which appears to have given this kind of materialism a wearingly persistent legitimacy. A writer of anxiety for whom questions of moral and historical agency were always uppermost, West pulls late modernism into the post-war period with a devastating demonstration of its political and moral limitations.

The question of where post-war politics could go also worried Jacques Lacan as he trod his way through the debris of wartime London on VJ day. My final chapter opens with Lacan's account of the work of Wilfred Bion who had tried to restore some kind of agency to war-ravaged soldiers by getting them to share a special kind of hallucination that Bion called 'the group'. Bion's group, however, is premised neither on the democratic principle of listening to the voices of others, nor on the submission to the voice of authority that underwrote the totalitarian fantasies that shadowed the period; rather Bion is experimenting with a model of agency that understands – and can therefore do without – the power of its own fantasies about authority. Muriel Spark and Penelope Fitzgerald capture the comedy, as much as the pathos, of this stance in post-war fictions which understand the seductions and the ridiculousness of authority in equal measure. That comedy, I suggest finally, is not to be taken lightly.

This book opens with a scene stolen from the archives of Mass Observation, but which might have come from one of Bowen's short stories. Gripped with persecutory anxiety, a woman lies in her bed wondering whether opening her blackout blinds would give the bombers enough light to blast her husband out of existence. It ends with the death of a character from Penelope Fitzgerald's novel set in wartime London, *Human Voices* (1980). Jeffrey Haggard dies because of the way objects are distorted in the blackout (fatally, he mistakes a parachute bomb for a taxi). Unlike the woman from the Mass Observation archives, however, Jeffrey is no hysteric. Or rather if he is a hysteric, he is one who well understands the anxiety that comes with having to answer to a historical moment when it is claimed that democracy can only be defended by the exercise of authoritarian means. It was the illusion that civilization offered some time of protection against punitive barbarism that Freud believed had been shattered by the First World War. Writing in the wake of the second, Fitzgerald's novel is an elegant late reminder of how wartime waylays our fantasies about ourselves as agents of history and culture.

1
Anxiety at a Time of Crisis: Psychoanalysis and Wartime

Some time in the autumn of 1939, somewhere in London, a woman sits bolt upright in her bed gripped by anxiety. She blinks into the darkness searching for some familiar shape that might pull her back from the abyss of her dream world into the real world. But it is black, pitch black. Not for the first time, she curses the blackout. She hates the dark. Closing her eyes against the night, she fingers her throat and recalls her dream. It is a familiar dream: one of those arms that come to strangle her with regular monotony in the night is right now lying heavy across her thighs; it belongs to her husband who has not yet (why not?) been called away. Her analyst calls this persecutory anxiety. All she knows is that her head throbs and that all this has to end. It could end, were it not for this blackout. If there were no blackout then the bombs could come and find him – or her, it wouldn't really matter who – and then it could end. She gently removes her husband's arm from her body, clicks on the bedside light and makes her way towards the window.

Readers of 1940s fiction might recognize something familiar in this story of barely concealed menace on the home front. Annexing realism with the sub-genres of gothic, melodrama and fantasy, late modernist writers such as Elizabeth Bowen, Rosamond Lehmann, Henry Green, Patrick Hamilton and Graham Greene flesh out their troubled epoch with dark cartographies of the human psyche in wartime. These anxious narratives for anxious times turn the self inside out: characters are shattered as much by the forces of their erotic lives as those of war, as the blackout emerges as a kind of dream screen for unconscious desire. Not only are the private imaginations of quietly driven characters 'invaded' by war, these fictions also try and understand what it means for the psyche to be shaped by a history that it cannot assimilate. As recent work on mid-century British literature has demonstrated, writing like this gives us a different kind of historical perspective on the strained psychopathology of wartime Britain.[1] Indeed 1940s writers frequently present history itself as an affective charge that can only barely be comprehended by the imagination. A strange sort of dissonance, for example, is at the heart of both Bowen's and Henry Green's wartime work: the 'brittle film' that makes everything opaque in Bowen's *The Heat of the Day* (1948) gums up the eyes of the reader as much as it does those of the novel's much deceived and deceiving characters; while Green's three great wartime novels, *Caught* (1943), *Loving* (1945) and *Back* (1946), all feature characters whose precarious presence in the world rests only on the most curious and often torturous of self-imaginings. More conventionally, but with a violence that can only just be contained within the romance genre, Lehmann's wartime characters are driven by a desire that finds its metaphorical correlatives in the bombed-out basements of dingy London flats (*The Echoing Grove*, 1953); while the similarly driven fugitives of Graham Greene's wartime 'entertainments' are subject not only to historical forces, but to a capricious God. And George Harvey Bone, the gentle psychotic murderer of Hamilton's *Hangover Square* (1941), set in 1939, lumbers through his persecutory anxiety with a historical pathos that more than matches my opening story of the homicidal fantasies of a woman discovering that 'the war' might also be one way of killing off her nightmarish spouse.

But this story of one woman's night terrors doesn't come from fiction. The facts of this case of paranoid anxiety on the domestic front were first reported in September 1939 by the psychoanalyst R.A. Macdonald in a report commissioned by Tom Harrisson of Mass Observation and destined for the Ministry of Information. Macdonald's analysis of civilian morale is based on his reading of the 'anxiety dreams' recorded by mass observers (the two files labelled 'male' and 'female' containing the typescripts of these dreams, as well as the writer, Naomi Mitchison's dream diary, can be found in the enticingly titled 'Dreams Box' in the Mass Observation archives).[2] This woman, however, is not an observer, but one of Macdonald's patients drafted into his report to show how dangerous cases of persecutory anxiety can be for national security. Only death can bring an end to this anxiety and such an ardent desire for death, Macdonald argues in earnest but deadpan prose, is clearly not good for morale. This woman is dangerous, he suggests, not so much because she might actually light up the blackout (however much her anxiety drives her towards the window), but because she is likely to delight in unpleasant rumours; when you are crazy enough to welcome your own death, the thought of imminent invasion smells sweet amid the rubble of the Blitz. In this narrative of domestic misery, then, anxiety has gone astray; Macdonald's patient's own psychic defence against anxiety (death) has become fatally muddled with national defences against a possible air-raid attack (blackout). Such shattered anxious selves posed more than a risk to national security; to the extent that their private misery set up an uneasy relation with public panic, they also threatened to take pathology into the public sphere.

The prospect of a public space overrun with disordered and patholo-gical mentalities was a prevalent and popular concern during the late 1930s: what was food for fiction was deeply worrying for a culture relat-ively newly appraised of the potential for psychological disarray. In 1938, for example, a voluntary committee made up of different psychi-atric experts focused on three major preoccupations: the likelihood of a devastating air attack on London, the possibility of widespread civilian panic and an 'epidemic of shell-shock' similar 'to that observed during the war of 1914–18'.[3] Although Freud's work had greatly influenced many of those psychiatrists and psychologists who worked with the trauma victims of the first war outside of the Army (which played ambivalent host to the brilliant, but sometimes maverick, abilities of analysts such as Wilfred Bion, John Rickman and other members of what became known as the 'invisible college'), psychoanalysis had only a marginal role in official thinking and planning for the psychic casu-alties of the second war. Despite repeated offers of help by the British Institute of Psycho-Analysis to the Ministry of Health, '[a]ll these offers' the leading psychoanalyst, Edward Glover, lamented at the time 'were rejected without ceremony'.[4] These dusty answers did not prevent the London Clinic of Psycho-Analysis from acting on its own initiative and setting up a 'War Emergency Clinic' at 96 Gloucester Place in 1939 offering short-term treatment for those whose psyches were ravaged by war. Nor did it stop Glover from using the clinic as an 'Obser-vation Centre' and gathering together a group of twenty analysts to monitor reactions to the war among their own patients. Macdonald was one of those analysts, as were Donald Winnicott, Melitta Schmideberg (Melanie Klein's daughter, who at that time was implacably opposed to her mother's work), Paula Heimann (Klein's supporter), John Bowlby and Ella Freeman Sharpe, one of the founders of British psychoanalysis.[5] Some sort of psychopathology of the home front of sorts, then, did exist in Britain, but its influence and its work were limited by what Glover saw as official conservatism and reticence. In his three reports on 'The Psychological Effects of War Conditions on the Civilian Population' (published in two parts in the *International Journal of Psycho-Analysis*) Glover is clearly exasperated at the lack of opportunity for a psychoanalysis of the Blitz. Patients such as Macdonald's simply did not get into the national story and neither, as Glover points out, did they get into the statistics.

The response to Glover's complaint might well have been – and it might well still be today – that Britain did not need psychoanalysis because it did not have a national trauma on a scale to cause an increase in cases of neurosis. Most histories of the war in Britain will confirm that early fears of national panic and civilian air-raid psychiatric casualties were grossly over-exaggerated, and Glover himself notes that only one genuine case of 'bomb neurosis' was reported to the British Psycho-Analytic Society. But he also points out that lack of uniformity of research methods and the difficulty of observation under wartime conditions made these low statistics practically meaningless. By 1942 'The Mass-Neurosis Myth' – the myth that 'air-raids would give rise to wide spread "war neurosis"' – Glover argues, had been replaced by 'way of reaction' with a 'No Neurosis Myth'.[6] Today, the kind of psychoanalysis of anxiety that Glover sought is probably best found in the fiction of the period – the compelling strangeness of the 1940s novel, perhaps, is a measure of the difficulty of the task Glover was setting himself (how do you write the case history of a 'population'?). But returning to some of the psychoanalytic texts on anxiety of the period can also give us an insight into how trauma came home to Britain in this period. At the same moment as the battle front became the home front, psychoanalysis was also establishing a new home, literally in so far as Britain became the Freuds' home in exile, and theoretically and clinically in the turn to child analysis. In this chapter, I want to begin to address some of these themes, first by backtracking a little to Freud's later work on anxiety, and second by turning to the wartime work of two of his most significant legatees, his daughter, Anna Freud, and her professional and theoretical opponent, Melanie Klein.

I

Trauma not only scars history, its interpretative and narrative models – the 'aftermath effect' (*Nachträglichkeit*) which shows how our belated representations of trauma are never congruent with the shocking event itself – also impact on the way we represent history to ourselves – in dreams, nightmares, phobias, fantasies, fiction and narrative. Much of the attraction of current trauma theory rests with the way that it renders the unconscious effects of history newly visible. But trauma, of course, has a powerful affective, as well as effective, history. Indeed, this, to an extent, is what anxiety is for psychoanalysis: an affective charge that, while it plunges the subject into helplessness, also gives its own particular narrative to trauma and the ways in which we try and cope with it. For Freud, writing in his 1926 text, *Inhibitions, Symptoms and Anxiety*, while the subject who is gripped by anxiety might be speechless in one respect, in her anxiety she is also powerfully eloquent on the subject of trauma. As Freud puts it: 'Anxiety is [...] on the one hand an expectation of trauma, and on the other a repetition of it in a mitigated form.' Anxiety then both tells trauma's history and attempts to give a new narrative to its future. It is a 'signal' (Freud's word) which both prepares us for a real danger to come, and repeats a shocking traumatic event from the past. Anxiety 'says' to the subject – the haunting ventriloquism is Freud's: 'The present situation reminds me of one of the traumatic experiences I have had before. Therefore I will anticipate the trauma and behave as though it had already come, while there is yet time to turn aside.'[7] Except of course this narrative is told to us silently: only the unconscious listens and takes appropriately defensive action. All the subject knows is that she is taking down the blackout blinds in the middle of the night; or carefully but a little compulsively reading endless wartime newspaper cuttings (Louie in *The Heat of the Day*); or threading together pieces of furniture with string, like a demented spider retrospectively weaving its web around the corpses of its victims (George Harvey Bone in *Hangover Square*). Anxiety, then, tells us secret stories about ourselves. Add this to the distinctive temporality that Freud gives to anxiety – it looks both forwards and backwards; it is, as Theodor Reik argued, 'Janus faced' – and it perhaps becomes possible to begin to argue that anxiety for Freud, as for the 1940s novel, offers something like what we could call an affective historiography of trauma.[8]

If wartime Britain was an anxious culture, it was because this kind of affective history was being told on so many different levels. Gripped by the anticipation of a trauma to come, haunted by the traumas of World War I and witness to the mass civilian bombing of the Spanish Civil War (as I discuss in the next chapter), the British population certainly had enough to be anxious about. But, as Freud points out, we are not actually anxious about the things we know (the wars of the twentieth century, even by the 1940s, were all too familiar); because anxiety has a distinctive 'quality of indefiniteness and lack of an object' it also tells the affective history of a life that is not consciously known – the life of the unconscious and of fantasy, what we can perhaps describe as the traumatic childhood of the real dangers of the present moment.[9] 'If you think about it', said Edward Glover, sending out his own (anxious) signals across the BBC airwaves at the beginning of the war:

> the whole atmosphere of modern war is likely to revive those unreasoning fears that the human race has inherited from its remotest ancestors: gas masks that make us look like strange animals; underground shelters; rumours and suspicions; enemies overhead and unseen; wailing sirens; screaming air bombs, and vast explosions in the night. Small wonder, then, that we are afraid lest in the face of a real danger our first impulse should be to behave like little children [...] We are afraid of being afraid.[10]

The surreality of war makes infants of us all: from our own strange animal faces, Mickey Mouse gas-masks and babies in what look like bell-jars; to the dark red-rimmed eyes and human smells all crammed into the subterranean spaces of the London Underground; to the unseen but overheard (in both senses) noises that threaten from a sky dappled by the silver of barrage balloons that look as though they could have been snatched from the hands of the balloon-seller in Hyde Park – the iconography of wartime Britain is also the stuff of childhood nightmares. Small wonder, indeed, that our first impulse might be to behave like R.A. Macdonald's anxious patient. Or as the two firemen, Pye and Roe, discover in Henry Green's 1943 novel, *Caught*, set in the period leading up to the first London Blitz, that to be gripped (or 'caught') in anxious expectation of a real danger to come is also to bear witness to the return of traumas from the past (childhood incest in the case of the working-class Pye, the death of his wife and the abduction of his son in the case of middle-class auxiliary, Roe).

The point about anxiety then, as Glover puts it, is that it is not rational; which is a strange thing to say, perhaps, about a response to a war that people had every good reason to be extremely fearful about. Inasmuch as psychoanalysis might be charged with finding monsters where there are quite simply tanks, here, however, what Freud was also trying to do in 1926 was to find a way of describing how anxiety is inscribed within the deepest contours of the psyche – in a place where one can only make sense of the tanks if one understands how it is that they can also be monsters to an ego that no longer knows whether to be anxious about what is happening in the world or about what seems to be threatening it from within. Indeed, it is the ego itself, as much as the drives which both define and challenge it, that is at issue for Freud in

1926. Freud's earlier economic theories of the psyche had conceptualized anxiety as an effect of the transformation of libido – pleasurable drives, once inhibited, turn into the unpleasurable affect of anxiety (Freud's example in this early work was how the practice of *coitus interruptus* was bad for sex but good for anxiety).[11] With the inter-war advent of his second topography, Freud moved on to a more complex reading of anxiety: what he now had to do was marry this economic theory with his new topography of psychoanalytic agencies (ego, id and super-ego). Famously, the ego now becomes what Freud calls the 'seat' of anxiety. It is the ego that both gives the signal for anxiety, but which at the same time is essentially helpless in the face of that anxiety. Anxiety thus both guards the ego against future shock *and* has the potential to plunge the psyche into disarray: 'anxiety is not only being signaled as an affect' writes Freud, 'but is also being freshly created out of the economic conditions of the situation'.[12] As Samuel Weber has noted, it is difficult to decide here whether Freud sees anxiety as protecting the psyche or whether it actually causes the psyche's destruction. Freud seems to want it both ways; which is also why, as Weber's reading reveals, *Inhibitions, Symptoms and Anxiety* is a text which is at least as anxious as the anxiety it is trying to describe.[13]

What is certain is that Freud's final theory of trauma puts anxiety at the centre of psychic life. This move also entails another significant shift of emphasis. Freud is not only concerned with castration anxiety in *Inhibitions*, but also with its more primitive prototype, separation anxiety: it is no longer just the father who provokes anxiety, as Freud had insisted in his earlier work on sexual difference, but 'the absence of the mother that is now the danger; and', Freud adds, 'as soon as that danger arises, the infant gives the signal of anxiety, before the economic situation has set in'.[14] There is a familiar psychoanalytic paradox about causality at work in this sentence: the infant is anxious *before* the traumatic 'economic situation' has occurred; before, that is, according to the temporality of anxiety that Freud himself describes, he has experienced 'the' trauma which will allow him to anticipate all future traumas. The temptation here is to send the small ego back on a journey of infinite regress; but significantly Freud stops short of tracing the first separation back, for example, to birth itself (which, to Freud's disapproval, was precisely where Otto Rank had located it). Rather, what Freud is trying to narrate here is a process by which the ego comes into being out of an anxiety which can only protect the ego from loss retrospectively; as if, as Winnicott will later put it, before anxiety there is no temporality in which the ego can exist in the first place, no narrative, that is, that can locate it in a series of traumas which are always about to happen.[15] What is 'signalled' by the absence of the mother, then, is the beginning of a process through which the ego comes into a precarious kind of being through its anxiety. This turn to the mother is also a sign of Freud's renewed concern with infantile sexuality in the late 1920s (two of his most important essays on sexuality were published while he was working on his final theory of anxiety).[16] When we are anxious it is not only the castration of the subject that is being recalled (Lacan will later describe how anxiety puts the subject herself into question[17]); there is also a darker type of anxiety emerging in Freud's writing of this period – one that pushes trauma to the imaginary limits of subject-formation itself.

At the same time, Freud's interest in traumatic anxiety in *Inhibitions* also originates with his dissatisfaction with the psychological theories of shell-shock that emerged during World War I. For Freud it simply did not make any sense (as it did for many of his contemporaries, such as, notably, W.H. Rivers, who began to take Freud's work seriously at this point) to remove the sexual component from theories of war neurosis and to insist, instead, that the traumatic shocks received on the Western Front were caught up in a self-protective anxiety about death and destruction. The unconscious, Freud insisted in his introduction to a collection arising from the first post-war international symposium on war neuroses, does not recognize death; it has no experience of mortality, no knowledge of absence and no means to represent its own annihilation. What the unconscious does know about, however, is traumatic loss (be it that of castration or separation) and *that* is what is signalled by anxiety – not death itself but its affective psychic prototypes and substitutes.[18] It is thus precisely because anxiety raises a threat to the integrity of the ego, and, in particular, to the self-love or narcissism that for Freud keeps the ego precariously intact, that the libido still has a part to play in the war neuroses.

Take these two concerns together – the turn to infantile psychic life and the psychoanalysis of the war neuroses – and *Inhibitions, Symptoms and Anxiety* also begins to appear a historically anxious text: it both looks back to the traumas of World War I and forward, not directly to World War II, but certainly to the increasing dominance of child analysis in what was to become Freud's home in exile. In this sense, Freud's final reworking of the problems of anxiety and trauma runs parallel with shifts in history: just as his economic theory of trauma cast a shadow over readings of World War I, so too are psychoanalytic theories of anxiety in the light of Freud's second topography contemporary with

World War II, with the turn to child analysis in Britain, and with what Anna Freud was to describe as the 'war raging in the nursery'.[19]

II

It is perhaps no coincidence, then, that the famous battle between the two leading exponents of child psychoanalysis – Anna Freud and Melanie Klein – can be traced back to Freud's *Inhibitions, Symptoms and Anxiety*, and that the 'Controversial Discussions' set up to debate the differences between the two women took place on the war-torn British home front – as if by the 1940s it was the mother (the mother not only at the centre of psychoanalytic theory, but the future 'mother' of psycho-analysis itself) who was indeed now at the centre of anxiety.[20] Much of Klein's first published book, *The Psychoanalysis of Children* (1932) is an extended reading of Freud's *Inhibitions, Symptoms and Anxiety*.[21] Klein later wrote in a letter to Ernest Jones that she thought that Freud had reached his 'climax' in that book but, she adds pointedly, he 'only did not go further, but rather regressed'. She then concludes, even more pointedly, 'I am concerned that Anna's influence was one of the factors that held him back.'[22] Strictly speaking it was Klein who in fact 'regressed' in her theoretical contribution to the theory of anxiety by tracing anxiety back to the very beginnings of psychic life, to early Oedipal phantasies and to the aggression and guilt that, for Klein, engulf the young child. Anna Freud, as far as Klein was concerned, would have held her father back because, unlike Klein, for whom phantasy is all for the young child, she insisted on the importance of the external world, the environment and the role of the parents in the analysis of children. Anna Freud's own work on anxiety is sketched out in her 1936 book, *The Ego and the Mechanisms of Defence* which is also heavily indebted to her father's *Inhibitions, Symptoms and Anxiety*. By the beginning of the war the battle-lines between the two women had already been drawn then, across, we might say, Freud's final theory of anxiety.

As they circled one another in what was to become an increas-ingly acrimonious dispute, the positions the two analysts adopted both replayed the dilemmas that Freud left behind him, and began to offer a form of anxious commentary on the traumas of their own time. Thus Anna Freud's concern in *The Ego and the Mechanisms of Defence* is with 'objective anxiety': for her, the task of the analyst is to demonstrate to the child that there was really nothing to be anxious about and she deliberately (and partly in response to Klein) avoids any analysis of 'instinctual anxiety'. Such a far-reaching analysis she points out risked further weakening the anxious ego and leaving it exposed to even more traumatic anxiety.[23] Klein could not have disagreed more vehemently. There is always something to be anxious about, especially for the child, she insists, not least one's self and one's own primary instinctive and frequently murderous aggression. Anxiety floods Klein's earlier work. For her, there can be no ego in the first place without there being enough anxiety to worry it into being. What many people continue to find so shocking about a case history such as, to take a famous example, 'Little Dick' is the extent to which Klein's play technique works partly by generating anxiety in the child. Without anxiety, for Klein, there can be no meaning, no phantasy and, by implication, no ego: a 'sufficient quantity of anxiety is the necessary basis for an abundance of symbol-formation and phantasy', she writes of Dick, before plunging him into a bewildering play world, through which, Klein claims, Dick learns to tolerate anxiety.[24] ('Nurse coming?' Dick asks repeatedly after one such session, with a comic timing lost on his analyst.[25]) The task for the Kleinian analyst, then, is not to reassure the child but to make it anxious, to compel it to recognize the force of its own instinctual anxiety and to convert this anxiety into symbolization – to turn affect into meaning, indifference into difference, and to generate a narrative in which it is possible for an ego to emerge. Thus while Anna Freud goes about the business of educating anxiety, Melanie Klein incites it; and while Anna Freud turns the anxious ego to face the outside world, Melanie Klein twists it inwards to meet the trauma arising from within.

In their choice of wartime career, each analyst also seems to follow her own idea of where anxiety seems to be coming from and goes to meet it, so to speak, on its own ground. Anna Freud tracked the public and social consequences of anxiety with her work with Dorothy Burlingham in the Hampstead War Nurseries, and later on with her work with child refugees.[26] By contrast, Melanie Klein spent one year of the war in Pitlochry, Scotland, analysing just one child, 'Richard', the precociously gifted evacuee whose wartime obsessions Klein painstakingly analysed as evidence of his own early infantile anxiety. While the one analyst goes public with anxiety, the other goes private. But, as Macdonald's persecuted housewife demonstrates, there is no such thing as 'private' wartime anxiety; by the same token, there is no wartime anxiety, as Glover warned, that does not also live in the heads of those who experience it historically. With this in mind, the famous differences between Anna Freud and Melanie Klein that were to rip apart the British Psycho-Analytic Society during the war, begin to emerge as perhaps less significant than their similarities.

If the children living in the residential nurseries (at 13 Wedderburn Road and 5 Netherhall Gardens in London and the Barn in the country) under the care of Anna Freud and Dorothy Burlingham are anxious, for example, it is not (or not only) because bombs are dropping from the sky. As Anna Freud notes in one of her monthly reports to the US charity that funded the nurseries, although 'the picture of the "bomb-shocked" child is one sure to elicit sympathy', among her readers, it is not one she is familiar with in her professional work in Britain. The war children Anna Freud lives with are simply not traumatized in the same way as soldiers were in the first war. On the contrary, they seem cheerfully impervious to the danger of air-raids. Examples of this indifference abound in Freud and Burlingham's epic account of the day-to-day lives of the children in their care, which they describe with an utterly compelling attention to detail. One instance is particularly piquant. The children are watching an aeroplane circle the sky from their Hampstead garden. 'Some adult said: "Look it is writing!", a statement which one of the children corrected by saying "only scribbling". None of the children seemed to connect the sight of an airplane with the idea of possible danger.'[27] If anxiety is 'signalling' here, it is not doing so in a code the children recognize. For them, the planes are merely doodling insignificantly. In their wonderfully insouciant indifference, it is as if the children are quite literally refusing to 'read' the danger (the 'writing') in the sky. They play on regardless, finding other things to amuse themselves (such as a visit from Stephen Spender in his auxilliary fireman's uniform: the rhymed proximity of 'Spender' to his 'suspenders' sends the children into fits of unnervingly joyous hysteria).

But these displaced children are nonetheless anxious. What they fear does not fall from the sky, but comes from somewhere much closer to home. However much their carers might try and reassure the children by teaching them to read the writing in the sky, there is a more tenacious anxiety at work in the Blitz that proves difficult to educate. Symptoms of anxiety are on the rampage in the war nurseries, kicking at the furniture, causing night terrors, buttoning the lips of normally garrulous children. In Freud's 1926 account, the mother is both the cause of traumatic anxiety and the figure who can restore meaning and psychic continuity to the child. In Anna Freud's account, infants lose their mothers (they are as the title of her account of her work at the nurseries states *Infants without Families*). It is not just, however, that separation anxiety afflicts these children; it is more the case that object-loss in wartime makes it difficult for them to contain this anxiety within themselves. If the children are frightened of circling planes, it is because they are loaded not only with bombs, but with a potentially explosive freight of infantile anxiety. As Anna Freud notes, in a passage that sounds almost as if it might have been written by Klein, '[w]hen the child has only just learned to curb his own aggressive impulses, he will have real outbreaks of anxiety when enemy bombs come down and do damage around him'.[28] In other words, the children respond to external aggression just as if it were internal aggression – and vice versa. Their bombs come from inside as well as outside: which is what makes their anxiety all the more devastating.

In the summer of 1940 Melanie Klein had made a very similar point. Concerned about the possibility of invasion and of psychoanalysis itself being destroyed, in the hot and turbulent June of that year (France had just fallen, the Battle of Britain was raging), Joan Riviere, one of Klein's most loyal advocates, invited her mentor to speak about the war. What Riviere wants, she says in a letter to Klein, is for her to talk to a small group about the psychological causes and effects of war. Her letter ends with the words 'I am so looking forward to Saturday – psa is a great anodyne in all this anxiety!'[29] In response to this request Klein drafted a paper that was to remain unpublished, 'What Does Death Represent to the Individual?' War, for Klein in this paper, fleshes out the phantasy lives of her analysands in vivid and violent ways. As for Anna Freud's young charges, this reinscription of outside into inside and vice versa can lead to psychic catastrophe. As Klein puts it: 'If the feeling that external war is really going on inside – that an internal Hitler is fought inside by a Hitler-like subject – predominates, then despair results. It is impossible to fight this war, because in the internal situation catastrophe is bound to be the end of it.'[30] But if anxiety 'blitzes' the ego into catastrophe, crucially it is only through anxiety, Klein also argues, that the war-ravaged psyche can overcome its despair. Klein does not simply interpret war anxiety in terms of instinctual anxiety: the historical referent is not subsumed by the ahistory of phantasy; the relation between the two, in this paper at least, is more subtle. The pressure of war anxiety, she says, throws 'light on former material' and hence is also able to 'remove much anxiety and despair'. The only way to remove anxiety, for Klein, is to go through anxiety. Analysts must, she tells her group on that Saturday in June, be constantly mindful of the interplay between the real dangers of the external situation with the internal one and with the past. Anxiety for Klein then, as for Freud, articulates a kind of affective historiography: it looks both forwards and backwards. But in 1940 what is also crucial for Klein is the extent to which anxiety reveals how it is that psychic destinies are predicated upon the lived traumas of the present war. This then is not only the kind of anxiety that traumatizes or 'blitzes' the ego; it is also a kind of anxiety that makes meaning possible as a kind of repetition of the past in anticipation of the future. If Anna Freud's anxious children reveal the extent to which historical traumas are experienced psychically, Melanie Klein's 1940 paper attempts to speak of how it might be possible to live with these traumas, not only in the present, but also in the future.

Twenty years after her analysis of 'Richard', the boy evacuated with Klein in Pitlochry, Klein finally published her epic account of their sessions together, *Narrative of a Child Analysis* (1961). Reputedly the longest case history published in the history of psychoanalysis, it is not only the excessive length of this book that makes it difficult to read (or to contain). On the one hand, it is as if there are too many phantasies emerging in too many different places in the *Narrative*: in the musty village hall where the two meet daily, in their games, in Richard's numerous illnesses and, most graphically, in Richard's extraordinary seventy-four drawings which map out a world in which the mother's body is a kind of ground plan for Richard's war phantasies. There is a claustrophobic feeling about Klein's account of this war-driven phantasy world; as though there is simply too much to fit into her overarching psychoanalytical master-plot. On the other hand, curiously there is nothing menacing about the anxiety represented in these pages; not least because there seems to be nothing left to hide between Richard and Klein. Indeed it is tempting to read the *Narrative* as the unexpurgated nightmare behind 1940s fiction. This is what it really looks like to discover a fascist in the heart of the one you thought you loved more than life itself (Stella's plight in *The Heat of the Day*): here is Richard's drawing of 'Mrs K', with Hitler's eyes looking out from her breasts; his trade-mark moustache at the belt of her skirt, his mouth forming a 'no' between her legs (Figure 1.1). 'Through her', Lacan wrote of Klein, 'we have the cartography, drawn by the children's own hands, of the mother's internal empire.'[31] At the heart of this particular map of darkness is a cartoon Hitler. As John Berger observed of Francis Bacon's paintings from the same period, what is striking about Richard's drawings and Klein's reading of them is not, in fact, the shocking sadism of the phantasies they depict, but the sense that we are operating in a culture where such violence is so readily present. Berger compares Bacon's figures to Disney's, and although Klein, committed filmgoer that she was, doesn't say it, it is surely Disney too who works his way into Richard's maternal phantasies, along with the U-boats, train maps and barrage balloons. Oddly, it is almost as if Klein has generated so

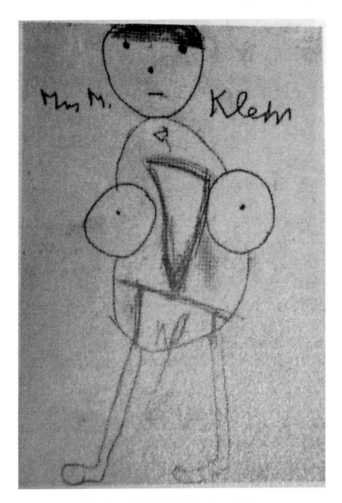

Figure 1.1   Drawing of Melanie Klein by Richard, aged 10

much anxiety in her young analysand, that there is nothing left to get worried about; which is also precisely what is so disturbing about Klein's account of Richard's analysis. A world without anxiety is a terrifying place to be.[32]

This is probably why, however, at other moments in the *Narrative* both Klein and Richard work hard at producing the kind of regenerative anxiety that preoccupied Klein in her unpublished 1940 paper; as a kind of counter-offensive, as it were, against the emergence of a world that has lost the potential for meaning (and against the emergence of what Lacan would call the real). In the forty-fifth session, for example, Richard starts to draw his former home:

> He drew a house and said it was their home (in 'Z') which they had left when the war broke out. The shape on the right was Oliver's house. At the bottom (indicated by a few lines) was the rose-garden and other parts of the garden. He made a dot to show the point on the wall where the bomb had fallen. A square nearby was the greenhouse which had been destroyed. Leading up from the roses to the left he drew a path. On the first floor were his parent's bedroom, to the left his room; on the ground floor the drawing-room which was little used, and to the right the lounge which was much used. Richard said he liked best the lounge and his bedroom, and he put circles round these windows. He liked his room so much because of his electric train which he missed very much and wished it could have been brought to their present house (in 'Y').[33]

This painstakingly careful cartographic return to a home in ruins is beautifully evocative of a sense of loss that runs through narratives of the period. Bowen's characters also frequently give themselves up to reverie in the fallen debris of their former homes; Charley Summers, Henry Green's returning soldier caught in the endless returns of *Back*, rediscovers sexual redemption in the rose garden of a similarly abandoned ruin; while the writer Rose Macaulay will go on to construct a new post-war poetics out of the debris of the City of London.[34] 'We were back in our old house', announces Richard with a piquant melancholy to match the best of the war's elegists. For Klein, predictably, the lost and now re-found house, is also the lost and re-found mother. She interprets quickly, pushing the former site of trauma into a narrative which speaks to Richard's present anxieties: 'the now unprotected, deserted house stood for Mummy, left alone at night and unprotected against the tramp-Daddy, and also for Mrs K. when she was in London and exposed to Hitler's bombs'.[35] Richard's now depressive anxiety, for Klein, allows the ruined house to become a symbol of the mother and of herself. There is a dizzying loss of reference here, as symbols seems to shuttle from past to present; gathering meaning not from what appears to be happening in the world but, increasingly it seems, from each other. Yet within this tight-fit imaginary hermeneutic, Klein also insists, exactly as she did in her unpublished 1940 paper on death, that it is still the 'interplay' between contemporary events and psychic ones that generates the relationship between anxiety and meaning. 'We must remember', she writes in her notes to this session, 'that at the time we were living in constant actual danger.' Richard's narrative is a story not just about a child who acts out his phantasy life through the iconography of war, in a more important sense he is a child who actually 'lives', that is, who gives his ego a form of narrative, through the anxieties of wartime. 'The present session', Klein concludes, 'illustrates my contention that fears of external dangers are intensified by anxieties rising in the earliest stages and that therefore the anxiety aroused by actual dangers can be diminished by analysis.'[36] Knowing that you are homesick for your lost house because you are also passionate about your mother, knowing that you fear for the safety of your analyst because you have learned to love her as though she is your mother, at least makes narrative meaning possible in the place of paralytic inhibition.

More than one commentator has drawn a parallel between the narrative that Richard constructs through his drawings, and the work of modernist painters.[37] In 1945, writing about another modernist painter for whom the relation between fantasy and abstraction was all important, Merleau-Ponty offered the following defence of psychoanalytic interpretation:

The psychoanalyst's hermeneutic musing which multiplies the communications between us and ourselves, which takes sexuality as the symbol of existence and existence as a symbol of sexuality, and which looks in the past for the meaning of the future and in the future for the past, is better suited than rigorous induction to the circular movement of our lives, where the future rests on the past, the past on the future, and where everything symbolizes everything else. Psychoanalysis does not make freedom impossible, it teaches us to think of this freedom concretely, as a creative repetition of ourselves, always, in retrospect, faithful to ourselves.[38]

The artist is Cézanne whose 'schizoid temperament', in Merleau-Ponty's reading, is indistinguishable from his work. According to her French translators, Merleau-Ponty lectured on Klein's work in the 1950s.[39] Merleau-Ponty's immediate reference in this passage is to Freud's famous interpretation of Leonardo da Vinci; but it is not difficult to read here something of what Klein understands about what it might mean to create a 'narrative' for the ego out of the anxiety through which it first goes to meet the world and through which the world leaves its indelible symbolic imprints. To this extent, in his anxiety Richard, like

Anna Freud's troubled evacuees, is a most eloquent historian of his troubled times.

On the other side of the English Channel, a group of six young children were having a very different kind of war from Richard's. Orphaned, some within days of being born, six German-Jewish infants entered the 'Ward for Motherless Children' in Terezin Concentration Camp, Theresienstadt, before they were twelve months old. After the war they were flown in bombers to a reception camp in Windermere, Westmoreland, among the first of the 1000 children to whom the British Home Office had permitted entry. Mindful of the children's close-knit group identity, the authorities decided that they should be kept together for at least a year. So it was that they ended up in Bulldogs Bank, an outer 'colony' of the Hampstead Nurseries, under the watchful eye of Anna Freud. If Richard's narrative gives a sense of what it meant to live through the war, the Terezin children's story is, more poignantly, one of sheer survival. What so impresses Anna Freud about the children, however, is their group behaviour. Unlike most three-year-olds these children are not locked in a constant battle for attention and possession. They share things, they look after one another; the only time they really display any sense of anxiety is when one of their number is absent. They are not, in short, like any other three-year-olds their carers have encountered. Having had, quite literally, no mother to lose in the first place (and no ready mother substitutes in the camp), the children's anxiety has led to a new kind of narrative: as if the group itself is the 'mother', and its threatened dissolution the signal of anxiety. But this is no utopia: although strongly attached to one another, these were, as Anna Freud puts it 'children for whom the object-world had proved disappointing' (only a psychoanalyst, perhaps, would describe early infancy in a Nazi concentration camp in these terms).[40] Where Richard, far away in Scotland, had too many objects to cram into one narrative; the Terezin children, as close to the heart of Nazi violence as it is possible (or bearable) to imagine, have too few objects – and one another.

What all these war children share, however, is a powerful unconscious drive to make new histories emerge out of the debris of their times; to turn anxiety, as it were, into a form of possibility. Like Klein, Anna Freud is curious about the apparent mismatch between historical anxieties and inner ones. Indeed, what intrigues her about the Terezin children is, once more, what might look like an inexplicable indifference to historical violence: 'It remains an unanswered question', she writes of the children, 'why the atmosphere of anxiety and terror in which the children had spent their first years had not predisposed them to more violent anxiety states of their own.'[41] Why weren't the children more crazy? In part, Anna Freud argues, because the camp was so familiar to the children (they had never known anything else), they didn't know there was anything to be objectively anxious about (like being born into a Francis Bacon painting – or a Disney movie): but, by Anna Freud's own admission, the children are 'realistically' anxious – they can't bear the sight of black vans, for instance, dogs or, less explicably, feathers. Neither does Anna Freud's second argument, that because they had no mothers they had no one to 'catch anxiety' from, really work: the children are perfectly capable of infecting one another with their symptoms and inhibitions. Only Anna Freud's final explanation really seems to fit with the evidence she herself gives of the children's behaviour: the children, she says, 'possessed strong defences against anxiety in their close relationship to each other which acted as reassurance and protection'.[42] If Freud's pre-war work on anxiety had located a narrative of the anxious genesis of the ego in a story of primary object-loss, post-war his daughter discovers the contours of a rudimentary socialism in a narrative about the overcoming of anxiety: the most creative possible response under the circumstances, one might think, to a cruelly enforced 'experiment' (Anna Freud's word) in anti-Oedipalism. Some symptoms are more worthwhile than others. Anna Freud would continue to insist that anxiety could be educated: likewise, Klein would never give up the idea that the most significant of anxieties were those buried deep in psychic history. But at the same moment as these two analysts were locked in a public battle about the future of psychoanalysis, off-stage (in the nursery, in the playroom, in private meetings and unpublished papers) what they share is an acutely brilliant sense of how it is possible to live both in and through wartime anxiety. Historians of the traumas of their age, both women testify powerfully to the workings of anxiety at a time of crisis.

***

The fear that the British civilian population would be as shell-shocked as the soldiers of 1914–18 turned out to be unfounded. As Richard M. Titmuss and Tom Harrisson later argued, this was, by and large, an official fear that grossly underestimated the British people.[43] For Harrisson and others, this condescension was compounded by the baleful lack of official and governmental understanding of the kind of social and welfare support needed by a civilian population at war. In this respect Glover's 'No-Neurosis Myth' not only had a wartime propaganda value but was, perhaps, also an important component in that crucial 'myth' of the British people as a collectivity of steadfastly sane survivors who deserved much more in the way of social justice than they had had before the war and certainly more than they got during it. For those concerned with securing the right to social welfare, the kind of psycho-analysis of the Blitz that Edward Glover desired may well have looked (at least in the 1940s) politically inexpedient. Tom Harrisson certainly thought so and in his retrospective account of the work of Mass Obser-vation during the war, *Living Through the Blitz* (1976), he has little time for Glover's psychoanalytic pronouncements.[44]

But does conceding that Britain did have its own anxious history in the late 1930s and early 1940s necessarily strip the period of its political and historical expediencies? What I have begun to suggest in this chapter is that psychoanalysis not only had a part in this history, but also has something important to say about how we represent it to ourselves. In 1926 Freud demonstrated how anxiety was one of the ways in which the subject represented trauma to herself and in so doing he taught us to think of anxiety in concrete terms. Both Anna Freud and Melanie Klein extend this thesis and, in so doing, they also tell a story about how psychoanalysis is shaped by history at the same time as it makes the affects of history visible and interpretable. There do not seem to be any records telling us what happened to R.A. Macdonald's case of persecutory anxiety; so we don't know whether she did light up the blackout and invite in the bombs from the outside so as to allay the anxiety that was bursting in from the inside. If a small part of me wishes that she did, it is not only because of any morbid preference for tragic endings, but because of the way that such a denouement would 'explode' the false distinction between the psychic and the social. Indeed, if this woman's story still affects us now it is perhaps because her exorbitant and melo-dramatic anxiety so evidently resists the privatization of history. In her own way, she too is what we might call an anxious historian.

2
The Childhood of Anxiety

> In time of war you know much more what children feel than in time of peace, not that children feel more but you have to know about what they feel. In time of peace what children feel concerns the lives of the children as children but in time of war there is a mingling there is not children's lives and grown up lives there is just lives and so naturally you have to know what children feel.
>
> Gertrude Stein, *Wars I have Seen*[1]

> Twas the voice of the Wanderer, I heard her exclaim,
> You have weaned me too soon, you must nurse me again,
> She taps as she passes at each window pane,
> Pray, does she not know that she taps in vain?
>
> Stevie Smith, 'The Wanderer'[2]

As we saw in the last chapter, psychoanalytic narratives about childhood anxiety found a new and powerful resonance in wartime. There is also a sense, however, in which children in this period come to represent the childhood *of* anxiety; as if the labours of constituting a world in which the fiction of the ego might at least endure, signalled so poignantly by the psychic trials of the infant, become a sort of working metaphor for the anxiety of trying to imagine a world at war. Writing about how one imagines oneself in wartime, I want to suggest in this chapter, begins to share a vocabulary with descriptions of the effort of imagining oneself as separate, as 'weaned' or, in the most intense historical literalization of separation anxiety in the 1940s, 'evacuated'.

For a few, the nursery became the place where the horrors of civilian-targeted warfare were experienced at their most unbearably intense.

Describing what it felt like to try and comprehend the newly visible violence of the Spanish Civil War while looking after her first baby in her 1984 memoir, *I Meant to Marry Him*, the writer Jean MacGibbon recalled feeling 'a growing stress under the burden of responsibility for world events which we could not influence [...] The stress was like an illness. The pain of Guernica was a bodily pain, one with the pain of weaning.'[3] MacGibbon's 'pain' is indiscriminate – she suffered a breakdown only six years later. Neither can her pain be taken as representative: while we are all to a greater or lesser extent 'weaned', we are not all 'bombed'; there are important differences in the ways it is possible to become lost and helpless in the world. But there is something more than merely unfortunate about MacGibbon's awkward analogy here. Her experience of alienation, of having an affective identification with a history in which she can actually play no part, is rendered all the more moving precisely because it takes place in the nursery. The image is primarily one of pathos: the cries of the newly weaned babe expressing the pain of a first frustrated longing that will go on to define all future pain – 'You have weaned me too soon, you must nurse me again', as Stevie Smith's poem has it. But it also speaks to a sense in which the post-psychoanalytic child – the child of the 1940s and 1950s – starts to carry a perhaps more troubled – and troubling – set of meanings about trauma and imagination in wartime.

I want to begin by looking at some of the images of children that so disturbed MacGibbon and her contemporaries, as a prelude to asking in the second part of this chapter how thinking about children also became a way of thinking about war for psychoanalysis. When the war in Spain 'broke' (her metaphor) into MacGibbon's nursery, it did so on a wave of violent images: 'bloody cobblestones and running gutters [...] civilian life somehow going on [...] air-raids, people sheltering in the Metro, photographs of children's corpses'.[4] These last photographs were not simply one more appalling image among many. Taken after a Nazi raid on Getafe, an airport town just outside of Madrid in 1936, these particular photographs of children occupy a significant place in the history of modern war photography. Among the most horrific photographs from the Spanish Civil War, they were first published in November 1936 in the paper MacGibbon herself delivered, the *Daily Worker* (they were also published in the French paper, *Regards*).[5] Published under the headline, 'Nazi Bomb Kills Seventy Spanish Children', the five photographs taken by the Republicans to identify the children after the raid are juxtaposed with a picture of an English girl playing in her garden. The caption reads: 'She is English. She plays in peace, now. But fascist aggression, unchecked, carries its threat of death for our children too.'[6] As Caroline Brothers points out in her illuminating account of their publication, the photographs were a blatant contravention of the codes governing the representation of death in the British press at the time.[7] Not only were the pictures violently horrible in themselves (the children were 'laid out under numerical labels like laboratory exhibits'[8]), their publication also must have felt like a kind of violation: while some may have imagined a place where the corpses of small children awaited identification by their parents in 1936, one would not have expected to *see* those bodies.

In many respects the anxiety provoked by the Madrid pictures was specific to their medium: these were not just images of dead children, but were what Virginia Woolf at the time called 'pictures of actual facts; photographs'.[9] As Elena Gualtieri has demonstrated, it is quite probable that Woolf was looking at precisely the same photographs as MacGibbon when she made this claim to the veridical power of photography in her classic anti-war essay, *Three Guineas* (1938).[10] Woolf chose not to publish the photographs with her final text, which was instead embellished with images of the vainglorious frippery of the patriarchal institutions which, in Woolf's at the time controversial analysis, make wars happen. These photographs of men in fine frocks and silly hats (judges, soldiers, dons and one bishop) are part of Woolf's argument against war; the missing Madrid photographs, however, are not, which is precisely Woolf's point. 'Photographs, of course', she writes, 'are not arguments addressed to reason; they are simply statements of fact addressed to the eye.'[11] This does not apply to all photographs: what Woolf means is that specific photographs, such as those of the dead children of Getafe, are not arguments; the daft patriarch photographs by contrast are absolutely rhetorical. Woolf does not say why some photographs bypass argument and head straight, as it were, for the nerves: it is as if she doesn't have to, such is their power to shock. As with MacGibbon's, Woolf's response to the photographs is bodily, almost visceral. 'These photographs are not an argument', Woolf repeats, 'they are simply a crude statement of fact addressed to the eye. But the eye is connected with the brain; the brain with the nervous system. That system sends its messages in a flash.' The photographs' sheer indexicality cuts through direct to the nervous system, 'in a flash'. Woolf's language here recalls Freud's famous description of how when consciousness can no longer parry the shock of perceptual unpleasure, the traumatic moment – henceforth classified as a missed moment for consciousness – passes through direct to the unconscious.[12]

For Woolf then we cannot, it seems, hold on to the moment of 'shock'; the discontinuity, or sense of psychic dislocation, prompted by the moment of the photograph returns to us as a kind of lack in ourselves. We falter. We 'fail', as Susan Sontag puts it in her gloss of Woolf's reading of the photographs, 'to hold this reality in mind'.[13] Much of this failure has to do with the specific ontology of the photograph; with the way it seems to offer us, on the one hand, brute reality (Woolf's 'crude statement of fact') and, precisely because of that appearance, generates a profound anxiety about 'reality', about keeping that reality in mind and, indeed, about truth and belief. Describing how the publication of the Getafe photographs eventually undermined their own propaganda value, Brothers notes that while 'the pictures themselves proclaim the reality of their horror – "this really happened, see for yourself" – horror itself invests them with no special veracity with regard to their production; indeed the reader's wish to disavow their contents promotes greater scepticism'.[14] By compelling us to look, the photographs really only tell us that we cannot, in fact, bear to look. But while this kind of disavowal has everything to do with the nature of photography, it is also clear that in order to understand how we look (or fail to look) at these images, as Woolf, MacGibbon and others writing at mid-century knew, we also need to understand who is doing the looking: who are we that can look and not look, hold reality in one part of our mind but disbelieve it in another? Psychoanalysis answers this question with a narrative about the anxious origins of psychic life, of the way, for example, a child cannot even begin to look at the world without, to some extent, substituting fantasy for anxiety.[15] I want to turn to this narrative, particularly to the version that emerged during the late 1930s and 1940s, in the second section of this chapter. For now, I want to dwell on something about the Getafe photographs that seems to have gone unremarked in the literature about them: they are photographs of children.

In some ways it is, of course, completely unnecessary to note that what is particularly horrible about these photographs is the fact that they are of child victims. Nothing is more eviscerating than the image of a dead child, and, for this reason, images of children function readily as a kind of currency for the unspeakable horror of war. Sontag notes that in the 1990s Balkan war the 'same photographs of children killed in the shelling of a village were passed around at both Serb and Croat propaganda briefings. Alter the captions', she notes, 'and the children's deaths could be used and re-used.'[16] It is as if the children die three times: once by shrapnel, twice by the photographs which mark their irreversible absence from the living world, and three times as their photographic images are lifted into rhetoric. Indeed, in the case of the Getafe children the whole point of publishing the photographs was to identify the children precisely *as* victims of fascist aggression. For this to work the pictures had to fall within the genre of photographic realism (even if Brothers is right to suggest that the 'reality' of the photographs might have been so extreme as to provoke disbelief, it still follows that they had to appear real in order to do so). Children occupied a particular place in the emergence of documentary photography in the 1930s, particularly in the United States where images of the starving and damaged children of the depression were central to endeavours such as the Works Project Association, and to the work of photographers such as Helen Levitt and Dorothea Lange. Famously Lange was expelled from the Works Project Association for altering the negative of the image for which she is most famous, her 1936 'Migrant Mother' photograph in which a mother, cradling her baby, an older child resting on her shoulders, looks away from the children, furrowing her brow in exhausted apprehension.[17] As Anne Higonnet explains in her history of child photography, the shocking power of such images did not come solely from their 'reality effects', but from their comparison with culturally dominant images of childhood innocence. 'All along', Higonnet notes, 'positively Romantic photographs of children have made possible negative images capable of evoking pity or outrage. Because the "normal" image of the child was Romantic innocence, and signs of deviation from innocence could be understood as violation.'[18] When the *Daily Worker* published the Getafe photographs next to a photograph of a young English girl playing in her garden, they were making precisely the same point, albeit with a possibly self-defeating lack of subtlety.

The contrast between innocence and its violation, particularly in relation to poverty, had been a familiar staple of representations of children since the late eighteenth century. But there is something particular about the poignancy of photographs of children in the 1930s that disturbs in perhaps newly alerting ways; ways that, I want to speculate here, also have a kind of isomorphic relation to psychoanalytic thinking about childhood itself in this period. To some extent the poignancy of looking at photographs of children is connected with the congruence between the naivety which we assume (albeit wrongly) belongs to both children and photography.[19] Whatever cultural overloading is going on, and it is fairly impossible for an image of a child not to carry some kind of symbolic or iconic value, there is something in photographs of children that touches us – that heads straight to the nervous system, to borrow Woolf's terms. (When in *Camera Lucida* (1980), Roland Barthes elaborated on this something – he called it the *punctum*, 'that accident which pricks me (but also bruises me, is poignant to me)' – it is worth recalling that he was prompted to do so not just by a photograph of his mother, but by an image taken of her when she was a child: Barthes' mother is five in the famous Winter Garden photograph which, like the Getafe photographs in Woolf's essay, was not published with the final text of his memoir.[20])

When we look at images of children, we are not only looking for our own origins (I was that child, or my mother was that child), but for that bit of ourselves that we feel we have lost: hence, in part, the fascination with childhood innocence. That innocence is also laced with a sugaring of lost potential: before I was, there was someone else and, therefore, there was also a person who I might have become, and who I am not now.[21] Fantasies about childhood, about those lost selves, always cling to images of children, but with the advent of popular photography, something in the way we are addressed by images of children starts to shift. While, on the one hand, the proliferation of photographs of children in the mid-twentieth century allows for an expansion in cultural fantasies about childhood – quite simply because there were more images on which to hang these fantasies – at the same time the seemingly stubborn referential nature of the photograph also works to foreclose these fantasies. This, it seems to me, is what is both piquant and anxiety-provoking about the most moving photographs of children from this period; the way they work by exceeding the cultural and representational terms through which children are seen, compelling us to linger, as it were, within the reference of the photograph. Some of the most affecting images of children from the 1930s and 1940s are arresting not just because they show the horror of children caught in war and poverty, but because they disrupt – 'violate' is Higonnet's word for it – both the way we think about children and also, crucially, the way we think about ourselves, particularly as agents of narrative. I think that wartime photographs of children dramatize the way that we cannot keep the reality of what we are looking at in mind, precisely because the frontiers of that 'mind' itself are constantly being violated. They generate anxiety in the place of fantasy.

I want to take a detour into a more detailed reading of some of these photographs (this time of living children) in order to try to think about precisely what kind of anxiety these images of children might have provoked – and, indeed, continue to provoke. There is another famous photograph of a mother with a baby in her arms (this time feeding) and children at her side, from 1936 (probably). Like the mother in Dorothea Lange's photograph, this woman is also furrowing her brow in what looks like anxious apprehension. As with Lange's photograph too, the image is also caught up in a controversy about authenticity.

David Seymour's ('Chim') photograph has been published under several titles: 'Air Raid over Barcelona, 1936' (sometimes 'Air Raid over Barcelona, 1938') and, somewhat less dramatically, 'Land Distribution Meeting. Estramadura, Spain, 1936', and, somewhere between the two, 'A Public Meeting in Estremadura, just prior to the outbreak of the Civil War. Spain, 1936' (Figure 2.1). As Sontag points out, despite this

Figure 2.1 David Seymour ('Chim'), *Land Distribution Meeting, Estremadura, Spain, 1936*

uncertainty about the photograph's specific history, it is possible to confer a retrospective stability on the meanings of the image, precisely because it is so iconic, even emblematic, in terms of its historical moment.[22] By the mid-1940s, images detailing an apprehensive look skywards were as common as, indeed, images of mothers and their children. While representations of motherhood were entangled with mythologies of transcendence through suffering (it was the *pietà* not the nativity that dominated wartime representations of maternal love) and pro-natalist national ideologies, the skyward look captured the awful resonance of an almost total global air war.[23] There is no problem with holding these culturally embedded meanings in mind then; they are a well-known part of the familiar repertoire of twentieth-century historical spectatorship.

But while this familiarity might transcend any quarrels about the photograph's entitlement, there is much in the image that falls out of its iconically representational frame. Two of the children stare not upwards but towards us, creating, as Clive Scott has pointed out, a completely different set of visual priorities from the other people in the photograph.[24] Their gaze, in fact, is far more arresting than that of the apprehensive mother: by looking directly at their photographer they also look at us, making the spectator the reference of the photograph as much as whatever it is that is happening overhead. There is an address in the children's eyes that demands some kind of response. If we think the photograph is of an air-raid, that response is likely to involve some kind of pathos; if we think it is a land distribution meeting, we might be charmed by the children's cheeky disdain for the intricacies of wealth distribution: not knowing exactly where the children are we are left with the demand itself – as though it is we who are being held in the gaze of the children, and not the other way around. Similarly, although the photograph is steeped in the symbolism of motherhood, just where one might expect an indivisible maternal embrace what really catches the eye about the feeding baby is the way that his mouth has fallen off the nipple, whether because the baby has fallen asleep, or because his mother's upward glance has pulled the breast away from him. There is an exquisite intimacy in this detail which – as in the way in which the shadows from his mother give the boy to her right the impression of fading out of the photograph – marks the photograph's utter contingency. Finally, in many reproductions of the photograph, the sleeve on the baby's arm seems to settle itself on his elbow into the profile of a skull, whose ocular cavity gazes emptily at the child into whose body the death-head nuzzles its bony nose. This isn't quite the same as the famous anamorphic ghost of Holbein's *The Ambassadors*, but its weird emergence does put into question the extent to which the meanings of the photograph are within our control.[25] When we start seeing death lurking in the arm of a nursing child, we know that the photograph has taken us far from the protective certainties of fantasy. It is entirely possible, then, to hold this image of Spain in mind so long as we read the photograph within terms that are set largely from outside the actual photograph (the rhetoric of aerial warfare, for example); but because the image insists on being more than that, it is equally possible to find oneself caught within the image itself; held, we might even say, in its 'mind'.

After the war, Chim, who was also one of the founders of the Magnum Photos Group, went on to take a series of photographs of European children for UNESCO. Many of these photographs are historically emblematic in a similar way to the controversial 1936 image. These children, once more, are the generic victims of war: look, the photographs say, at the staring eyes, the ragged clothes, the shorn heads, the ribs; this is what we have done to our children; look at the way they hide in their mothers' skirts, look at the war games they play. At the same time, in some of the most striking images the children obstruct this kind of narrativization. The photograph of 'Terezka' (the caption does not give us her full name), 'a disturbed child in an orphanage', taken in Poland in 1948, is one of the most disconcerting images from this series (Figure 2.2). 'The scrawls on the blackboard are her drawing of "home" ', the caption tells us. By 1948, Terezka's 'home' probably could never be presented in anything other than quotation marks. The drawings on the blackboard may be of what her 'home' looked like as it was being blasted apart by an occupying army, or they might equally be of what it felt like to have your home blasted apart by an occupying army: it is not difficult now, and neither would it have been by the late 1940s, to read what she has drawn on the blackboard as representing what Terezka has been able to hold of her past in some region of her mind. She is 'squiggling', Winnicott might have said.

But while the photograph is clearly *of* a war-traumatized child, what is so remarkable about this image is the way that it also projects its own anxiety onto the viewer. As with the 1936 photograph, Chim's use of distortion is telling here. Cover the right hand half of Terezka's face, and what you see is the face of a wide-eyed innocent child who might even be just about to smile. Cover the left and the image is horribly different: Terezka's brow is furrowed, the shadows cast ageing lines across her face, the pupil of her right eye looks smaller: without the bow, you could be

Figure 2.2   David Seymour ('Chim'), *Terezka, a Disturbed Child in an Orphanage, Poland 1948*; the scrawls on the blackboard are her drawing of 'home'

forgiven for thinking that this face was not that of a child at all (the bow, in terms of its size and exuberance is incongruous in itself). This striking visual effect is caused by lighting and the angle of Chim's camera; but what the photograph thus asks us to do is hold the image of an innocent child *and* a violated child in mind at precisely the same time (in a flash, Woolf might say). Compelled to see innocence and its violation at once, we lose the temporal dimension that would allow us to put the photograph in a chronological narrative (the little English girl playing in the garden *is* innocent; the Getafe children *have been* violated): in effect the photograph asks that we live in the time of the process of the violation itself, in two times, or perhaps in a kind of timelessness better known to the unconscious. But if it is the unconscious that is pricked by Terezka's face, then who – or what – is the image actually addressing? Or rather, how is it possible to be in a position where one *could* be addressed by this photograph?

There are two frames to the photograph, the bleed of the actual image and the blackboard upon which Terezka draws. She is caught between the two frames staring out, most unnervingly, not at the photographer and viewer, but somehow *through* us, as though we are not there. Whereas the gazes of the Estremadura children demanded some kind of response, however hard you try it is actually impossible to meet Terezka's gaze: neither Chim nor the photograph's later readers are, so to speak, 'there' for her. 'I am nobody's nothing', says John, a small melancholic resident in Anna Freud's wartime nursery, and another child for whom 'home' could only ever appear in quotation marks in the 1940s.[26] Terezka's absent gaze says something similar; beyond the pathos of her look there is an even more uncomfortable truth – we are the 'nobody' for whom she is 'nothing'. What is really anxiety-provoking about Terezka's photograph is not just her all-too evident distress, but the way the image also challenges the integrity of the person who is looking at it.

Put in more aggressively psychoanalytic terms, the discontinuity of these photographs of children directly addresses a discontinuity at the core of the person doing the looking. In wartime 'we are ourselves', Freud had written in his famous 1915 essay, 'Thoughts for the Times on War and Death', 'waylaid by the significance of the impressions that overwhelm us'. As Samuel Weber notes, translate Freud's 'we are ourselves waylaid', back in to its original German, and you get an even stronger sense of the depth of this turmoil:

> *Werden wir selbst irre.* Irre means both 'crazy' in common parlance, and, more generally, 'to lose one's bearings, become disorientated'. In German, this state is attributed to a reflexive subject: *wir selbst*. 'We,' the subjects, are not just disorientated by things that are going on outside us, these events make us lose our bearings with respect to ourselves as well.[27]

If the impressions given by children such as Terezka make this disorientation perhaps even more extreme, if they make us feel all the more unnervingly disconsolate, it is not least because part of the strong appeal of images of children rests in the way they speak to that lost part of 'ourselves' (*wir selbst*) which is so significant to our understanding of modern subjectivity. As Carolyn Steedman has provocatively suggested, when Freud theorized childhood, he gave it another name, the unconscious.[28] When that lost object returns to us in a manner which we least expect, in a manner, says Freud, that is totally overwhelming (a 'whirlwind' [*Wirbel*] was how Freud described the collective shock of World War I in the same essay), what is signalled by our anxiety is a very fundamental kind of un-housing of our place in the world. This is what many British psychoanalysts were calling 'separation anxiety' – at precisely the same moment as the photographs from Getafe spilled onto Woolf's desk and onto the pages of the *Daily Worker* – when they tried to describe what it meant to keep your 'home' in mind in a world at war. It is to their version of this story that I want to turn next.

Why is it that images such as those of the dead children of Getafe more often than not defeat their own anti-war propaganda purpose? Propaganda works, wrote the feminist writer, philosopher and Fabian, Amber Blanco White in *The New Propaganda* (1939), by finding objects that justify otherwise irrational anxieties, by, as she puts it, creating a 'consistency between feeling and belief'.[29] Propaganda thus gives us narrative fantasies that rationalize our anxiety: this works well, White argued, for the fascists (there's nothing easier than turning irrational hostility into ideology) but less well for 'left-wing propaganda' which has an unfortunate habit of provoking anxiety and, hence, of evoking a paralysing sense of guilt in the place of where there might be, in White's terms, political outrage or a sense of justified entitlement (more often than not, one might counter, guilt and political outrage are felt at the same time). Nothing, writes White in 1939, plays 'a greater part in what may be called the politics of unreason' than the forces of anxiety and guilt.[30] As for MacGibbon, as well as for many other progressive women who had successfully put childhood onto the political agenda in the first part of the twentieth century, for White the psychopathology of modern political life begins in the nursery – it is to the helplessness of the infant that we must look for our failure to hold the realities of the world in mind. The small boy who howls and hits because his mother refuses him his chocolate, says White, embodies 'a prototype of all dangerous situations': furious yet helpless to deal with what he perceives to be her withdrawal of love, too young to deal with his anxiety and guilt, he projects his hostility onto his mother, an act for which he then feels even more guilty. Unable to tolerate the anxiety which comes with the loss of his love object, the infant is poised to wage his own war of psychic terror on the world – this is the same mechanism, writes White, with that incredible confidence that characterizes early 'applications' of psychoanalysis, that drove the paranoiac madness of Marat.

White's young terrorist replays the plight of baby Rita in Melanie Klein's 1936 essay, 'Weaning', first published in the widely influential collection of essays, edited by John Rickman, *On the Bringing Up of Children* (1936) (no doubt read by Klein's analysand-to-be, MacGibbon, and certainly read by White who is explicit in her debts to Klein and Rickman, as well as to Ernest Jones, Joan Riviere and Karin Stephen). Rita's weaning is traumatic, in Klein's reading, because it confirms the phantasy that she has lost – because she has *destroyed* – her mother (notoriously, the mother in this case was Klein herself). It is not the missing breast that makes this baby anxious, but the thought of what might emerge in its place. Rita has both failed to hold on to the reality of her mother (it is what Klein later calls the 'depressive position' that might reconnect her with that 'reality', such as it is in the Kleinian imaginary) and become entangled in a series of phantasies in which she is attacked both from within and without.[31] When, some twelve years after the 'Weaning' essay, Klein controversially describes anxiety as coming from an unconscious fear of the 'annihilation of life' itself, she is also describing what it feels like when the world seems to return one's own hostility in the form of a persecutory and primitive super-ego. For Klein, then, it is not merely the absence of recognizable objects in the world that makes for anxiety, but the sudden appearance of objects which turn back on the ego itself – challenging it with a lethal combination of fantasy and moral authority (moral authority *as* fantasy). In wartime such objects start to appear with an alarming alacrity: one way, Klein notes, that people dealt with the anxiety 'stirred up by air-raids, bombs, fire, etc', one way people tried to stop themselves going crazy, was by manically denying the war situation itself (Klein's version of the British 'Blitz spirit') – although Jean MacGibbon's experience might suggest that denial was not in fact a bad strategy.[32]

For the Kleinians then it was not a lack of imagination that was the problem when trying to comprehend the horrors of a world at war, but a terrifying *over*-imaginativeness. We do not so much see the atrocious image (or 'hold it in our mind') as witness the return of an object which challenges the fantasies we hold about ourselves. When Klein describes the process of weaning in 1936, like Freud writing about wartime in 1915, she is also giving an account of what it feels like to be waylaid by oneself; to be overwhelmed (or 'violated') not only by the impressions or objects that emerge in a world that, for the unconscious at least, is all too vividly real, but by fantasies that seem no longer to know their place. 'With fantasy', Renata Salecl glosses Lacan in her brilliantly illuminating discussion of contemporary wartime culture, 'the subject creates for him- or herself a protective shield against the lack, while in anxiety the object which emerges in the place of the lack devours the subject – i.e. makes the subject fade.'[33] With fantasy, we can cope with as many atrocity photographs as our war-torn cultural repertoire allows; while in anxiety there is something returned to us in these images which threatens to be completely overwhelming. It is in this sense too, perhaps, that we can say that images such as those of the dead children of Getafe were quite truly anxiety-provoking in 1936.

By June 1937, however, the newly anxiety-provoking experience of looking at pictures of atrocities happening elsewhere was joined by another new affectively-charged historical phenomena: the arrival in Britain of children from the Basque country, the first evacuees in a period that was soon to be haunted by images of displaced, war-torn children (such as, ten years later, Chim's Terezka). 'These children', MacGibbon wrote in her 1984 memoir, 'had been exposed to traumatic experiences which, today, is the lot of a majority of the world's children. At the time', however, she notes 'the full terrible truth of what had happened to them was new, at least to us.'[34] Arguably, what was also new was the idea of psychically, as well as physically, traumatized children (MacGibbon describes how some of the children 'went wild with grief' when they heard about the fall of Bilbao). In her contribution to Rickman's *On the Bringing Up of Children*, Susan Isaacs had urged her readers to acknowledge what at the time was largely unacknowledged, that small children can indeed be traumatized by what happens to them (precisely because, Isaacs argues, of the violence of their own emotional worlds).[35] One year later, here they were, the traumatized children, spilling out of buses in south London. By the time Britain began to evacuate its own children from major cities into the countryside, for psychoanalysis at least, 'the pain of weaning', the anxiety of separation, was furnished with a historical signifier that was to transform the social and political standing of psychoanalysis in Britain.

With the evacuation, Blanco White's chocolate-deprived howling child, baby Rita's wretched sense of persecution, the separating and weaning of children that had figured in psychoanalytic literature since the late 1920s, were no longer 'prototypical' anxiety cases; in the 1940s they became the embodiment of anxiety itself. And not only for psychoanalysis: the evacuation of what one estimate put at 734,883 children, was an 'experiment' that made the figure of the war-traumatized child newly visible for a culture that was rapidly having to get used to the idea that the small English girl playing in the garden pictured in the *Daily Worker* might well be the next target of fascist aggression; having to get used, that is, to the idea that 'home', with all its vexed political and historical connotations, was no longer inviolate (if it ever was).[36] For many psychoanalysts involved in the evacuation, notably Donald Winnicott and John Bowlby, the experiment was a bad one. Writing to the *British Medical Journal* in 1939, Winnicott, Bowlby and Emanuel Miller warned that the experience of separation 'in fact can amount to an emotional "blackout", and can easily lead to a severe disturbance in the development of the personality which may persist throughout life'.[37] 'For me, any success the scheme can claim', Winnicott noted bitterly in 1941, 'is that it could fail.'[38] The evacuation forced a kind of untimeliness on these children who by being separated from their mothers were also, most analysts agreed, 'weaned' too soon: ' "War" ' wrote Anna Freud of her nursery children, 'above everything else signifies the period of time for which children have to be separated from their parents.'[39] War, that is, signifies not so much trauma as a shock or breach to the psyche, but trauma as untimely separation. Too young to mourn for the loss of their parents, the children are unable – and the phrase is used again and again in this literature – to hold the reality of the absent parent in mind; 'the younger the child the less his ability to keep the idea of a person alive in himself', Winnicott writes in 1940.[40]

On the one hand, psychoanalysis in this period takes what might look like a somewhat un-psychoanalytic turn: famously, Bowlby, and to a lesser degree, Winnicott, began to insist on 'environmental trauma', that is, on a kind of 'reality' of object-loss that the evacuation seemed to dramatize all too vividly. At the same time, however, the kind of anxiety I have been trying to describe in this chapter, the anxiety that comes not so much from literal separation from a loved object, as that which takes over when the world seems to slip its imaginary moorings, re-emerges in descriptions of these brutally un-housed children. Thus Carol from Anna Freud's nursery, who

would at first let herself be fondled or held only by an unseen person. She would sit on somebody's lap, turn her head away, enjoy the familiar sensation of being held, and probably added to it in her own mind the imaginary picture of her own mother. Whenever she looked at the face of the person who held her, she began to cry.[41]

The point here is not that the return of Carol's real mother would end her torment; like the children who Anna Freud also describes as staring at their mothers with 'stony indifference', but who greet 'lifeless objects' from their past with joyful recognition, Carol is fending off anxiety by keeping 'imaginary pictures' in her mind. What is particularly anxiety-provoking about being away from home in wartime is the way these imaginary frames of reference cease to provide a way for these children to be in the world. Winnicott gives one of the most poignant descriptions of this kind of un-housing in a radio broadcast given at the end of the war:

> It is one thing for a child at home to fight battles round the whole of the house, and then at one o'clock to go in and have dinner. It is another thing to stand on one's head in the street for the pleasure of seeing your house upside down before turning in, and it is quite another to be two hundred miles away, feeling convinced the house is on fire or falling to pieces.[42]

It is one thing to have fantasies about your home as long as you are in it; and it is a joyous thing to be able to turn that home upside down just for the sheer hell of it; but if you are too young to keep that home in your mind, to take it with you as you go, what once looked like home is not so much held by fantasy, as devoured by it.

For writers such as Blanco White, MacGibbon, Klein and Winnicott, then, the anxiety of the separated – 'weaned', 'evacuated', 'displaced' – child was the most meaningful place to begin to understand the psychopathology of living in wartime. For the children they wrote about, the pain of weaning was very precisely 'at one' with the pain of trying to hold the image of a world at war in mind. But the figure of the evacuated child in this period does something more than provide justification for a theoretical analogy, whatever the historical force of that analogy. In the first part of this chapter, I argued that photographs of children from this period had a way of projecting the anxiety they represented back onto the viewer. The child victims in these photographs are not just images of pathos, but figures which embody an anxiety that, perhaps, is always threatening to engulf us when we try and hold the reality of wartime in mind: Terezka in Chim's photograph, like John in Anna Freud's nursery, is not just a 'nothing', a small child whose eerie vacancy is testimony to the brutality of war, she is a 'nobody's nothing'. The traumatized children of the late 1930s and 1940s speak to an anxiety – maybe we could even say that they became symbols of an anxiety – about what it means to exist at all in wartime. This, I think, takes us to a much darker place than perhaps is usually allowed when we think about representations of childhood and war.

Quite how dark this place can be is glimpsed in one of Winnicott's most famous and controversial papers, first read to the British Psycho-Analytical Society in early 1947, 'Hate in the Countertransference'. The anxiety that most concerns Winnicott in this paper is psychotic anxiety. As he describes in his interpretation of a dream of his own in which he has no right-hand side of his body, this is the anxiety that is generated by the psychotic who demands that his or her analyst supply an early environment that was totally lacking in infancy: thus, Winnicott's patient demands that he has no body, because she hasn't got one either; what she needs is for their two minds to communicate alone. In this kind of anxiety the analyst can find himself devoured by his patient which is partly why, Winnicott argues daringly, the analyst also needs to know what to do with his own hate. For Winnicott it is not unreasonable to resent someone for insisting you mirror their craziness; and nor is it a bad therapeutic aim for a person to understand that their behaviour is loathsome. For the psychotic in analysis, as for the child learning what is real to it through fantasy, what needs to be returned is not more psychotic anxiety (what use is an analyst with only half a body?), but what Winnicott calls 'objectivity' or, more precisely, 'objective hate'. 'If the patient seeks objective or justified hate he must be able to reach it', urges Winnicott, 'else he cannot feel he can reach objective love.'[43]

But at the centre of Winnicott's account is another evacuee; a nine-year-old boy who had been sent to one of the hostels Winnicott was overseeing in his position as Consultant Psychiatrist to the Government Evacuation Scheme, not because of the bombs, but because of his repeated truancy. When he turns up at a police station near Winnicott's home, his wife takes him in for 'three months of hell'. 'He was', writes Winnicott, 'the most lovable and most maddening of children, often stark staring mad.'[44] What the child needed, argues Winnicott, was not just a loving home; what this stark staring mad little boy needed was to be objectively hated, as Winnicott describes vividly in what I think is one of the most unnerving pieces of writing in psychoanalytic literature:

> Did I hit him? The answer is no, I never hit. But I should have had to have done so if I had not known all about my hate and if I had not let him know about it too. At crises I would take him by bodily

strength, without anger or blame, and put him outside the front door, whatever the weather or the time of day or night. There was a special bell he could ring, and he knew that if he rang it he would be re-admitted and no word said about the past. He used this bell as soon as he had recovered from his maniacal attack.

The important thing is that each time, just as I put him outside the door, I told him something; I said that what had happened had made me hate him. This was easy because it was so true.[45]

What is disturbing about this scene is surely not just the idea that one can, or indeed that sometimes one should, hate a child, albeit granted that Winnicott's frank anti-sentimentality is pretty shocking. For me this image of a nine-year-old boy being repeatedly put out the door, 'whatever the weather', is upsetting because it seems to repeatedly, and achingly calmly, replay a trauma in which adult and child are both at the very edge of craziness. By telling the boy that he hates him, it may well be true that Winnicott is returning to the boy some kind of certainty about his self, hateful bits and all; but in the chilling way he describes the gesture ('This was easy because it was true') it is almost as if Winnicott is putting the boy outside of himself again and again, as if the only way one can stop oneself being as crazy as a child in wartime, the only way to stop oneself being irreversibly waylaid, is to keep on putting him on the doorstep – to keep on, as it were, evacuating him. Whose psychotic anxiety are we actually dealing with here? 'In time of war', wrote Gertrude Stein in the quote with which I opened this chapter, 'you know much more what children feel than in time of peace.' It is also possible, as Winnicott seems to demonstrate here, to feel as if you know *too* much of what children feel in wartime. Indeed, perhaps what Winnicott calls his 'hate' for this nine-year-old boy is also the point at which one can no longer tolerate keeping the realities of other people's pain, and other people's separations, in mind.

In a recent essay on the preoccupation with childhood in the fiction of writers who first published just after the war, N.H Reeve has written of the way in which children became vehicles for understanding the psychical and existential meanings of conflict. Childhood, Reeve argues, emerges not just as a 'symbol for whatever has been torn away or cast adrift, but as a condition of being and responding in which event, idea and sensation are only dimly distinguishable'.[46] Reeve's emphasis is on the way that post-war fictions use children to picture the 'perplexingly excessive immediacy' of the very recent past, but as I have tried to suggest here, children had started to become figures for wartime anxiety as early as the Spanish Civil War. In a fascinating discussion of an early short story by Elizabeth Taylor, Reeve presents a scenario which could almost function as a kind of dark post-war literary codicil to the *Daily Worker*'s juxtaposition of the dead children of Getafe and a small English girl playing in her garden. 'A Sad Garden', first published in 1945 as 'Study', as Reeve notes, does not directly evoke the war but it is deeply implicated in a heavily oppressive sense of bereavement and pain. Sybil has lost both her husband and young son, Adam, and is visited in her autumnal garden ('filled with the smell of rotting fruit'[47]), by her sister, Katy, and niece, Audrey. Prim Audrey is no match for her vibrantly wicked dead cousin (when Sybil recalls smacking Adam for gouging out his initials on the garden bench, she remembers how 'he had stared at her in hatred, wild, beautiful, a stain on his mouth from the blackberries'[48]). As Audrey plays on Adam's old swing, Sybil begins to push her with a steadily mounting sense of menace: 'I'd push him out into the world. Push him!', she thinks, recalling Adam's shouts, his 'wickedness and devilry':

> She gave a vehemence to her thought and Audrey with her hair streaming among the branches flew dizzily away. Frantically now her aunt pushed her, crying 'There you go. There you go.'
> The child, whiter than ever, was unable to speak. She sensed something terribly wrong, and yet something which was inevitable and not surprising. Each time she dropped to earth, a wave of darkness hit her face and then she would fly up again in a wild agony. A strand of hair caught in some twigs and was torn from her head.
> Sybil stood squarely on the grass. As the swing came down, she put up her hand and with the tips of her fingers, and yet with all her strength, she pushed. She had lost consciousness and control and cried out each time exultingly:
> 'There you go. There you go' – until all her body was trembling.[49]

'There you go'/'I said what had happened had made me hate him': in Taylor's short story the violence implicit in Winnicott's endless putting his evacuee out of the door erupts. 'There you go' – what primitive, explosive feelings does the aunt send up into the sky with the terrified girl? Caught in a cycle of expulsion and return, Audrey and her aunt's demented grief are figures for a trauma that even the sharp intensity of Taylor's prose has trouble containing. 'In a space of a few words', Reeve writes of this scene, 'we seem to swing from childhood and puberty to wartime loss and grief and back again, in the experience of being seized by an overwhelming force and having no option but to cling on and ride with it until it settles.'[50] A whirlwind, recall, was how Freud had described a similarly 'overwhelming force' in 1915. In 1940s Britain, it was not whirlwinds, but children who came to figure this potentially calamitous anxiety about the frontiers of the mind.

I want to end with one more child evacuee, again from Taylor's fiction. In 'Plenty Good Fiesta', collected in *Hester Lilly and Other Stories* along with 'A Sad Garden', Fernando, a refugee from the war in Spain, comes to stay with the narrator's family after having been teased because of his 'nervous habits' by other children in the nearby refugee camp. With his bag of donated girl's underwear, a Fair Isle jersey and a pair of heavy borrowed boots, Fernando has, says his host, achieved a 'jaunty gaiety to cover up his naturally clinging disposition'.[51] At a local fête (the 'fiesta' of the title), Fernando's gaiety finds overdetermined expression as he rides on a bicycle on an (aptly named in this instance) merry-go-round. Once more, as with so many of the images of children that I have been tracking in this chapter, there is a pathos in Taylor's description of the incongruities of the innocent in wartime. Taylor's narrator opens the passage with a scene that could be describing one of Chim's UNESCO photographs:

> I think that one of the most touching things I have read about a war was by Gertrude Stein who remarked how the look of her French village altered in 1939. The elder brothers and the fathers went off to the front, and suddenly the lanes were full of little boys riding bicycles too big for them, standing on the pedals, their elbows in the air. I do not know if Fernando's brother [who had been killed by the fascists] had a bicycle and there was not the same brief period of riding it, but it was now revealed to us that the great force and passion of Fernando's life was to own one [...] Ignoring the rest of the fair, he made for the children's roundabout, where, among peacocks, racing cars, airplanes, and gilded horses, he could see a stationary bicycle with moveable pedals.

But as the roundabout gains speed, Fernando gives himself up to his fantasy ride. Furiously pedalling nowhere, Fernando stays in one place, but also moves somewhere pointedly out of the imaginative reach of the watching adults:

At first Fernando waved as he passed us, but later forgot. He gazed into the distance pedalling rapidly, grave, absorbed. His eyes narrowed, and leant to an imagined camber of the road.

What distances in Catalonia, we wondered, did he cover? What goal achieve? Sometimes, impatiently, because of fool drivers, he rang the bell, sometimes seemed to stiffen his whole body, bear down on the pedals, braking for unseen obstacles, though the roundabout took him merrily on [...]

Each time the roundabout ran down, the bronchial music wheezed off into a trailing sigh, he would hand in another penny in a peremptory, irritable way, checked in his dream, and sit steady, tense, waiting. Once, catching my eye, he looked quickly aside, as if the sight of me violated his privacy.[52]

The haunting repetitiveness of Fernando's roundabout ride speaks to a trauma that can only be registered in its belated effects. But there is also something else particularly striking about this child as he spins round and round, curiously at one with the mechanized rhythm of the roundabout. Fernando exists intact *in* his dream. 'Once', writes Taylor's narrator, 'catching my eye, he looked quickly aside, as if the sight of me violated his privacy': note that it is 'the sight of *me*', the onlooker, the witness to Fernando's story (his 'pain'), who has 'violated [Taylor's word this time] his privacy'. Like the children in some of Chim's photographs, Fernando keeps his own, weirdly vacant but nonetheless powerfully challenging integrity by returning the gaze of the adult; it is the image of the onlooker herself that is being rebuffed; it is her presence that is threatening Fernando's new-found propriety. Who is the more anxious here? Fernando, staying so doggedly, so joyfully, in his dream as he circles around? Or those of us who watch, with Taylor's narrator, this small whirlwind as he passes through a dilapidated English fairground, we ourselves who are the unwelcome and unreal figures for a small boy intent on pedalling his bicycle?

***

There is a scene that recalls Fernando on his bicycle in the 1947 film, *Hue and Cry* (directed by Charles Crichton).[53] The first 'Ealing Comedy', *Hue and Cry* is a schoolboy romp crossed with a campy noire-ish detective story. It is a funny film, with a strongly authentic period flavour. The menace of the immediate war years, however, persists through Crichton's striking use of the bombed-out landscape of post-war London. Frequently shot from either above – looking down, for example, into bomb craters and smashed up ceilings – or from below – looking up through the lattice of beams and rubble to the now clear skies – the film's frequent scenes of ruin and debris evoke a strong sense of vertigo. In one such scene a small boy is filmed from below, sitting atop the rubble, against a vast expanse of sky. He is playing war games: ack, ack, ack, he goes, parroting the anti-aircraft fire that once punctured London's nights. Vroom – another plane swishes down across the sky. The scene disturbs precisely because of the proximity of the boy's play to a form of traumatic repetition: is he playing or is he somehow possessed by the recent past? ' "Go to the fwont!" ', Freud reported his grandson saying furiously as he threw his toys – and so his soldier father – away in the first war.[54] By the end of the second in much of Europe the 'fwont' had come home; leaving the children to play beyond the pleasure principle in the blasted debris of their former homes.

By the mid-1940s children's war games had become a common trope for registering the psychic fallout of war. The war craziness of children, after all and in all its pathos is preferable to the spectacle of fully-blown adult psychosis. The anxiety of children is understandable because they are so clearly stuck in a situation that they cannot comprehend. Adult helplessness – the helplessness of political identification without political agency – is more troubling. This might be why, as I have tried to argue in the first section of this book, psychoanalysis turned to the figure of the child in the 1930s and 1940s to find a model of a situation in which the world is unmanageable. Indeed there is perhaps a sense in which it possible to claim that in this period at least, all babies were to some extent war babies.

The war babies grew up to be war delinquents. *Hue and Cry* was one of the first representations of the youth gangs that were to irritate the popular cultural imaginary of post-war Britain and fascinate its psychoanalysts and new sociologists. By the late 1940s and early 1950s the lawlessness of youth had become a metaphor for the largely unacknowledged lawlessness of the war that had just passed. But as they hover between, so to speak, craziness and history, Crichton's boy playing on the rubble, like Taylor's boy on the roundabout, are more than just symbols for the anxiety of wartime. Running the past into the future, both boys disclose something of what it might mean to find a way of being in history without being subsumed by it. We can also read them, that is, not only as embodying the persistence of trauma in the madness of their games, but as back-pedalling into the past so as to keep the future possible. In the next two chapters, I examine what this kind of 'dreading forward' in the vertiginous spaces of wartime Britain meant for literature and art.

3
Bombs and Roses: the Writing of Anxiety in Henry Green's *Caught*

(The firemen saw each other's faces. They saw the water below a dirty yellow towards the fire; the wharves on that far side low and black, those on the bank they were leaving a pretty rose [...] They sat very still, beneath the immensity. For, against it, warehouses, small towers, puny steeples seemed alive with sparks from the mile high pandemonium of flame reflected in the quaking sky. This fan, a roaring red gold, pulsed rose at the outside edge, the perimeter round which the heavens, set with stars before fading into utter blackness, were for a space a trembling green.)

Henry Green, *Caught*[1]

War, she thought, is sex.

Henry Green, *Caught* (119)

Roses are not generally thought to be objects of anxiety. They are objects of desire, or perhaps sometimes objects that arrest desire by their invitation to aesthetic contemplation, but only for the phobic could a rose really be said to be an occasion for dread. Writing during World War II, Henry Green ('a trembling green') suggests otherwise. In this description of the London Blitz from his 1943 novel, *Caught*, everything comes up roses. First among literary clichés, roses lend themselves to this kind of effusive figurative estrangement, and Green is certainly by no means the only British writer in World War II to note that the fire and the rose are one.[2] In *Caught*, however, Green's roses wreathe desire and dread together so tightly that the psychoanalytic cliché – war is sex – snaps back into the tautology that Freud, perhaps, always intended.

The idea that war could be sex was also the scandal of Freud's theory of the traumatic neurosis during World War I. When the psychiatric casualties from that war limped into the history of psychiatry, although many began to accept Freud's theory of the unconscious, the idea that sexuality might have a role to play in trauma was roundly rejected. Only a desexualized version of psychoanalysis was admitted into the field hospitals and officers' convalescent homes that sprung up in upper-class houses all over Britain. One of these was Green's childhood home which, he later said, like the homes of many of the over-privileged, opened up its doors to the wounded and traumatized in a calculated act of class preservation.[3] One does not have to think too hard to appreciate why, for some at least, it was preferable to see these torn and shocked bodies as seized by a dreadful – but after all perfectly understandable – fear in the face of war, rather than gripped with a less comprehensible anxiety that carried with it a dangerous and potentially lethal sexual charge.

But from a psychoanalytic perspective, the antagonism of sexuality and sexual difference is right at the heart of trauma, and this, especially in the recent alliance of psychoanalysis and history, necessarily causes some cultural and critical awkwardness. One of the strengths of contemporary trauma theory lies in its articulation of a nuanced and subtle historicity, read through both psychoanalysis and literature, which allows the humanities to reconnect with historical violence, without (supposedly) falling into the pitfalls of a naive historicism.[4] The awkwardness comes because sexual antagonism is both clearly historical (the violence is well documented) *and* structurally necessary to psychoanalytic theories of trauma. The two, the historical and the psychic, are clearly not analogues, but they remain stubbornly and infuriatingly intertwined in complicated ways.[5] Faced with this theoretical tangle, two options present themselves. The first is to privilege historical trauma over sexual trauma. In this version, trauma theory uses psychoanalysis to provide an account of the multiple difficulties of historical representation while escaping the age-old accusation of sexual determination. War, thus, is not (only) sex. The second is to insist again on the structural necessity of sexuality and, in particular, of sexual difference, not as the ahistorical referent that lurks beyond representation but, as Slavoj Žižek puts it, as the 'very obstacle' to symbolization and representation.[6] This approach has the distinct virtue of keeping sex in trauma theory and of insisting that the labours of historicity will always, de facto, be a matter of sexuality in some form. War, thus, is (still) sex. But what kind of sex is war? Is the kind of sexual antagonism that causes us to stumble over the representation of historical trauma always and invariably the same? Not so much ahistorical as unhistoricizable?

In this chapter, I want to approach some of these questions by taking a step back to the London Blitz and to Henry Green's novel, *Caught*, written in the early stages of the war. War both threatens and provokes narrative. It threatens, as Walter Benjamin pointed out famously, because it degrades experience to the extent that narrative communication itself is thrown into crisis; and it provokes for precisely the same reason.[7] Silence from the writer during wartime, thus, is often less a sign of pious reticence and more a mute token of exasperated difficulty. Not so for Green, who wrote three novels during World War II.[8] A writer who insisted from his schooldays until his death that art was emphatically *not* about representation, Green was one of the handful of British writers during the war to risk an encounter with the limits of the novel form.[9] Fascinated by the misheard, the unspoken and the oblique (his word), Green is a trauma writer not before, but very much of his time. He is so, foremost, because like those of other modernist writers, Green's novels are not so much monuments to historical consciousness, as poetic elegies to historical unconsciousness. It is precisely what cannot be consciously realized in wartime that attracts Green; and it is from the wounds in time and experience – anxiety, death and sex – that his writing draws its understated power. Green's writing, however, is in no sense some pained lament to the inexpressible; what is registered as traumatic in his work is also, and often exuberantly, erotically charged. War – bizarrely, achingly, stupidly – is sex, not just for the inappropriately named Prudence from *Caught* (from whom I quote above) but for Green too. To this extent, Green offers us an opportunity to consider how it is that there can be no trauma writing that isn't caught up with sexuality; and how it might be – and this is perhaps a more difficult proposition – that it is precisely what appears so non-historicizable about sexuality (as drive not gender) that becomes the precondition for a way back into history amidst the rubble of the Blitz.

I

It has become something of a commonplace to note that war is a threat to narrative memory. Anxiously waiting for war, however, is another matter. In his autobiography, *Pack My Bag* (1940), written in the crazy days of the Munich Crisis, Green notes: 'there must be threat to one's skin to wake what is left of things remembered into things to die with'.[10] To anticipate death in the company of one's memories is, at least, to have something to give form and place to what otherwise would be the nowhere of anxiety. But, as Green observes, such memories are not just cushions of existential support; in shock we awaken memories from yesterday so that we can die with them tomorrow. The past runs into the unthinkable future; narrative chronology gives way to an anxious historicity: '*a rose blossoming into a bud*' (emphasis in original) is how Maurice Blanchot later describes it.[11] This anxious historicity is the thematic and structural principle of *Caught*. Conscripts to the defence of the Home Front, Green's auxiliary and regular firemen, cooks and members of the ARP (air-raid precaution) are caught in the interminably anxious time that came to be known as the 'Phoney War'. This was the irreal space between the declaration of war and the first air-raids on Britain between the autumn of 1939 and the summer of 1940. The lines of civil defence were drawn up in Britain's major cities and the papier-mâché coffins for the anticipated thousands of air-raid victims were made to order: for ten months the civilian population looked to the sky, but still the bombs did not fall; whilst from the east and south the relentless destruction and Nazification of Europe moved closer. It is, writes Green in his frontispiece to the novel, 'the effect of that time that I have written into the fiction of *Caught*'.

For the novel's two central characters, the working-class, newly promoted Fire Station Officer Pye, and the middle-class, volunteer auxiliary fireman Roe, the effect of that time of waiting is the incursion of the past into the anxious present. Both are caught by memories – memories of incest, in the case of Pye ('I got a fit of rememberin' back' [166]), and for Roe, of the death of his wife and the abduction of his son ('absorbed by what was left to him of the sights and sounds' [63]) – that flare up in the text in intense and vivid image-clusters. It is these persistent image memories that come to index the horror of the future, barely disguised in the two characters' much noted anagrammatical py(e)ro(e)technic coupling in the technological hellfire that was the London Blitz – narrated only twice in the entire novel. To write 'the effect of that time', hence, is not to be understood as producing an epic account of how war affects people, but as a way of registering the effects of a suffocating national historicity. One must look to the montage techniques of a film such as Humphrey Jennings's *Fires Were Started* (1942) and perhaps not, say, to the wholly successful tragi-pathos of *Mrs Miniver* (1942) to find the visual equivalent of Green's literary practice. *Caught*, then, is not only a psychoanalytically-informed genealogy of trauma, an exploration of the belated effects of the past upon the present lives of war-anxious characters who are all, in their way, markedly different neurotic 'types'.

It is also a text which, in the tradition that Benjamin associated with Baudelaire and Proust, gives poetic form and shape to the trauma, not of the told, but of the telling.[12]

How can one tell an anxious historicity? What does it take to imagine a rose blossoming into a bud? A passage towards the end of the novel suggests how (and what it might take), and is worth looking at in some detail, not only because it hints at how *Caught* might be read, but also because it prompts certain questions about that reading. On sick leave, recovering from the effects of the first London Blitz ('A bomb came too close. It knocked him out [...] They called it nervous debility' [172]), Roe tries to explain to his evacuated sister-in-law, Dy, what it's like to live through a Blitz:

> 'I never felt so alone in all my life. Our taxi was like a pink beetle drawing a pepper corn. We were specks. Everything is so different always from what you expect, and this was fantastic. Of course, we couldn't hear for the noise of the engine, and we had shut the windows so as to get more inside [...] Yet I suppose it was not like that at all really. One changes everything after by going over it.'
>
> 'But the real thing', she said, getting her teeth into this, for she liked arguments, and the bit about the beetle had drawn her attention because she thought it vivid, 'the real thing is the picture you carry in your eye afterwards, surely? It can't be what you can't remember can it?'
>
> 'I don't know,' he said, 'only the point about a blitz is this, there's always something you can't describe, and it's not the blitz alone that's true of. Ever since it happened I feel I've been trying to express all sorts of things.'
>
> 'I expect that's the result of your being blown up.'
>
> 'No,' he said, exasperated suddenly, 'there's an old fault of yours, you're always trying to explain difficult things prosaically.'
>
> 'What's prosaically?' she asked. She did not understand. (179–80)

This quarrel will be familiar to anyone who has attempted to track debates within trauma theory. Dy wants a referential theory of experience, Roe replies that the point about traumatic experience is that it is *not* something that can be immediately understood.[13] Dy clings to the idea that the 'real thing' is the perceptual photographic picture 'that you carry in your eye' after the event; for her, Roe's problems with expression are the predictable outcome of the mechanical violence of shock ('I expect that's the result of your being blown up'). But for Roe, the image – far from being a handy retinal mnemonic imprint awaiting later development – was compromised to begin with. It is not only that 'one changes everything by going over it'; just before this exchange, Roe has already explained that to witness an event is not to have any unmediated access to the 'real thing': 'one's imagination is so literary', it is 'more like a film, or that's what it seems like at the time' (174). This common modernist complaint about the already-written nature of experience opens up a place for a kind of writing that traces the residues and negatives of that experience; a writing that begins with what 'you can't remember' and 'what you can't describe'. For, the point about a blitz – and the point about trauma – is that it marks the difficulty of catching 'the real thing' within the limits of whatever representational means are at hand, in this case, the filmic and the literary. This much is as familiar to contemporary trauma theory as it is to modernism and psychoanalysis. But why (to ask perhaps a prosaic question) is it a woman who gets to play the naive referential historicist here? How come it is she who can't get the point about the eloquent historicity of the unspeakable in trauma?

One would indeed have to be literal-minded to miss the point that it is precisely the filmic image ('We were specks') and the literary imagination ('Our taxi was like a pink beetle drawing a peppercorn'), or the 'vivid' parts of Roe's account, that draw Dy's attention in the first place. Both accounts of the Blitz in *Caught* are similarly vivid rosy colour-fields; the burning London docks, for instance, are 'a mosaic aglow with rose' (181). It is the intensive build-up of colour words that gives the text, and the war, its erotic charge. It would have been better, the narrator notes at one point, for the Admiral grey fire engines to have been painted 'pink, a boudoir shade, to match that half light which was to settle, night after night, around the larger conflagrations' (149). In this, it is not only the Blitz that is a mosaic of rose, but *Caught* itself. Green (a chosen pen name) was by no means the only modern writer to fold experience into chromatic pockets.[14] Freud had already suggested that while 'the linear outlines like those in a drawing or in a primitive painting' cannot do justice to the characteristics of the mind, 'areas of colour melting into one another as they are presented by modern artists' can.[15] Benjamin too, as Howard Caygill has demonstrated, looked to 'chromatic infinity' as an internal limit point within the modern organization of experience.[16] Green shares Benjamin's fascination with word and image and with the distinction between colour in painting and colour in fantasy. He shares with Freud the idea that chromatic melting can index the non-temporality of the unconscious and, by implication, of unconscious desire – which is why Green's roses can, within the same verbal space, light up the horror of a blitz and turn boudoir pink. What I referred to earlier as an anxious historicity emerges in *Caught* as a chromatic montage that flowers into the text at periodic intervals, turning narrative time into erotic space. But what has such brilliantly chromatic montage got to do with prosaic women?

Where contemporary trauma theory is concerned, in Cathy Caruth's phrase, with 'permitting history to arise where immediate understanding may not'[17] (another version of the eloquent historicity of trauma) in Green's writing women arise where history cannot (eloquence purchased at a gendered price). Female flesh, as translucent as a rose petal, stretches over the absence of historical experience. To be 'caught' in anxious expectation, to wait for war, is to flesh out the gaps in 'immediate understanding' with a fantasy of sexual difference. In this sense Roe is not only the sophisticated theorist of the unspeakable in trauma, he is also something of a fetishist. Roe supplements the threat to his skin, the aching 'dreading forward' towards a war which stubbornly refuses to unfurl into an event, with graphically *imagistic* memories of his dead wife.[18] He 'could not keep his hands off her in memory [. . .] the touch of her rose petal skin' (33). Like a fetishist, Roe substitutes over-evaluation for absence. He also has a penchant for the banality of the sexual, as well as of the literary cliché. Lawrentian passages dehisce into exuberant profusions of roses:

> he thought he saw the hot, lazy luxuriance of a rose, the heavy, weightless, luxuriance of a rose, the curling disclosure of the heart of a rose that, as for a hornet, was his for its honey, for the asking, open for him to pierce inside, this heavy, creamy girl turned woman [. . .] the opulence his darling had carried about in her skin, sheathed for his display to his sense, in the exuberance of his mother's garden. Her bare legs had been the colour of the white roses about them, the red toenails, through her sandals, stood out against fallen rose leaves of a red that clashed with the enamel she used, the brick paths had been fresh, not stained, as the walls here, by soot-saturated rain. (65)

This is less Rilke colour-musing with Cézanne than Green giving a literary reply to the thick brushstrokes, the rich build-up of oil on canvas, of his friend, and at the time his rival in love, the painter Matthew Smith.[19] Just as in Smith's paintings from this period, where a thickly expressive surface texture lights up the colours of his series of paintings of women accompanied, in various ways, by their metonymical roses,

here too perceptual mimesis is arrested by opulence.[20] These painterly and literary surfaces are as much part-objects as roses and painted
toenails. Sentimental author of his own desire, Roe faces the threat of
the future by erecting an image-memorial to the past. But such 'things
remembered' also reveal the traces of the threat they are intended to
conceal. Barely two pages later, Roe is called to his first fire-drill of the
war. Again, he recalls his wife, but this time her image is only barely
distinguishable from the future menace he anticipates:

> They were mute in a vast asphalted space. The store towered above,
> pile after dark pile which, gradually, light after light went darker than
> the night that was falling. For twenty minutes at dusk the scene was
> his wife's eyes, wet with tears he thought, her long lashes those black
> railings, everywhere wet, but, in the air the menace of what was yet
> to be experienced, the beginning. (37)

A rose blossoms into a bud, the yet-to-flower terror of the Blitz.

Green, then, makes time flow backwards and forwards in *Caught*
through a flowery chromatism that turns images of anxiety into images
of desire – and vice versa. But for Roe, the middle-class male hopelessly
socially adrift in the homosocial class-mix of the fire brigade, this anxious,
tenacious (and occasionally tedious) heterosexual desire is wholly self-
referential: rosy pictorial memory-making, as the missing 's' in his own
name indicates, is an act of narcissistic self-making. Sexual difference,
in this instance, is a structure that allows this self-authoring to work: by
incorporating the dead other into the self, Roe also subsumes the threat
of difference, which is also the menace of the war, into the logic of the
same. The relation between war and sex here is not so much tautological
as supplementary: the menace of war, the nowhere of anxiety, is sup-
plemented by the dead woman and the somewhere of heterosexuality.
This heteroerotic memorializing is about as non-historicizable as literary
or aesthetic form, or indeed, fetishism. Roe's voluntary memories made up
of surface texture and cliché are clearly embedded within the necrophilic
tradition of literary modernism – but this isn't necessarily what makes
them historical. What makes both Roe's sentimental authoring and *Caught*
itself symptoms of their time is, as we will see, the *failure* of these opulent
image memories and, so the failure of sexual difference, to make up for the
absence of meaning occasioned by war.

Where Roe's roses swell up, so to speak, from the inside, for the working-
class Pye, sex, or more precisely, sex *as* traumatic memory, comes at him
from the outside. In the anxiety of the present, Pye is 'caught' by the

revelation of incestuous sex with his sister (currently locked up in a mental asylum, charged with having abducted Roe's son). No more than Roe, can Pye live in the present; but where his bourgeois underling takes fetishistic solace in the past, Pye compulsively imagines forwards by constructing fantasy situations in which he has the authority denied to him in real life – what one does in one's head in *Caught* is a matter of class as well as of sex. Half-asleep, dreaming up a scenario in which he goes to visit his sister (taking with him 'a comb with rose briars painted on top'), Pye 'pictures himself' in a confrontation with the asylum doctor: ' "Is there any history in your family, Mr Pye?" ', asks the doctor; to which Pye responds, ' " 'Istory, what d'you mean by 'istory?" ' (87) – a question that might well be asked of the text, as well as of Pye. Pye does have a history, but he doesn't encounter it in his dream which, as with so many of Green's characters' anxious imaginings, gives Pye a curiously opaque kind of storytelling capacity. Only towards the end of the novel does Pye keep this belated appointment with historical truth:

> Without any warning, and with a shock that took all his breath, Pye saw the dry wood shaving creep, bent in the moonlight, the back way to their cottage. He saw it again as though it were before his eyes, which he now tried to draw away from the doctor's [...] In a surge of blood it was made *clear*, *false*, that it might have been his own sister he was with that night. So it might have been her voice, thick with excitement and fright and disgust that said 'Will it hurt?' So in the blind moonlight, eyes warped by his need, he must have forced his own sister. (My emphasis)(140)

In contrast to Roe's memories, Pye's revelations are not illuminated: the memory is 'clear, false' in the *blindness* of the moonlight. That cognitive equivocation is inherent in the traumatic act that is half-revealed here. Incest, famously, is taboo because it thwarts the means by which cultural meanings are made. In this context, incest is like war; not because they are both taboo (war clearly isn't), but because both cause problems for instantiation: neither the meaning of war nor the meaning of incest resides in concrete acts, but outside of them, in symbol formation (or in the symbolic exchange of women and signs).[21] Roe's trauma-theory-as-fetishism is one way of keeping something like a symbolic exchange going: as war is to woman, so dread is to a rose, so the threat to one's skin is to an enamelled toenail, so formlessness is to aesthetic opulence, so blindness is to vision. By contrast, Pye's exchange mechanism fails him completely. Nothing is illuminated. It is misperception, not perception, that prevails in the blackout: ' "What" ', he asks Roe just before his death, ' "d'you make of this moonlight, I mean the black-out? [...] D'you mistake objects in it, 'ave you taken one person for another?" ' (157). Here then the tautology – war is sex – is grotesquely operative; wandering through the blackout, 'too disturbed to notice the invasion of Norway' (133), Pye finally sticks his head in a gas oven before the first bombs fall.

II

Green was not the only observer to note that surreally particular to the British home front was the uncanny way in which the anxious space of a nation under siege, ghosted by phantoms half-glimpsed in the blackout, exteriorized the unconscious, made fantasy look like reality and war look like sex. Many psychoanalysts too worried about this erotically-charged public sphere. As in *Caught*, this worrying desiring anxiety manifests itself most clearly, as we saw in the previous chapter, in terms of vision: war, like sex and, indeed, like art, is a matter of the image, of what can and ought to be seen. The psychoanalyst, Melitta Schmideberg, Melanie Klein's daughter, for example, noted how scopophilic impulses played their part in the Blitz in the following description:

> During the day, ruined buildings revealed to the curious their inmost secrets. Here two walls were gone, but a table laid with cutlery and glass stood intact. There nothing remained but a single wall with a suspended bath aloft. A patient was astonished because so many nice houses looked so incredibly dirty, and he gleefully described a house of which only one wall was left and where, above the mantle-piece one could see a number of pornographic pictures.[22]

War blasts apart the home to reveal its sordid secrets to the world (this, too, is Pye's tragedy). The ruins of a city and the rubble of its civic life are, of course, powerful metonymies for the death and wounding of its inhabitants. In descriptions such as this, however, as in *Caught*, it is as if sex, in the form of the image, begins to arise at the precise moment when the phenemologization of the wound – or the 'Blast' – becomes, apparently, impossible. There is a correlative moment to Schmideberg's account of the pornographic imaginary of wound culture in *Caught*. Ducking down to a shelter amid the chaos of the first raid on London, Roe is 'gleefully' astonished to stumble across a couple in rapt, forgetful, union: 'He had been kissing her mouth so it was now a blotch of red.' That 'blotch of red', however, quickly begins to bleed into other images and to literally spew out of the wounds that the pornographic image (or primal scene) connotes, but cannot contain: 'The twisted creature under a blanket coughed up a last gushing, gout of blood', 'Two police brought past a looter, most of his clothes torn off, heels dragging, drooling blood at the mouth' (97).

Just as in the first war, when the response to this eroticization of the wound was to take the sex out of trauma theory, so too in the second. In radio broadcasts and in the medico-psychiatric press, the advice was to separate 'realistic' anxiety from 'neurotic anxiety', to pin anxiety to a proper 'empirical' referent and, hence, to sweep fantasy off the streets.[23] Ego psychology, with its influential ideology of adaptation, found a foothold here. Britain, Anna Freud suggested some years later, found a way of 'adapting' to its trauma.[24] By contrast, when Lacan visited Britain at the end of the war what he thought he found was a 'rapport véridque au réel', 'a more truthful relation to the real, that [Britain's] utilitarian ideology barely understands [and] that the term adaptation betrays completely'. This is not (yet) the Lacanian real that is so important to contemporary trauma theory, but in this period Lacan was beginning to think about psychoanalysis in a way that was to take it well away from the normative restraints of ego psychology, and what he saw in wartime British psychoanalysis was to inform that thinking.[25] It would be a clumsy over-simplification to argue that it was the war that finally radicalized psychoanalysis. Far from it, in fact; for many, the symptomatic response to the overwhelming experience of trauma was a renewed faith in the so-called 'reality principle'. But, for others, the experience of the Blitz (in Britain) and the blitzkrieg (in the rest of Europe) served to confirm what they had long suspected: that anxious desire cannot be authorized under the corrective will of an educated ego, but comes at the ego from elsewhere. In anxiety, one does not 'adapt' to the real; like Pye, one is 'caught' by it – just as one is caught by a picture or (which may be more disturbing) by an image.

This 'anxious elsewhere' is precisely where Green's perspicacity about sexuality and the image ends up, as hopefully will I, after a short psychoanalytic detour. So far we have seen war turn into 'sex' in two different ways. Roe, the anxious fetishist, supplements the thought of death with a kind of compulsive citation of literary and painterly rose-coloured images that turn anxiety into desiring memory. Where Roe recollects pictures in order to collect himself, his anxious alter-ego, Pye, is subject to traumatic memory images which shatter meaning and identity by bringing desire and anxiety together. Green is not, however, comparing anxious 'character-types': *Caught* itself resembles what it describes. The text compulsively assembles image-clusters, pockets of chromatic prosody, as if to give some kind of temporary stability to a narrative that otherwise risks the same dissolution of meaning and identity that it adumbrates. For good reason perhaps: Green wrote the novel while serving as an auxiliary fireman on the home front between, as the last words of the text inform us, June 1940 and Christmas 1942. Like many, Green was convinced that he would not survive the war. One way to approach *Caught*'s anxious textual production, then, is as a meditation on the extent to which the anticipation of death can be folded into narrative representation. I've begun to suggest this anxious anticipation emerges as a kind of sexualization, or eroticization, of lost and anticipated experience.

Caught shares much with Freud's final theory of trauma and, in particular, with his key inter-war text, *Inhibitions, Symptoms and Anxiety*. To some extent, the Freudian theory of anxiety can be read as a meta-psychological companion to Green's text – not because it interprets *Caught*'s manoeuvres but because, in a backwards sort of repetition, it anticipates them. Anxiety, as I described in Chapter 1, cuts in two directions for Freud. On the one hand, it is a 'signal', a protective action which warns the ego of a potential danger to come: the signal – like an air-raid siren – announces 'I am expecting a situation of helplessness to set in.'[26] But this warning, on the other hand, is efficacious because it is predicated on the repetition of a past trauma: anxious anticipation thus has the potential to plunge the ego into traumatic anxiety anew and to devastate its defences. 'Dreading forward', for Freud too, carries the seeds (or the bud) of a past trauma; one which can either protect the ego (Roe) or shatter it (Pye). André Green later describes that traumatic anxiety in terms of 'real instinctual impulses from the id which have broken the ego's barriers and are advancing in force toward the heart of the ego in the manner of a *Blitzkrieg* [his word]',[27] thus neatly underscoring the way in which, although it might appear that Freud is trying to set up an opposition between 'realistic', 'signal', adaptive anxiety, and 'neurotic', traumatic, drive-invested anxiety – an opposition between war and sex, no less – anxiety continually calls into question the oppositions that are set up to contain it.[28] It is precisely because the id can advance on the ego in the manner of a blitzkrieg, and, for that matter, because a blitzkrieg can advance on the ego in the manner of an id, that an apparently realistic anxiety can flower into an eroticism, as Green (Henry) has demonstrated. What is more important for some of the arguments I've been trying to advance here, however, is Freud's definition of that traumatic anxiety – a definition that turns on death, sexuality and the image.

Traumatic anxiety cannot arise out of a fear of death, for the well-known reason that there is no representation of death in the unconscious.[29] As Freud puts it in *Inhibitions*, in yet another rebuttal of the unsexing of trauma theory in World War I: 'The unconscious seems to contain nothing that could give any content to our concept of the annihilation of life.'[30] The thesis that the shell-shocked soldiers of the first war were reacting to death threats to their instincts of self-preservation falls to the ground, as Freud pointed out as early as 1918, once it is understood that our relation to ourselves is libidinalized, that is, narcissistic.[31] The image of the absolute annihilation of the self is simply off limits for the subject of psychoanalysis: if I picture my own death, I am still there, still watching and so representing myself to myself and, therefore, I am not dead.[32] This may be why when we feel a threat to our skin we awaken memories to die not only with us but, perhaps, *for* us – vicariously. Anticipating death, therefore, is not what traumatizes the subject; rather it is the mitigated repetition of an experience that feels *like* death that overwhelms the ego. Thus, says Freud, 'fear of death should be regarded as analogous to the fear of castration'[33] – and this may be why imagining things to die with reinstates sexual difference with such forcefulness. If the signs of anatomical difference for the heterosexual male are taken as proof positive of the reality of castration, one way to fend off the threat to oneself is by demonstrating – over and over again – that it will not happen to you, because it has already happened to her. The fetishist takes a less prosaic and less murderous approach: finding roses in place of wounds, he affirms sexual difference at the point at which he denies it ('for', as Freud puts it, barely one year after *Inhibitions*, 'if a woman had been castrated, then his own possession of a penis was in danger').[34] Both reinstating and muddling the terms of sexual difference, in other words, are also ways of dealing with death.

But castration anxiety itself has another prototype in Freud's history of the anxious ego, in the trauma of 'separation anxiety' or 'object-loss.' As Freud is careful to point out, it is not so much the loss of the mother *qua* object that causes traumatic anxiety, but more precisely 'the loss of the perception of the object (which is equated with the loss of the object itself)'.[35] This distinction is crucial because it allows us to understand why anxiety and trauma can never be 'realistic' (or prosaic), but will always be a matter of the image in relation to the ego or, as Weber puts it, of 'the production and maintenance of stable cathexes, in particular of a visual nature'.[36] Neither is the lost perception to be understood as referring directly to the presence or absence of the object (to 'the picture you carry in your eye afterwards', as Dy puts it): anxiety has what Freud calls 'a quality of indefiniteness', because although its presence can be signified or imaged, its object cannot be represented. Images or 'perceptual identities', for Freud, are far from veridical: rather they betray the extent to which the subject of anxiety is always at one remove from its objects. That 'at one remove' is also the mark of sexuality: the first situation of helplessness – separation anxiety – is also the first articulation of the gap between the intolerable tension of neediness and the hallucination of the image of the object that (or so we fondly imagine) can fill that need. As Jean Laplanche has argued, this misperception at the core of the ego is the very definition, not only of anxiety, but also of the sexual drive.[37] Thus it is not only the case that sexuality somehow gets into the image: traumatic anxiety ('drive attack', Laplanche calls it) both makes – and breaks – the images by which the ego constitutes itself. As well as thinking of images *of* sexuality (as pleasant as that is) it is also, therefore, just as important to understand how anxious sexuality itself becomes the condition of the image in the first place.

What, then, might be erotic about the image-clusters that swell up in *Caught* is not only their content, but the way – as if obeying the synthesizing laws of Eros – they give form, re-cathect as it were, the image as a protective reaction against the loss of perception signalled by anxiety. And what might (more accurately) be fetishistic about Roe's opulent rose-memories is the way in which their artifice works to retain perception, to erect the image only through (as Freud puts it in 'Fetishism') a 'very energetic action'.[38] The thickness of the painterly surfaces of these images lets us know that object is not so much perceived (perceptual mimesis) as actively made, just as the citation of cliché tells us that this active making is also an active repetition. One might be tempted to call this relation between sexuality and the image non-historicizable, always arising in the constitutional trauma of sexed subjectivity. But that would be to forget where we started. If sexuality looks non-historicizable here it is surely because it is doing the historicizing – giving us images not *of* historical violence, but which respond to the threat of that violence. The 'fear of death should be regarded as analogous to the fear of castration'. 'War, she thought, is sex.'

III

I too was not, nor my understanding, that resolves things out of the images of the senses. I was not the one who saw, but only seeing.

And what I saw were not things...but only colours. And I too was coloured into this landscape.

Walter Benjamin[39]

To be 'caught' in anxious historicity, then, is to be caught up in a relation to the image. Actively remembering things to die with is also a protest against death or, at the very least, part of an effort to master it through the authoring of images. Much of the pleasure of reading *Caught* derives from the way that, psychoanalytically speaking, its symptoms are also its sublimations: the sensuality of the novel's images offers a temporary aesthetic resolution, small moments of sense-making, in a novel which – quite literally – has no image of a future in which its tensions could be resolved. But as much as Green is as caught up in the lure of fetishistic image-making as his character, Roe, *Caught* also undoes its own, already tenuous, claims to authority. In the same way that the image can only arise in relation to trauma, there is a wound in the rose which, Green suggests, has to be allowed to bud if there is to be an alternative to a fetishistic form of historicization. In this sense, it is Pye's fate – the fate of one who is traumatically caught by images not of his own making, whose 'eyes are warped by need' in the 'clear, false' blindness of the London blackout – that thematizes a more troubling and difficult relation to the image than we have seen so far.

Just as object-loss lies at the core of Freud's theory of trauma – the loss that underwrites the difficulty of living historical trauma and the sexual trauma that follows from that difficulty – so too in *Caught*. The novel opens with Roe trying to imagine the abduction of his son, Christopher, by Pye's sister. It is this act of violent separation which wreathes the lives of the novel's characters together in a melodrama of unhappy coincidences; without Pye's incest, there would have been no abduction, whereas for Roe himself the abduction prefigures the death of his wife and so is caught up with his rose-memorializing. By opening a war novel with the abduction of a child, Green confirms what Freud sixteen years earlier had begun to explore: that trauma is less the effect of shock than an anticipated repetition of primal separation. By 1940, as we saw in the last chapter, this thesis had not only been accepted by psychoanalysts and psychologists, but for many it was also being lived historically: 'this separation that war had forced into their lives'(10) as Green puts it elsewhere in the novel, a separation that feels *like* death, was repeated again and again all over mainland Europe. And in Britain the evacuation of children away from the city centres was felt by many to be at least as violent as an abduction.[40]

But Green is not thematizing history here: once more, he writes the 'effect of his time' into the fiction of *Caught*, through a meditation on the historicizing potential of the image in relation to anxious sexuality. So far we have seen how images in *Caught* eroticize anxiety; how a dreaded absence turns into a rose, then into a woman, and finally into a picture that can make sense out of anxiety. In the opening scenes of the novel, however, Green runs this series backwards, and returns us to what can be described as the origin of the image in relation to anxiety – to a kind of vertigo of the image. If roses are Roe's fetish, fear of falling is his phobia. Roe joined the auxiliary fire service because 'he had for years wanted to see inside one of these turreted buildings and also because he had always been afraid of heights' (27). In classic psychoanalytic terms, of course, the taboo on the desire to see (inside one of these turreted mothers, Melanie Klein might say; inside one of those blitzed buildings, her daughter might add) is the motivating force behind the fear of heights. The anxiety of vertigo is above all an anxiety about the image – note again, not about what the image denotes, but about a drive that might overrun the sense-making properties of the image. It is not the mother we fear, but her loss – which we equate with the image – coupled with our overwhelming need.

It is significant then that in a text where all the mothers are either dead, deranged or dangerously bogus, Roe imagines his way into his son's trauma through his own vertigo. What, Green notes, was 'fatal' about the scene of Christopher's abduction was that the department store in which it took place 'had been lit by stained glass windows in front of arc lamps which cast the violent colours of that glass over the goods laid out on counters' (11). As for the son, so too for the father who falls into this chromatic violence by recalling a childhood vertigo attack during a visit to Tewkesbury Abbey, where

he had that terror of the urge to leap, his back to deep violet and yellow Bible stories on the glass, his eyes reluctant over the whole grey stretch of the Abbey until they were drawn, abruptly as to a chasm, inevitably, and so far beneath, down to that floor hemmed with pews, that height calling on the pulses he did not know why to his ears, down to dropped stone flags over which sunlight had cast the colour in each window, the colour it seemed his blood had turned. (12)

The terror of the urge to leap lies not in the death that awaits one on the stone flags beneath ('The unconscious [contains] nothing that could give any content to our concept of the annihilation of life'). The terror, rather, lies in being 'caught' between the 'deep violet and yellow' of the windows, and the reflection of the colours on the stones; of being caught, in other words, between two images. What is 'traumatic' about the image here is not what it denotes but the extent to which it dissolves the opposition between a perceiving subject (one who gives form to the image of colour) and a perceived image. As the light on the stone flags turns into 'the colour it seemed his blood had turned', Roe's body bleeds into the image he not only sees, but is 'caught' or seen by. It is as if the connotational properties of the roses that elsewhere flower up *in media res* are sucked dry: only a kind of visceral colour – the zero-degree point of signification of any image – remains. One cannot catch these colours, actively perceive them as a whole image, erotically bind them into pictures to fend off death; one is caught between them.[41] This too is Christopher's fate who, while 'held to ransom by the cupidity of boys', 'lost in feelings of this colour' (13) thrown by the light of the department windows onto goods laid on the counter, is abducted, not so much by a woman posing as a mother, but by phantasmatic colour:

> Words were not means of communication now [...] when she pulled at his jacket, he did look up and saw nothing strange in how she was, *caught* full by the light from those windows, so that her skin was blue and her orbs, already sapphire, a sea flashing at hot sunset as, uneasy, she glanced left, then right [...] At the angle she now held herself she lost those rose diamonds in her eyes, these were shaded and so had gone an even deeper blue. He became dazzled by the pink neon lights beyond her features. *Caught* in another patch of colour, some of her chin was pillar-box red, also a part of the silver fox she wore [...] she *caught* full at him with her eyes that, by the ocean in which they were steeped, were so much part of the world his need had made, and so much part of it by being alive, then he felt anything must be natural, and was ready to do what ever she asked. (My emphases) (14)

'So much part of the world his need had made', and yet Christopher is dazzled, caught, by the infinite, vertiginous, contrast of colours that only barely let the form of Pye's sister come into focus.

If, as Mark Cousins has suggested in a reading of Hitchcock's *Vertigo* which could also work as an analysis of the overtly pictorial and filmic qualities of *Caught*, pictures are defences against the return of traumatic images, then in the opening scenes of the novel it is as if Green is diagnosing what will later become the text's own defence mechanisms.[42] The threat that such images pose is that of not being able to 'occupy' them with a representation – with a rose, for instance. And if that trauma, psychoanalytically speaking, marks the heterogeneity of the sexual drives in relation to representation, so too, for Green at least, does the violence of a blitz. The abduction scene ends by firelight. Christopher yells. 'She put both hands over her mouth, which was wide open, and so left, in the shadow, a dark hole between firelit fingers over a dark face' (16). Compare this to the passage with which I began:

> They saw the water below a dirty yellow towards the fire; the wharves on that far side low and black, those on the bank they were leaving a pretty rose [...] This fan, a roaring red gold, pulsed rose at the outside edge, the perimeter round which the heavens, set with stars before fading into utter blackness, were for a space a trembling green.

The 'dark hole between firelit fingers' now 'pulses rose' in the fires of the Blitz; just as the 'blotch of red' in the scene in the air-raid shelter haemorrhages into the wounds of war. Green's colour words beat a circuitous path between the body and the world, thwarting the opposition between the two. This dissolution of boundaries is repeated in the organization of the text. *Caught* begins with an abduction scene and ends with a description of the Blitz: the two blocks of narration are typographically and stylistically equivalent; both cut up Roe's free-indirect discourse, for example, by putting areas of text in parenthesis, not in order to establish a narrative hierarchy, but to mark off (to cite Freud once more) 'areas of colour melting into one another'. These chromatic pockets do not 'make sense' in the same way as Roe's opulent rose-memories. They are, rather, assaults on the senses. What the Blitz and Christopher's abduction share is a break-up of images – a kind of anti-cathexis, to use psychoanalytic terms. Words, the psychoanalyst and army medical officer, Wilfred Bion, noted later, can be hallucinations; images which appear, he says, as 'evacuated objects' (there were more ways than one of being evacuated in World War II as much of this book has tried to argue).[43] The point about a blitz, Green seems to be saying here, and what perhaps makes it so difficult to describe, is the way its lurid sensuality sends those 'evacuated objects' back to us, destroying the opposition between inside and outside (evacuating the subject) and thus attacking the ability to categorize or describe experience. Another name for such an attacking force is the death drive – 'the extreme of sexuality'.[44] 'War, she thought...' Leaving 'a pretty rose' beyond the synthesizing powers of Eros, Green (trembling) finally gives us something to die with. Unlike Céline, whose work he admired intensely, Green here is not, I would argue, aestheticizing the death drive. Rather, he writes 'the effect of his time', by marking a moment when it no longer becomes possible to fend off the effects of history with a fetish. This, it seems to me at least, is a thoroughly historical endeavour.

IV

Green's meticulous attention to the workings of anxious desire and the image might be thought of as a late chapter in a modernism which (certainly since Baudelaire) tracks the peripateticism of human sexuality as a way of marking the trauma of modernity. It is as if Eros began to falter at some point; or perhaps it is more accurate to say that psychoanalysis – like the literary history it parallels – has provided us with a language that can make that failure visible and, to some extent, intelligible. It was World War I that prompted Freud to consider what kind of representational economy lay beyond the synthesizing powers of Eros. The speculative daring of *Beyond the Pleasure Principle*, its stops and starts, its leaps and equivocations ('What we cannot reach flying we must reach limping'; Freud closes his book with a version of the *Maqamat* of al-Hariri[45]), means that it has a justifiably canonical place in contemporary trauma theory. It should not be forgotten, however, that the concept of the death drive has had something of a chequered history over the last eighty years. Rejected at the time by the majority for its speculative excess, and embraced by others because it seemed to offer psychoanalysis a new foundation (for the Kleinians) or means of critique (for the Surrealists), the death drive's various manifestations – as the repetition compulsion, as the Nirvana principle, as aggressivity, as the 'extreme of sexuality' – are always partly contingent upon the historical exigencies it is brought on to account for or answer to.

With this thought in mind, one final word about Henry Green. Green's next novel, *Back* (1946) tells the story of a returning soldier's anguished and deluded mourning for his dead lover. Her 'name, of all names, was Rose'.[46] Coincidentally, Green's anti-hero, Charley Summers, limps because he 'had lost his leg in France for not noticing the gun beneath a rose'.[47] Whereas Roe in *Caught* erected rose-memorials to his dead love in order to imagine an unimaginable future, in *Back* Charley is unable to make a fetish out of his Rose's absence. Rather, as he begins to 'awkwardly search for Rose, through roses', her name comes at him from the outside world: from shop windows ('in a second-hand booksellers with a set of Miss Rhoda Broughton [...] his eyes read a title, *Cometh Up as a Flower'*, 'also in a seed merchant's front [...] "Carter's patent Rose" ', 'from a wireless shop, a record through loud speakers of "Honeysuckle Rose" '[48]); in the words of others ('Mrs Frazier spoke of rising prices. "Why," she said, "they rose, they've rose..." '[49]); in time itself ('only to find roses grown between the minutes and hours and so entwined that the hands were stuck'[50]); and finally in the form of Rose's half-sister, Nancy Whitmore, who Charley doggedly pursues convinced that she is his lost love.

There is no space for interiority in *Back*: no imagistic memorializing as self-authoring. Charley's fate is wholly determined by the agency of the roses that relentlessly pursue him through the text. Lovers, like the workers and the tools in the wartime industry that Charley helps administer, can be replaced. The unconscious in *Back* is structured like the language of a wartime economy – a language of rations, shortages, rising prices and of dead, missing and evacuated persons. But the most striking aspect of this novel is Green's commitment to a sense of the ordinariness of the trauma of the missed encounters that get tangled up in the letters of his novel. In the end it simply doesn't much matter if Charley's life is scripted beyond his conscious desires. That script, in this sense, *is* what lies beyond Eros (or beyond Rose). To live a life in which one's history and fate are so cruelly beyond the limits of one's wishes (beyond the ego, Lacan would say) is painful, but the results are not always fatal. The death drive can play comedy as well as tragedy, as Charley finally explains to Nancy:

> 'Anyway, it took a bit of forgetting, but I've forgotten now alright.'
> 'All's well that ends well, then.'
> 'Least said, soonest mended,' she agreed.[51]

4
Bombs, Birth and Trauma: Henry Moore and D.W. Winnicott

One morning I walked back through the park, and saw the highest branches of a tree draped with bits of marabout, with some sort of silk, with two or three odd stockings and, wrapped around the top of the tree, like a cloak quick-thrown over the shoulder of some high-born hidalgo, some purple damask. Below it, balanced on a twig as if twirled around a finger, was a brand new bowler hat. They had all been blown across the road from the bombed hotel opposite. A surrealist painter whom I knew slightly was staring at this too. He said: 'Of course we were painting this sort of thing years ago, but it has taken some time to get here.'

Inez Holden, *It Was Different at the Time* (1943)[1]

Anxiety is perhaps what one feels when the world reveals itself to be caught up in the space between two frames: a doubled frame, or one that is split, who can tell?

Samuel Weber, *Return to Freud*[2]

Inez Holden's painter friend was not the only one to note that the war had turned the world surreal in 1940s Britain. 'No dream is worse than the reality in which we live', thundered a special triple issue of the *London Bulletin*, the journal of British Surrealism in its call to arms against Hitler in June 1940. 'No reality' it added 'is as good as our dreams.'[3] This issue of the *Bulletin* coincided with the exhibition, 'Surrealism Today', held in the Zwemmer Gallery in London between June and July 1940. The show included photographs of Max Ernst's House at St Martin d'Ardèche, 'rebuilt and decorated in collaboration with Leonora Carrington', and work by Roland Penrose, Eileen Agar,

Edward Burra, Len Lye, Paul Nash and Lee Miller. Two of Henry Moore's reclining figures were also there, one lead and one elm, along with five more of his sculptures, including *The Helmet* and *Fire-Engine*. France had just fallen. Barely three months after the opening of the show the blitzkrieg turned into the Blitz and the war – which had taken some time to get there – had finally arrived on the British home front.

The experimental film-maker, Len Lye, called one of his contributions in the exhibition *Pre-History Figments*. It is worth hanging on to this phrase if only to note that the 'pre' here does not necessarily vanquish history altogether, but rather sets up a tension between the kind of history that can be represented and its other. Pre-history is not only what precedes the telling of the past, it is also what, so to speak, 'falls out' of historical representation: the unconscious, the sublime, myth and form are all, in this sense, 'pre-history figments'. Freud, for example, talked about the 'prehistoric epoch' brought about by childhood amnesia; while some versions of surrealism insist that, however we imagine them, such pre-historical figments need to be forced into dialectical engage-ment with the present.[4] The art and writing of World War II is full of pre-historical turns. 'So', noted the writer, Bryher, as she trod through the ruins of London towards the end of the war 'this was what the war was making of us, it was giving us hallucinations and driving us back to the blank spaces of our beginnings.'[5] History, a visitor to the Zwemmer gallery might have concluded, was often a matter of being in two places at once. Indeed, what may have been really threatening about finding that your world had turned into a surrealist painting in the summer of 1940 might have been a kind of disconcerting doubling of the temporal and spatial frames that keep the world in check. The problem is not only that the dream becomes reality (which, as we saw in Chapter 1, was what bothered Anna Freud and Melanie Klein's anxious young charges), it is that it becomes impossible to position oneself securely inside or outside reality or dream, history or prehistory. In this chapter, I want to suggest that for one wartime artist, Henry Moore, and for one psychoanalyst, Donald Winnicott, the pre-historical turn was also a step into such an anxiety-provoking space.

British wartime culture is commonly understood less in the context of the anxiety-provoking spaces of surrealism and psychoanalysis, than in terms of myth and monument. Angus Calder has done much to dismantle the 'myth of the Blitz', the historical fantasy of fearless collective endurance that still clings to the British imaginary. Equally pervasive, but a little more sly, is the cultural belief in art's capacity to redeem the trauma of war and newly reconcile humanity to the world;

it is this version of the wartime myth that Henry Moore's wartime work and, in particular, his post-war sculptures in Britain, Europe and the United States are usually associated with. In the first myth Britain appears eerily free of anxiety, and in the second trauma is harnessed and ennobled in the name of art, humanity and so on. Both offer only partial versions of British wartime art and culture. As Andrew Causey has argued, however, Moore's drawings from the late 1930s to the 1940s reveal the extent to which the surrealist in Moore persists alongside the developing sculptor of monuments to human suffering.[6] In other words, there is a sensibility that cuts across Moore's work that is rather less enamoured of redemptive myth-making than his popular image might convey. It is something like this kind of surreal sensibility that I think Adam Phillips also has in mind when he suggests that Winnicott's style is closer to that of Lewis Carroll and Stevie Smith than to that of his psychoanalytic predecessors.[7] Together these figures do not really make a major contribution to the surrealist tradition (Moore was always marginal to British Surrealism); but at the very least, this work betrays an instructive struggle with its own (so to speak) pre-historical terms. It is the story of that struggle that I want to tell here.

I

The Zwemmer gallery in 1940 then is a deliberately unconventional place to start. Most accounts of Moore's war work begin neither with connections with surrealism nor with his early 'primitive' enthusiasms, but with the famous Shelter Drawings that Moore, an anti-fascist but initially reluctant war artist, began three months later. The story of how Moore came to make the drawings is often told in Moore scholarship. Returning home from a dinner party on 11 September 1940, four days into the first London Blitz, Moore breaks his usual habits and takes the Tube. In the bowels of Belsize Park Station he finds London's underground shelterers, refugees from governmental indifference and incompetence.[8] He begins to draw. Published by Editions Poetry, London, in *Lilliput* alongside some of Bill Brandt's photographs in 1942, exhibited throughout Britain during the war and widely cited as testaments to the living hell of the home front, Moore's Shelter Drawings became, and still are, a crucial part of the cultural mythology of wartime Britain (Figure 4.1). Moore later remarked that it was this work that allowed him to reconcile his primitivism with what he called his 'humanist side'.[9] Indeed, although he had begun to experiment with a more naturalist approach two years earlier, most agree that it was in

Figure 4.1   Henry Moore, *Study for 'Tube Shelter Perspective: the Liverpool St. Extension',* 1940–41, pencil, wax crayon, coloured crayon, watercolour wash, pen and ink, *Second Shelter Sketchbook*, p. 24, AG. 40–41.92

the Shelter Drawings that Moore really began to put naturalist empathy back into what throughout the 1930s was a fairly sustained attention to forms of abstraction. The Shelter Drawings then mark the end of a relatively obscure modernist reputation and the beginning of Moore's second career (as John Russell put it) as one of 'the keepers of the public conscience'.[10]

War, indeed, in these drawings drives us back to our beginnings: in fact at first glance there seems to be hardly anything in them to mark their modernity or sense of time and place at all. Moore's chthonians, mouths open, shrouded by blankets, tangled in one another's arms, hover somewhere between death and secure repose in underground shelters that are at once mass tombs and, oddly, spaces where domestic life persists (the undead in these images are knitting). This sort of out-of-time uncanniness owes as much to the repetitive nature of the drawings as it does to Moore's empathetic eye for human suffering. Figures multiply vertiginously, down tunnels and up escalators, in an iterative familiarity: this, one could argue, is primitivism as citation. It is then perhaps not surprising to discover that what Moore thought he had found in Belsize Park Station was Henry Moore: 'I saw hundreds of Henry Moore reclining figures stretched along the platforms [...] even the train tunnels seemed to be like holes in my sculpture.'[11] Moore, in other words, had been sculpting this kind of thing for years but it had taken some time to get there. Or as one of his later critics put it: 'History put in Moore's way precisely those images of envelopment and protectiveness which had been thrust on him in earlier years by the shape of the block, or by tendencies implicit in art history, or by his own unconscious memories.'[12] The implication being that art history and Moore's psyche had had nothing to do with history before it started to resemble them so strangely; before it so fortuitously fell in their path, as it were, conveniently on hand to consecrate the notions of art and indi-vidualist history at the very moment when both were called to account. History is enveloped by pre-history, and it is partly this envelopment – and its persistence in the way Moore is viewed – that I also want to question here.

Obviously, the sketches could not have been drawn anywhere other than in London in 1940, yet this same historical immediacy seems to place a sense of mythical profundity on the way they have been read. The drawings, goes a familiar argument in the critical commentary, transcend the history they at the same time convey. 'These motionless swathed figures belong to no accidental setting of time and place', an early reviewer in *Penguin New Writing* noted in 1943, 'Rather they are memorials to the enduringness of things, of stone and human patience and courage.'[13] Later Erich Neumann, Moore's influential Jungian critic, took the enduringness of things one step further:

> In these Shelter Drawings Moore was given a unique opportunity to see his inner image of the archetype of the feminine as the sheltering cave in the earth realised all around him in actual fact. With the collapse of the modern civilized world an archaic, primitive world of

cave life suddenly appeared in its very midst, and the long forgotten situation of human beings crawling for shelter, like worms, into the womb of the earth and being swallowed in its abysses became an all too typical reality.[14]

War is birth the wrong way round. Being born and being bombed here amount to pretty much the same thing. Neumann's archetypism is not unusual for its time (he is writing in the late 1950s), nor is the predictable way in which he universalizes the figure of the mother (Moore's? Myth's? The collective unconscious's? The nation's?).[15] But for all his questionable archetypes, I suspect Neumann is responding to something that is suggested in Moore's work itself as much as it is by the fantasies of the Jungian analyst. The slippage from moment to myth to monument is captured perfectly in Moore's 1944 sculpture, the Northampton *Madonna and Child*, commissioned by Canon Hussey who had seen and admired the Shelter Drawings. Moore used the Shelter Drawings as a basis for the sculpture (figures which, we remember, were already repetitions of his pre-war work). Alone the sculpture betrays little of its vertiginous facsimile origins, but is rather a monument to a fantasy about security and permanence (about the 'enduringness of things'), as much art as reaction formation.

It is not the intrusion of the archaic into historical time that is worrying here, far from it. What is troubling is the apparently effortless way that the pre-historical figment and the historical document become the same thing. As David Sylvester has remarked, albeit in a different context, Moore's genius for revealing similarities between disparate things makes such symbolic equations appear natural and inescapable: 'the revelation is like that of some elemental truth', Sylvester notes, 'once recognised, it seems inevitable'.[16] In the Shelter Drawings, Peter Fuller once wrote, making a similar observation to Sylvester's with very different implications, Moore 'mythologised, and therefore made comprehensible the experience of ordinary people'.[17] While it is of course true that myth can make experience intelligible, underwriting the turmoil of the present with a guarantee that this experience belongs, eventually and inevitably, to 'some elemental truth' that can only be located out of history also risks cancelling out historical experience at the precise moment it claims it as it own.

This kind of reading turns art into something that ennobles trauma even as it acknowledges it. It also remains indifferent, I would suggest, to another altogether different way of registering historical trauma in Moore's drawings in this period. Partly because the war made sculpture projects difficult, Moore produced a great many drawings during the war. Some continue the subterranean theme of the Shelter Drawings, such as the sketches of the Castleford miners, while in others he pursues the exploration of the sculptural possibilities of space that had preoccupied him in the late 1930s. The curious shapes in pinks, yellows, greys and green that so distinguish the Shelter Drawings are both anticipated and repeated in drawings that remind us that the Henry Moore associated with surrealism was never that far from the side of the war artist. Moore's first comment on the war, *September 3rd 1939*, for instance, owes more to the spirit of the Zwemmer gallery than to his alleged turn to a newly reconciled humanism. Eight women bathers bob up and down in the sea under the cliffs looking anxiously across to France and mainland Europe (Moore was on holiday in Dover, on the south-east coast of England, when war was declared) (Figure 4.2). It is the worried women's heads as much as the familiar wartime trope of the English coast, that call for comment. These weird double interiors, heads-within-heads, recall, among many other similar explorations of enveloping forms he made

Figure 4.2 Henry Moore, *September 3rd 1939*, 1939, pencil, wax crayon, chalk, watercolour, pen and ink on heavyweight wove, 30.6 × 39.8 cm, AG. 39.35

during this period, Moore's *The Helmet*, produced at the same time and exhibited in the Zwemmer show in 1940, and his earlier 1939 lithograph, *The Spanish Prisoner*.[18] As with so many of Moore's drawings and sculptures from this period, these figures – victims and subjects of fascism and war – are claustrophobes and agoraphobes, trapped within themselves (heads-within-heads) and lost in expansive space. They could almost be illustrations of Freud's second topography; egos within super egos, 'frontier creatures' anxiously doubled within and against the world.

It is of course hardly surprising that Moore the sculptor should produce drawings that overdetermine the ways in which we inhabit space or, for that matter, the way in which it inhabits us. In his widely influential modernist classic, *Abstraction and Empathy*, Worringer noted that the task of the artist was to use abstraction in order to win the object back from anxiety-provoking space. Abstraction, for him, like the hysterical symptom for Freud, marks our discontent; it is the trace of an archaic attempt to master the caprice and stubborn recalcitrance of the external world. It is this type of anxious relation to space that Moore seems to be exploring in his famous 1942 *Crowd Looking at a Tied-Up Object* produced during the lull between the two large-scale bomb attacks on London (Figure 4.3). If one reading of the Shelter Drawings demonstrates how Moore was able to incorporate history into mythic vision, *Crowd* seems to evacuate history, the war, altogether. Some have read this drawing as Moore's retreat into his own imagination; a sort of personal Dunkirk, a run for cover back into the strangeness of the surreal and abstract – back to blank spaces – and away from not the chaos but the stultifying over-order of wartime Britain (Moore got bored with the underground shelters when the authorities stepped in and started to tidy them up).[19] Clearly, the drawing is not about the war in the same sense that the Shelter Drawings are. If anything, Moore's main concern here is art itself. But if *Crowd* is an allegory about the relation between sculpture and its public, it is one, I think, that reveals an unconscious structure of feeling that is as eloquent on the subject of wartime experience as the Shelter Drawings.

Moore's tied-up object is anxiety-provoking and bizarre at the same time: turn it 90 degrees, suspend it a little higher and it could almost be one of surrealist photographer Lee Miller's barrage balloons hovering incongruously over the English countryside. Menace often verges on the comic in images of Britain at war. Similarly surreal is the ordinariness of the crowd of women; although there is something undoubtedly intimidating about the object's sheer size, at the same time it almost looks as if the women could be waiting at a bus stop. Like, as Moore

Figure 4.3 Henry Moore, *Crowd Looking at a Tied-Up Object*, 1942, pencil, white wax crayon, charcoal (rubbed), watercolour wash, pen and ink, 43.2 × 55.9 cm, private collection, AG. 42.174

himself said, a sculpture waiting to be unveiled, the shrouded object tells an understated story about the prehistory of an object's entrance into the world. However, this is an expectant birth only; the object's unveiling cannot be realized within the narrative frame of the picture. In much the same way as *September 3rd 1939, Crowd* suspends 'what happens next': the future becomes a blank space, something that can only be imagined negatively, the bus that doesn't arrive, the war that never ends, a tied-up object. Like a traumatic object, it signifies but it does not represent or reveal anything. As with the future and as, indeed, with the traumatic past for the neurotic patient in analysis, we know nothing about the object except that there is something to know. That, so to speak, is its point.[20] No wonder the women look apprehensive.

'[T]he group sense of communion in apprehension' is actually how Moore described the Shelter Drawings, a description that could equally apply to *Crowd*.[21] He also noted that what he was trying to get at was 'the feeling of people underground with the knowledge of something happening above'.[22] Obviously, Moore means the feeling of anxiety as one waits for the bombs to fall from above: a common enough experience between the autumn of 1940 and May 1941 and beyond. But note the curious disjunction between affect and space here. Moore's hasty syntax – 'the feeling of people underground with the knowledge of something happening above' – reveals a form of what psychoanalysts at the time were calling splitting: feeling is underground, knowledge above. Indeed, Moore's own account perhaps better describes his preoccupations in the first *Shelter Sketchbook* than Neumann's archetypes. At least ten of the drawings experiment with the juxtaposition of underground and overground spaces; some are cross-sections which contrast the bombed ruins above ground with the sheltering figures below, while others superimpose different spaces upon one another. Affect and cognition are as driven apart here as they are in *Crowd*. What comes across in both is an anxiety that makes itself present *as* a worry about topography: underground, overground; affect, cognition; inside the shroud, outside in the crowd; looming object, vast expanse of landscape; 'the feeling of people below with the knowledge of something happening above'. This anxious feeling, moreover, is disquietingly free-floating: does Moore mean the feeling we get when we look at the underground crowds, or is it *their* anxious feeling? Who is the subject of this sentence or, indeed, of Moore's drawings? Or to rephrase the question psychoanalytically, where is the ego in this anxiety?

II

Many of Moore's pre-history figments – phallic objects in barren landscapes, caves, wombs, tombs – echo the sort of symbolic spaces where psychoanalysis finds itself, so to speak, home from home. Indeed, it is perhaps no coincidence that during World War II when the British Society of Psycho-Analysis nearly split apart it was, at least in part, in an extremely bad-tempered debate about just how primitive psychoanalytic primitivism should be.[23] As more than one commentator has noted, the more history imposed itself during the 1940s the further back analysts such as Melanie Klein and her followers seemed to track the anxious origins of psychic life.[24] As for the Moore of the underground shelters, for some psychoanalysts too, the war seemed to be an occasion for the consecration of a life lived in the more liminal spaces of experience. As Adam Phillips has noted, for many of these analysts the 'war inside [was] ahistorical and beyond contingency', while 'the war inside [was] the truth of our being; the outside [was] merely history'.[25] The same mere history, perhaps, that Henry Moore stumbled across on the escalators in Belsize Park underground station.

I want now to return briefly to psychoanalysis to try and re-trace the logic of some of Moore's anxious spaces in a different cultural register. In particular, I want to look at a post-war paper by Donald Winnicott. Winnicott was as intrigued as Moore by our relations to the space we inhabit, primitive anxiety and, of course, mothers. Like Moore, he also bought these spaces to public attention: Winnicott's wartime radio broadcasts on evacuees and childcare are a key moment in the history of the popularization of psychoanalysis in Britain. Both artist and analyst, we could say, bring prehistory into history in literal as well as meta-phorical ways. Four years after the war Winnicott presented a paper to the British Psychoanalytic Society. His subject, appropriately enough for this period of national reconstruction and renewal, was 'Birth Memories, Birth Trauma and Anxiety'. One way to read this paper is as an elegy for the traumas of the Blitz, except that in it Winnicott barely mentions the war. 'I hardly noticed the blitz', he noted in his classic 1945 paper, 'Primitive Emotional Development', 'being all the time engaged in the analysis of psychotic patients who are notoriously and maddeningly oblivious of bombs, earthquakes and floods.'[26] Winnicott's choice of subject – birth fantasies – seems not only maddeningly oblivious to historical violence, but also appears to risk casting its author into the hinterlands of psychoanalytic speculation: the psychoanalytic establish-ment had been trying to rid itself of the mythic occultism of Otto Rank and Jung ever since the 1920s. In his book, *The Trauma of Birth* (1924), Rank had scandalized Freud with his insistence that it was the trauma of birth, the separation from the mother, that was repeated in the trans-ference and not, as Freud insisted, libidinal desire. 'The Unconscious', Rank had argued in what one might be tempted to read as a some-what prescient reading of the Shelter Drawings, 'can think of separation, departure, and dying only in terms of the wish-fulfilling regression to the womb, because it knows and can portray no other wish tendency.'[27] A tomb, for Rank, would have to be a womb-like thing. Winnicott is scep-tical about birth anxiety, but he finds himself increasingly convinced by the anxious feelings of some of the psychotic patients who come to him with examples of what he calls 'birth experiences'. '*While disbe-lieving the details described as memories I found myself prepared to believe in the accompanying affect*'[28] (emphasis in original), he says, implying that affect tells a kind of history that narrative memory ('details described as memories') cannot.

This affective history is related to Winnicott by patients such as Miss H, a nurse who has a special empathy with psychotic children. Miss H is looking after a little girl who suffers from a phobia of (of all things) the London underground. In an effort better to empathize with her charge, she starts to mimic the little girl's anxiety. Together they venture underground: as the little girl trembles, so too does Miss H, both fight for breath, both begin to suffocate. Winnicott comments that in the Underground 'Miss H [...] was herself reliving the birth experience along with the little girl.'[29] Shortly afterwards, Miss H also begins to suffer from what she calls 'blackouts' (remember how at the beginning of the war Winnicott, along with John Bowlby and Emmanuel Miller, had described the experience of some child evacuees in terms of 'emotional blackout').[30] My point here isn't simply to note how the landscape and language of war begin to inhabit the spaces and vocabulary of the psyche. It is obvious that whatever Winnicott is trying to describe it is not exactly a birth experience. Birth trauma and its fantasies – blank beginnings – are Winnicott's way of describing something else.

That something else has less to do with what it feels like to be born and everything to do with how it is possible to think of an ego or a self in the first place. Birth, Winnicott argues, is an impingement by 'an environment which insists on being important'.[31] To be born or to relive birth is to experience 'the feeling of being in the grips of something external'. This can feel all the more intolerable and so all the more traumatic because of the way that the infant experiences 'something without any knowledge whatever of when it will end'. The child being born is a child out of time and, Winnicott suggests, like a prisoner of war, suffers from an experience that appears to have no terminus. It is this type of impingement that makes birth feel like a form of persecution (Winnicott's word).[32] Later Winnicott will say something similar not about birth, but about what he calls the 'total setup', the environment and the processes by which the self, in his account, gets to be. In this later version, it is only through care or 'good enough mothering' that the baby actually becomes 'the baby'. Through care, says Winnicott, 'the shell becomes gradually taken over and the kernel (which has looked all the time like a human baby to us) can now begin to be an individual'.[33] But when these impingements from the outside world demand *too* much from the infant, this process can go hideously awry: by constantly having to react to the outside world the infant once more begins to resemble a shell. When Winnicott is talking about birth trauma then is he also talking about a primal displacement or exteriorization: traumatic anxiety in his account is 'the feeling that the centre of gravity of consciousness transfers from the kernel to the shell'. Like the women bobbing up and down in the Channel, Moore's *Helmet* and his *Spanish Prisoner*, Winnicott's self is redoubled in space: interiority begins on the periphery; the stuff in the middle, he reminds us, was once no more than a set of imprints on the surface. The self thus only establishes itself, only gets to have an interior 'kernel', in relation to a prior exteriority or to the space into which and through which it is born.

Or into which and through which is it is bombed. Here is a final example of a 'birth experience' from Winnicott's 1949 paper. The patient is another psychotic who has just read (rather inadvisably one might think under the circumstances) Rank's *The Trauma of Birth*:

> She dreamed that she was under a pile of gravel. Her whole body at the surface was extremely sensitive to a degree which it is hardly possible to imagine. Her skin was burned, which seemed to her to be her way of saying that it was extremely sensitive and vulnerable. She was burned all over. She knew that if anyone came and did anything at all to her, the pain would be just impossible to bear, both physical and mental pain. She knew of the danger that people would come and take the gravel off and do things to her in order to cure her, and the situation was intolerable.[34]

There were two places where one could be buried alive on the home front during World War II, in one's dreams or in one's home; once again Winnicott fails to make any connection. But what is striking about this passage is not so much the capacity of psychoanalysis to swallow the landscape of war into its own interior. Much more interesting here, I think, is again that sense of the difficulty of establishing the coherence of the self or ego – that horrifically sensitive skin surface – in relation to space. To feel that one is buried in a dream is already to be split between different spaces, between dreamer and dreamed, and between the rubble of fantasy and that of history. For this woman, as for the child being born and the prisoner of war, the 'situation was intolerable'.[35] Perhaps what also cannot be tolerated here is the sense of a self that no longer knows where it is.

Between being born and being bombed then, between myth and history, there is always this problem of how the self gets to be itself in relation to a kind of primordial spatial dislocation: ontogenesis for Winnicott is foremost a matter of topography or 'environment'. If war gets into psychoanalysis in the 1940s, as I have been suggesting, it perhaps does so not only as historical content but by posing these kind

of questions about psychic topography. This is not exactly new: psychoanalysts had been talking about psychic topography in terms of modern
war ever since the 1920s and Freud's division of the mind into ego,
id, super-ego. In *Inhibitions, Symptoms and Anxiety*, Freud describes the
ego as a 'frontier station' and mixed garrison.[36] At the height of the
war Melitta Schmideberg described the 'situation of being attacked from
above and of being unable to retaliate' as resembling 'that of a small
child whom an adult can strike from above'.[37] For Klein herself writing in
1946, anxiety comes from the fear of one's own destructive impulses that
'is experienced as the fear of an uncontrollable overpowering object'.[38]
(An uncontrollable, overpowering object...?) Winnicott does not share
Klein's insistence that all anxiety is experienced as aggressivity. His overpowering objects, so to speak, are often as comic as they are menacing.
Indeed, it is perhaps because he is less inclined to think of the psyche as
a form of warfare in itself that Winnicott manages to say more about the
difficulty of imagining ourselves historically. In 1949 Winnicott wanted
to give an account of what it felt like to be born; to have, that is, an
experience totally out of history, to begin at a place, he says, 'before the
word anxiety can be usefully implied'.[39] What he ended up with was a
theory of anxious spaces, both persecutory and nurturing, which also
describe what it feels like to be totally and intolerably in history.

III

In 1938, one year before war was declared, Max Ernst visited Henry
Moore's studio in Hampstead, London. What he particularly liked,
apparently, were Moore's tied-up objects; the drapes that swathed
Moore's half-complete sculptures, yards of white muslin settling over
the studio like a thick mist.[40] Ernst had a very different sort of war
from Moore, and it is unlikely that he saw *Crowd Looking at a Tied-Up
Object*; but he would have appreciated its surreal qualities, the way in
which, for example, the object, at once persecutory and alluring, threat
and gift, stands upright unexpectedly but expectantly in the landscape.
Had Ernst looked back over Moore's work he might also have identified with the persistence of his colleague's preoccupation with this
theme. Drapery is everywhere in Moore's war work. Alan Wilkinson
has argued that these folds and wraps, the shrouds and knots, unite
Moore's anti-representational work with the naturalist documentary
impulse of the Shelter Drawings; as he points out, the first *Shelter Sketchbook* is littered with examples of 'abstract done for drapery from a
purely sculptural point of view'.[41] Sometimes Moore's obsession hides

itself under the skirts of his naturalism, in the clothing of the female figures of the Shelter Drawings, for instance; at other times there is an almost ludic quality to the repetition of these draped objects. Ernst too was fond of repeating those kinds of objects which, as Rosalind Krauss has argued, point to the presence of a kind of optical unconscious in his work. Krauss's optical unconscious belongs to French Surrealism and the psychoanalysis of Jacques Lacan.[42] It is perhaps worth pointing out here that Moore's work appeared in the French Surrealist journal, *Minotaur*, about the same time as Lacan was first working out that alienating psychic space that he was eventually to call the imaginary.

Alas this does not mean that we can recast Moore as an avatar of the optical unconscious. But there were perhaps two Henry Moores in the 1940s, or at the very least two versions of Moore. In the first there is the Moore who transforms the experience of the Blitz into a mythic primitivism. The symbolic equations of the artist's vision make art appear where there is historical trauma ('I saw hundreds of Henry Moore reclining figures stretched along the platforms'). This is also a reading of Moore that liberal Britain felt very comfortable with; the conservative and arguably rather dull Moore of the 1950s and 1960s is not far behind. In the second version, Moore, like Winnicott, rediscovers not mythic space but anxious topography. Moore, of course, had been burrowing through these spaces before the war in his classic 1930s sculptures, but there is something in the early 1940s that produces a different kind of intensity: maybe precisely because the work bears the weight of the war. The world appears doubled in these drawings. Indeed, what might be really anxiety-provoking about *Crowd Looking at a Tied-Up Object* is not just that we, like the crowd, do not know what the object is (we fear what we know, we are anxious about what we don't), but the way the drawing refuses the distinction between perceiving subject and perceived object. What, in fact, the figures in the crowd seem to be seeing is an enlarged repetition of themselves, a redoubling of their own surfaces.

Moore returns to this theme four years later. *Girl Reading to a Woman Holding a Child* (*c.* 1946) contrasts an interior with an exterior (Figure 4.4). Out of the window, framed by the curtain, is a reproduction of *Crowd*. In the foreground are two women who look as if they had brushed off their clothes, come out of the shelters and begun to put their lives back together – this is 1946 and, like Winnicott's paper, this drawing speaks to the post-war period of reconstruction and national renewal. It is difficult, for example, not to see the ideology of pronatalist domesticity working here: a woman reading to a woman nursing

Figure 4.4   Henry Moore, *Girl Reading to a Woman Holding a Child, c.* 1946, pencil, wax crayon, coloured crayon, watercolour wash, pen and ink, 44.5 × 61.0 cm, private collection, AG. 46.53

neatly brings the twin themes of education and nurturing together into a domestic space. War (the 'group sense of communion in apprehension') has literally receded into the background. But this reading does not quite work. There is a precarious visual hierarchy of different spaces in the picture. What is a window frame could also be a picture frame, bringing the outside, the surreal landscape, the anxious object, the worried women, closer to the inside. This sense of dislocation is repeated in the errant gazes of the figures. No one meets the other's gaze here; note, for instance, the infant as it hangs precariously onto the breast of the mother almost refusing her gaze (another nice rebuttal for those who insist in finding maternal symbiosis in Moore). It is not the tied-up object here that provokes anxiety; but the implosion of the spaces themselves. Maybe it is the framing device of the curtain in this picture that causes most anxiety in all this. It is precisely because it won't fix the frontiers of the visual world for us that we notice it. The curtain disturbs our field of vision, intruding on it, refusing the perceiving 'I' a fixed place – perhaps in an echo of the kind of effects provoked by wartime photographs of children we saw in Chapter 2.[43] As if in a dream,

Moore's drawing, like Winnicott's bombed and born patient, asks us to consider what it feels like to be in two places at the same time.

Anxiety is foremost a feeling we have in relation to space: it is what we feel, to recall the quotation from Weber with which I opened this chapter, 'when the world reveals itself to be caught up in the space between two frames'. The Second World War made this space newly visible: 'war' wrote Elizabeth Bowen in *The Heat of the Day*, 'moved from the horizon to the map'.[44] A new and distinctly doubled form of spatial perception came into being. It was this space that Winnicott was describing four years after the war when he tried to work out what it felt like to be born. Moore's anxious topographies also map this space with, I think, a fidelity to some of its difficulties that some of his more mythic-minded critics obscure. Possibly it is this and not the timeless myth of human suffering that really makes his work a fitting memorial to the anxiety of World War II.

5
The Writing of Post-War Guilt: Rose Macaulay and Rebecca West

What would a guilty room look like?

Graham Greene, *The Ministry of Fear*[1]

It is a matter of indifference who actually committed the crime, psychology is only concerned to know who desired it emotionally and who welcomed it when it was done.

Sigmund Freud, 'Dostoevsky and Parricide'[2]

Morally speaking, it is hardly less wrong to feel guilty without having done something specific than it is to feel free of all guilt if one is actually guilty of something.

Hannah Arendt, *Eichmann in Jerusalem: a Report on the Banality of Evil*[3]

Writing in the wake of the Eichmann trial, and of the furore that had followed the publication of her controversial reports on the trial, Hannah Arendt perhaps had good reason to worry about the extent to which a cultural psychology of guilty feelings was interfering with the moral imperative to establish actual guilt. Despite the best efforts of justice, guilt never was going to remain within the walls of the 'Beth Hamishpath' in Jerusalem in 1961. As Arendt points out, Eichmann's odd willingness to stand trial after his capture in Argentina by the Israeli Secret Service, one of the many peculiarities of this hugely complicated event, was bound with his sense of a culture of guilt working beyond the demands of the law. Eichmann claimed that he actually wanted to stand trial (not that he had any choice in the matter) because of the 'guilt complex' emerging in Germany: by hanging himself 'in public', he said, he could do his part in 'lifting the burden of guilt from German youth'.[4] It was this kind of exploitation of a dangerously 'sentimental' guilt that concerned Arendt. For Arendt, this and the fact that Ben-Gurion's Mapai party tried to use the trial to demonstrate the rightful necessity of the Israeli state to a world – including most pointedly the world of the Jewish Diaspora – deemed guilty of passive collusion had threatened, but not succeeded, to turn this most necessary of historical acts into a show trial.[5] There is no moral or political use, Arendt cautions again and again, in crying over spilt guilt in this way. 'Only in a metaphorical sense can one say he *feels* guilty for what not he but his father or his people have done', she concludes.[6]

Writing about the famous trial scene in Dostoevsky's *The Brothers Karamazov* some thirty years earlier, Freud had argued that this kind of metaphorical sense of guilt for the crimes of others was crucial to an understanding of the trial's tension. For Freud there is absolutely no problem with saying that you can hate your father so much that you can feel as guilty over his death as your brother who actually murdered him. This is guilt by identification and desire, the two prime movers in psychoanalytical theory. Freud had already noted the extent to which guilty feelings can overrun the most modest demands of justice in 'Psychoanalysis and the Establishment of Facts in Legal Proceedings' (1906) where, in his first ever reference to a *sense* of guilt, he cautioned that the court 'could be led astray by the neurotic, who reacts as if he were guilty, although he is innocent, because a sense of guilt which already existed and lay hidden in him takes over the specific accusation made against him'.[7] Accusations do not so much establish guilt as rationalize an otherwise completely senseless sense of guilt; which is why, famously for psychoanalysis, criminals frequently act *from* a sense of guilt.[8] As Freud would later argue in his defence of a man convicted on the strength of his parricidal feelings alone, a sense of guilt hardly helps the court establish actual guilt: 'Precisely because it is always present', he noted of the Christopher Halsman case in 1930, 'the Oedipus Complex is not suited to provide a decision on the question of guilt.'[9] For psychoanalysis guilt is always going to be disproportionate in the ways that Arendt found so damaging. Indeed, when Eichmann used the language of psychoanalysis (the German 'guilt complex') to justify his own perverted political martyrdom, he also understood that for psychology it matters less who committed the crime than who feels emotionally responsible for it. No more than Arendt does Freud think that feeling guilty and being guilty are the same thing: for psychoanalysis, however, the spilling of guilt can neither be dismissed as merely, if dangerously, 'sentimental', nor easily put back into the judicial jar from which it has spilled.

To an extent Arendt is right to insist that justice and the law remain uncorrupted by the psychic and cultural dynamics of guilt – even as, or especially when, that corruption looks inevitable. It does not, however, follow that the question of what sort of cultural and historical fantasies guilt generates or preserves should not be asked; indeed, perhaps this question has to be asked if what remains of lawful guilt is to be protected.[10] In the immediate post-war context, fifteen years before Eichmann came to redefine war guilt for a new generation, that question was urgent. As Arendt's mentor, Karl Jaspers pointed out in his influential *The Question of German Guilt* (1947), based on the lectures he gave in Heidelberg just after the fall of the Nazi regime, and in which he painstakingly differentiates between types and contexts for guilt in an effort to head off the promiscuous generalizations that were later to worry Arendt, guilt took on a new significance in 1945. 'Today things are altogether different', Jaspers notes in a comparison with the punitive reparations demanded by the Treaty of Versailles after the First World War, 'The question of guilt has acquired a more comprehensive meaning. It sounds quite unlike before [...] "You are guilty" means much more than war guilt.'[11] Post-war, this 'much-more-than-war-guilt' guiltiness acquired a newly brittle prominence ('what used to count in the world has become brittle', Jaspers says elsewhere).[12] In almost direct proportion to the political necessity to protect and redefine the law, particularly international law, in the wake of both Nazi lawlessness and of the Soviet show trials, the call to guilt ('you are guilty') took on a new cultural, psychic and existential resonance: it sounded different.

In this chapter I want to ask how guilt 'sounds', or gets written, not only after the war but also after Freud and modernism, through a reading of Rose Macaulay's textually exuberant 1950 novel, *The World My Wilderness*, and Rebecca West's brilliant and densely figurative writings on the Nuremberg Trial, later collected in *A Train of Powder: Six Reports on the Problem of Guilt and Punishment in Our Time* (1955).[13] Writing after the war, but before guilt was swept up into the sort of discussions about the malaise of the human condition which, in part, set the stage for the reception of Eichmann, both Macaulay and West call on a certain modernist style of writing to find correlatives for a post-war situation in which the meanings of political and criminal guilt were, to say the least, overdetermined. How far the by then somewhat depleted resources of modernism were adequate to this task emerges as a crucial question in both women's writing. At issue here, then, is a question about a certain *way* of writing about guilt.

I

Literary guilt, almost by definition, is nearly always disproportionate in some significant kind of way. When William Empson, for example, described Coleridge's Ancient Mariner as a 'peculiarly grand case of "Neurotic Guilt" ', he was not only complaining about the mariner's self-pitying whining (it is, after all, only a bird), but about the extent to which Coleridge sold out to a Christian allegorical reading of redemption through suffering, when the poem's real moral was that the mariner could be redeemed through a secular 'return of spontaneous delight' in nature. The mariner's crime, that is, is of less consequence than the ideological use to which his suffering is eventually put in the poem.[14] For T.S. Eliot, famously, there is the even greater risk that the senseless mutterings of the neurotically guilty might prove to be of no consequence whatsoever. Guilty feelings, like other intense emotions, need 'objective correlatives', he warned in his essay on *Hamlet*; without the right set of objects, situations or chains of events, guilt can become aesthetically meaningless. Eliot is positively Freudian in his description of such affective waywardness: 'The intense feeling, ecstatic or terrible, without an object or exceeding its object, is something which every person of sensibility has known; it is doubtless a subject of study for pathologists.'[15] Much immediate post-war writing can be described as furnishing war guilt with its own literary pathology. Shoshana Felman, for example, has noted of Albert Camus' *The Plague* (1947) that Camus' choice of a doctor to 'bear witness' to the contagion is 'itself somehow a philosophical and ethical correlative of a situation *with no cure*, and of a radical condition of exposure and vulnerability'.[16] Post-war, it is the pathologists themselves who have got into literature.

Macaulay's *The World My Wilderness*, while lacking Camus' philosophical seriousness, is also trying to discover a new literary pathology for historical culpability. In this novel nearly everyone is guilty to some extent, or at least *feels* guilty. The novel's heroine, the aptly over-named Barbary, is banished from her home in south-western France by her mother who blames her for colluding with the Maquis in the death of her collaborationist stepfather, and finds a new home from home, away from the cold judicial eye of her KC father, in the ruins around St Pauls, London. Barbary's war guilt, however, is not so much the real focus of the novel as is a more general moral dereliction, signified by the smashed up churches and temples of law, and by the gang of adolescent delinquents who inhabit them; the post-war lawless who help Barbary and her step-brother Raoul into a feral life of petty crime. 'The novel's painful question', noted the novelist Penelope Fitzgerald (who was frequently dragged over bomb-sites by a ruin-obsessed Macaulay in this period), 'is what have we done to our children?'[17] In a trope that dominated the late 1940s and 1950s, for Macaulay too the post-war delinquent is the bearer for the moral failings of the wartime generation: we are guilty, goes this logic, for their criminality (neither John Bowlby nor Donald Winnicott would have disagreed – neither perhaps, chillingly, would have Eichmann). Thus Barbary's war crimes are set against her parents' failings and, in an oddly protracted denouement, her mother forgives her for the death of her stepfather while forced to confess that Barbary was not in fact the child of her first husband, but of a former lover. So in another trope hardly unfamiliar to either literature or psychoanalysis, a mother's guilt stands behind the excessive behaviour of the child. But this sense of an ending, the idea that blame can be apportioned and people reconciled to each other's failings, falls limp when set against the rest of a novel which finds redemption not so much in love and forgiveness, but in the stony rubbish of the post-war wilderness itself.

There is a significant tension here because, on the one hand, Macaulay clearly wants to indict the moral wilderness of her novel's title. Barbary suffers because she cannot find a context in which to make her war guilt meaningful. Lawless because all representatives of the law are, for her generation, simultaneously representatives of fascist brutality, Barbary laments the fact that her lack of faith also bars her from atonement: 'we others can't be forgiven', she muses as she wanders around the empty shell of a bombed-out church, 'because we sin only against people, and the people stay hurt or killed, or whatever it is we have done to them'.[18] As for the traumatized priest who interrupts Raoul and Barbary – as they perform, in a wonderful scene of early beatnik camp, a bizarre parody of a mass among the ruins (Barbary has painted the crumbling walls with a 'Judgement Day' picture, jazz plays on the radio, a black kitten is offered as a 'symbolic sacrificial offering') – with the cry 'we are in hell now',[19] for the novel too the horror of the post-war epoch is that it reveals a world of guilt without meaning. But whereas this all nods towards that sense of incurable existential malaise that was to dominate fiction in the later 1950s, Macaulay's novel still wants to make the guilt of her wayward heroine somehow redeemable and, in a recognizably modernist manner, calls upon both the resources of literary history and the novel's own repetitions and citations, its own considerable fictional density, in order to try and make it so.

For if, on the one hand, Macaulay wants to indict Barbary's lawlessness and the moral darkness of the post-war landscape, on the other the novel is in thrall to the ruins over which she scrambles and to the literary debris through which Macaulay tries to 'salvage', to borrow a term from Leo Mellor's reading of the novel, some meaning out of guilty despair.[20] From the citation from 'The Fire Sermon' on the opening page, to Barbary's upright brother Richie's shuddering recitation of the memorable 'rat's alley' line in the final chapter, the novel returns again and again to the empty chapels and windowless windy homes that are both Eliot's *The Waste Land* and Barbary's preferred habitat. Indeed, it is perhaps an incidental (if compelling) irony that the poem in which Eliot worked so hard to correlate the affective residues of the first war should find itself so awkwardly placed as the poetic touchstone for the emotional ruins of the second. 'I am very, very fond of ruins', sings Mavis, one of Barbary's gang, as she trips over the stony rubble and singing grass, 'ruins I love to scan'.[21] Mavis is singing a Marie Lloyd song, the same song that Macaulay will use to open her 1953 study, *The Pleasure of Ruins*. Ruins give us pleasure, albeit of a morbid or egotistical kind, Macaulay argues in this book, which is also a loving photo-essay to the romance of the historical remnant, because they signify a weirdly nostalgic permanence. The new post-war ruins, she notes, citing the work of Paul Nash – but she could have just as well referred to Henry Moore – may be for 'a time stark and bare, vegetationless and creatureless, blackened and torn', but it will not take long for them to yield up their hidden pleasures, once the ruin-poets have worked their magic and softened their 'resentful sadness' through art.[22] Something of a ruin-poet herself, in *The World My Wilderness* Macaulay accelerates the process of ruin dignification with an incantatory poetry that moves between the rubble of St Giles, Cripplegate, and the valued remains of a literary culture that can only whisper its despair between the lines (while Eliot is Macaulay's main source, he is joined by his own, and Macaulay's, best company: the Metaphysicals, Marvell and Thomas Traherne, the King James Bible and Shakespeare). But thus stuffed with historical and textual matter, Barbary's wasteland fails to be an objective correlative of the 'more-than-war-guilt guiltiness' that inflicts the novel's characters and becomes, instead, a kind of emulsifying cipher – all is guilty, all is waste, there is nothing left to do other than lovingly kick over the stony rubble, the 'quaint honour turned to dust', of a culture gone to the upside-down bats with the baby faces.

It is as if guilt in the novel has no place to go other than back into an aesthetics of the literary fragment which, like the ghosts of Cripplegate who gaze 'respectably down at' the police chasing the thieving Barbary and Horace over the rubble, 'lending the law the silent support of some eight centuries of property and substance',[23] work as a moral reproach to the lawlessness of the present. 'The crook in all of us is bursting out and talking possession', says Barbary's lotus-eating mother, Helen, 'like Hyde while Jekyll slowly dies of attrition.'[24] The war has made everyone guilty. Helen is well placed to know: her particular crime is not only sexual but literary deception. Voluptuously lazing beneath the bougainvillea in the garden of her Roussillon villa, she spends her spare time writing fake troubadour poetry. 'Fraud, forgery, plagiarism, falsification, theft, concealment and even destruction of documents, to win glory or prove a theory', she explains to Richie, 'scholars of all periods have done that sort thing.'[25] Making stuff up is hardly the same as colluding in a wartime execution (something Barbary has done twice), nonetheless in Macaulay's wilderness world the particularity of crime is subsumed under the spongy weightiness of a very generalized sense of guilt. Helen's self-indictment is doubly odd because nicking things and faking it up is also, of course, what Macaulay is doing in the novel. In her pink house with the trompe-d'oeil shutters of painted ladies and 'dado of sea creatures of the deep',[26] Helen, 'a comfortable, ironic hedonist'[27] partial to games of chance, has herself been filched from the Cleopatra of 'The Game of Chess' section of *The Waste Land*. Similarly criminal, the lines in the novel's epigram ('The world my wilderness, its caves my home, / Its weedy wastes the garden where I roam'), are not those of some anonymous seventeenth-century poet, as Macaulay's attribution suggests, but belong to Macaulay herself, Milton scholar and fabulous faker-upper of seventeenth-century poetry.

Winnicott might have understood this comparison between teenage and literary delinquency, between the salvaging that went on in London's bomb sites and Macaulay's own literary historical salvaging as a sign of hope perverted. As he pointed out in an address to magistrates in 1946, for the post-war delinquent being lawless and anti-social is also a way of demanding something better of society and the way it organizes its moral life.[28] It is tempting to say that Macaulay's novel is similarly demanding something better of literature. The stakes for Macaulay herself in this were high. She had had to pick her own way out of the ruins in the 1940s, not only out of her blitzed house with its precious library torn to bits, but out of the death of her long-term married lover, the former priest, Gerald O'Donovan. Like the later, more successful and much funnier *The Towers of Trebizond* (1956), *The World My Wilderness* catches Macaulay on her ambivalent return to the Anglican Church. Whereas the later novel, however, is about guilt and religion (and reads in part as a settling of the spiritual accounts of long-term adultery) the novel closer to the war could better be described as anxiously tenebricose, as it laments a universal guilt, but ultimately remains in the dark about what to do about it. Thus the novel ends by demanding something better than what it itself can do at the present time. In Eliot's poem, redemption is suspended: we never know whether the rains fall or not. Wandering around the ruins like a post-war Fisher King, it is Richie who gives the last word on the ruins in *The World My Wilderness*: 'It was a symbol of loathsome things, war, destruction, savagery; and earnest, perhaps, of the universal doom that stalked, sombre and menacing on its way.'[29] But it is a symbol too plump with writing and history to carry the weight of the moral authority Macaulay wants to give it, and in the end *The World My Wilderness* is a novel about a 'more than war guilt' guiltiness that has no place to go, except back into a hugely evocative but nonetheless historically brittle figurative textuality.

I have written at length on Macaulay's novel not to diminish its considerable intensity but to suggest that the peculiar way in which it fails, if indeed fail it does, is significant in two ways. First, the novel speaks to a culture in which guilt is emerging as the primary affective response to the war: not regret, shame or anxiety (there was no anxiety left in post-war Europe, noted the existential psychologist, Paul Tillich, because the unimaginable had actually happened), but a strangely proliferating culpability that reads the signs of moral dereliction in the wreckage of post-war culture, but does not yet know what to do with itself.[30] In the period just before guilt emerged as the universal post-war condition for a world horribly appraised of its own capacity for evil (and before, as Denis Hollier has put it aptly, existentialism became a humanism[31]), it is as if the acknowledgement of some kind of guilt – even for a minor crime, and even for a crime you perhaps only wanted to happen unconsciously – at least provided some kind of affective relationship to immediate history, albeit, in Freud's terms, an identificatory relationship only, or in Arendt's, a dangerously sentimental one at that.

Macaulay was not the only British writer who was revising recent history from the precarious prospect of guilty feelings. A ruthlessly simple Old Testament logic drives the plot of Nevil Shute's rather nasty *Requiem for a Wren* (1955) where the Wren in question, Janet Prentice, atones for the deaths of seven escaping Czech flyers by witnessing the deaths of the five people (and the one dog) closest to her and then making up the numbers by killing herself: 'it's fair enough', she notes in her diary, 'because if you kill seven people wantonly just to show how good you are with an Oerlikon you've got to be made to suffer for it'.[32] The war, notes Shute's narrator, 'like some infernal monster, still venomous in death [...] can go on killing people for a long time after it's all over'.[33] Disproportionate guilt here is the continuation of war by other means. For other writers, war permits the continuation of a ruthlessly theological guilt by other means. In Graham Greene's *Ministry of Fear* (1943), a relentlessly awful Christian pity ties Richard Rowe's 'war crimes' (his complicity in the death of a fifth columnist) with his earlier mercy-killing of his sick wife: both crimes are subsumed, albeit compellingly so, under a narrative which Richard can only submit to (the promise of atonement is forged in that submission).[34] By contrast, Marghanita Laski's undeservedly little read *Little Boy Lost* (1949), anticipates the existential turn in British fiction by compelling its anti-hero, Hilary Wainright, to recognize the child who may, or may not, be the son he lost in France in 1943. In Laski's novel, feeling guilty turns out to be a way of atoning for a history for which you may not actually be responsible.[35]

Each of these writers takes 'war guilt' as a starting point for forging some kind of relation with recent history. Macaulay does this too, but what is notable about her writing is the way that, unlike in the work of some of her contemporaries, this excessively more-than-war-guilt guiltiness is folded over, as it were, back into the novel's own literariness – which is the second way in which the novel is particularly significant to my argument. It could be claimed that in this way the novel is performing its own 'traumatic' relation to history: its figurative ruins, thus, would be not an attempt to represent post-war moral obliteration, but an affectively charged repetition, or enactment, of the break between referent and sign which, for some, marks a traumatic break in historical experience. The fact that war guilt has no place to go except into the novel's own overdetermined figures for modernist redemption would, for this reading, be precisely its point: it is performing (not reflecting) the moral dereliction of a pathologically guilty situation for which, to paraphrase Shoshana Felman, there can be no cure. In *The World My Wilderness* it would only be possible to feel guilt in a very literal 'metaphorical sense', for in the end it is only literary metaphors that circle around the nameless post-war anxiety that rests at the core of the text. Macaulay's novel, however, is not this profound. It is not so much the pathos of the unpresentable that drives this fiction, as an excited piling up of figures that is always on the verge of turning citation into cliché: indeed, Macaulay's novel's post-war moral wilderness only just stays this side of kitsch. But perhaps in this way it manages to say something more historically pertinent about the writing of guilt. For it seems to me that it is not some kind of unspeakable anxiety, but an *over-naming* of guilt that is the issue here. With this thought in mind, I want to turn next to Rebecca West.

II

A biographer of Augustine as well as the author of a study of Henry James, West is particularly well placed to address the question of what happens to guilt when it meets a writing that enacts its relation to history by being acutely conscious of its style. West's own debts to James as well as her sharp political moralism are apparent in fictions such as *The Return of the Soldier* (1918) and the belle époque family saga, *The Fountain Overflows* (1956). But it is in her journalism, and in her urgent sense that there is an acute relation between style and political-historical commentary, most compellingly developed in her epic study of Yugoslavia, *Black Lamb and Grey Falcon* (1941), that West most provocatively confronts the question of the relation between moral agency and writing. West's fascination with what she would later describe as the 'problem of guilt and punishment in our time' begins in Macaulay's wilderness world. Her coverage of the trial of the traitor, William Joyce ('Lord Haw Haw') in 1945, which triggered what was to be a long fascination with the workings of justice, opens in the bombed-out 'desert of charred stone' surrounding the Old Bailey where 'churches stood blackened but apparently intact' and 'birds [...] flew through the empty sockets of the windows and long grass grew around their altars'.[36] (You could incise this passage directly into some sections of *The World My Wilderness* without leaving even the faintest scar.) No more than Macaulay is West simply scene-setting: her blitzed ruins too are correlatives for a post-war moral dereliction which, for West the journalist, can be redeemed only by the reimposition of the law. That commitment to the rule of law led West in 1946 to the Nuremberg trials and resulted in a series of articles she wrote for the *New Yorker* and the *Daily Telegraph* which were later republished as the first of three essays on post-war Germany, 'Greenhouse with Cyclamens I', in *A Train of Powder* in 1955. The process of revision between the two versions itself has a story to tell about how the Cold War inflicted its own narrative on the spectacle of the trial. In the 1946 *New Yorker* version, for example, West describes the Soviet judges as well 'liked' despite international tensions: in the 1955 version, their behaviour is referred to as 'childish' and befitting 'part of a mock trial'.[37] The threat that the trial might degenerate into some kind of travesty of itself was already present in 1946. Whereas West's increasingly shrill anti-communism might later blame the theatricality of some of the proceedings on the cack-handed politics of the Soviets, her original reports are also extremely sensitive to their own 'showiness', as West's brilliantly evocative descriptions of the trial are piled high with images which announce, in a way not dissimilar to Macaulay's, their own literariness. For West, however, this is less a case of war guilt spilling out into a redemptive literary-theological aesthetic, as part of an effort to think about how it is possible to write about a crime that is insistently and horribly real. The issue here, then, is not only about the proliferation of a sense of war guilt; West's writing also raises questions about the relation between writing itself, particularly writing which self-consciously understands itself as literary, and a very real political, historical and moral criminality.

'It is ironical', West writes at one point, 'to cross a dreaded frontier in order to report the last convulsions of a German crime and find oneself housed in a German fairy tale.'[38] She is describing the Schloss in which many of the women correspondents covering Nuremberg were housed. 'Dropsical in whimsy', this grotesque fairytale of a villa is a warped monument to the 'primitive fantasy' of its builders which was eventually to 'force their country to the edge of an abyss.'[39] In 1946 that fantasy stands rebuked not only by the trial, but also by the likes of French Jewish journalist, Madeleine Jacobs, as she rushes down the corridors in her beach sandals: 'It would have been very hard for the builders of the Schloss to grasp the situation', West understates, 'to understand that these ink-stained gipsies had earned the right to camp in their stronghold because they had been on the side of order against disorder, stability against incoherence.'[40] Writing about Nuremberg, for West, is foremost a way of reinstating order against disorder, stability against incoherence. This strong sense of the political importance of the law is something that unites a venerable tradition of women war crime reporters from this period including, along with Madeleine Jacobs with her wild hair and espadrilles, Janet Flanner, Martha Gelhorn and Sybille Bedford as well as West and, of course, Arendt. But in 1946 it is not just West who with her colleagues is living temporarily in a grotesque fantasy turned horribly consequential, in many senses her writing is too.

Where Macaulay finds the correlative for war guilt in a post-war wasteland, West discovers it in the seedy fairytale that contributed to the crime itself. The first report West filed for the *New Yorker* is astonishing for its brilliantly macabre descriptions of a barely-there ghastliness of the defendants. 'Wreathed in the suggestion of death', it is as if the crimes of these people are so inhuman, so beyond the comprehension of an ordered and stable discourse, that all that is left to them is a brittle appearance that might crumble under the smallest of breaths. With the 'head of a ventriloquist's dummy' ('thick brown young hair, the coarse bright skin of an actor who has used grease paint for decades, and the preternaturally deep wrinkles of the drug addict'[41]), and the manner of a Marseilles brothel madam, for example, Goering is not only one of the last inhabitants of the giant Schloss which was once Nazi Germany, but reads like a character out of late modernist gothic: with his creepy theatrical femininity, he could easily belong to the repertoire of damaged souls in, say, Djuna Barnes's *Nightwood* (1936). Meanwhile, from an earlier gothic tradition, the Hitler Youth leader, Baldur von Schirach, looks like Jane Eyre, while Schacht, President of the Reichsbank, 'might have been [...] a disagreeable corpse who had contrived to aggravate the process so that he should be specially difficult to fit into his coffin'.[42] These are the dead in metaphor, 'visibly receding from the field of existence', as West puts it.[43] The most disturbing description is of the clearly mad Hess who, writes West, 'looked as if his mind had no surface, as if every part of it had been blasted away except the depth where the nightmares live'.[44] Hess in fact looks remarkably like what Freud might have described as the blasted remains of a psyche without its protective shield in *Beyond the Pleasure Principle*.[45] But if Hess can emerge as the frail emblem for a situation of total trauma in West's rhetoric, what then of his guilt?

It is possible that the guilt of the defendants at Nuremberg was so much a given that the drama of the slow unfolding of evidence, argument and counter-argument so central to trial reporting might well have seemed irrelevant to a writer like West; compared, perhaps, to a more urgent imperative to describe the overwhelming strangeness of such a historically unique event. At the same time, however, there is a kind of over-substantiality to West's writing that gestures towards something insubstantial at the heart of the trial itself: indeed in 1954 West herself will describe Nuremberg as 'one of the events which do not become an experience'.[46] This sense of an event that should have meant more than it eventually did might account for why West's writing is so heavily dependent on simile and metaphor, on things appearing as other things but never being quite of themselves. It is as if she is acknowledging the failure of the trial to somehow adequately evoke the guilt of the defendants in cultural or philosophical terms (as compared to the watertight criminal and political case) in the overdeveloped metaphoricity of her own writing. But this kind of writing does not only correlate with a moral situation which (once more) may have no cure: unhinged from the requirement to demonstrate actual war guilt, West's proliferation of metaphors also has moral consequences of its own.

In a text in which a grotesque theatricality so frequently tropes the moral dereliction of Nazi Germany it is perhaps not that surprising to find West worrying about the 'posed and theatrical air' of some of the atrocity photographs given as evidence (the use of photographs as evidence of historical crimes was significantly new in Nuremberg).[47] For West, this shared theatricality suggests an awkward equivalence between the nation that committed the crime and the evidence meant to indict its leaders: where, West seems to ask, in a world of brittle appearances, can we actually find the crime? She finds it eventually in the only piece of evidence for Nazi crimes that she actually writes about in her reports (compare, for example, Arendt's later painstaking reporting of the documentary evidence against Eichmann, or Sybille Bedford's less comprehensive, but equally careful following of the testimonial evidence in the case against twenty-two former Auschwitz staff members in 1963[48]). 'Somebody', writes West, 'had been collecting tattooed human skin, and it is hard to think where such a connoisseur could find his pieces unless he had power over a concentration camp. Some of these pelts were infinitely pathetic, because of their obscenity.'[49] This is an arresting moment in West's writing, not only because of the power of the image, but because of the way in which these pathetic human pelts exceed her frame of rhetorical reference. The grotesque horror of the image of the flayed skin itself is actually all of a piece with the gothic nightmare that West finds in Nuremberg: what is disturbing about the skin is precisely its status *as* evidence; the pelts are the visible signs of a crime – they are effects that have been caused by acts – in a text which is very much caught up in appearances which seem to have no direct reference. It is difficult, in other words, to turn the obscenity of the skin – what you could call its all-too-real-indexical status – into metaphor; and for a moment, West's writing stalls. Not however for long, for, in the next paragraph, this authentic evidence of criminal guilt is re-spun back into the text's dominant metaphorical frame. The skin, thus, becomes another emblem of the inexplicable nature of the moral and cultural guilt of the German people. In a moment of pathos, West observes the French doctor in charge of the exhibits turn 'in his hand a lampshade made of tattooed human skin'. He says:

'These people where I live send me in my breakfast tray strewn with pansies, beautiful pansies. I have never seen more beautiful pansies, arranged with exquisite taste. I have to remind myself that they belong to the same race that supplied me with my exhibits, the same race that tortured me month after month, year after year, at Mauthausen.'

'And, indeed', West adds, 'flowers were the visible sign of that mystery, flowers that were not only lovely but beloved.'[50] These beloved flowers weave their mysterious way into West's later drafting of the original reports and re-emerge in the title of her three 1955 essays – 'Greenhouse with Cyclamens'. West first discovers the greenhouse in the garden of the Schloss and is surprised to find it sheltering a burgeoning cyclamen business. Popping out of their pots like the roots that cling to the stony rubbish in Eliot's waste land, the cyclamens are an ambivalent sign of the tenacity of the German character; a drive to industry that powers on oblivious to history. 'It might seem that it would never be very interesting that somebody had started a brisk business in potted plants', West writes. 'But this was Germany, this was 1946, and it was as if one were in a lock, and saw the little trickle of water between the gates which meant the lock was opening.' But she then adds: 'The war had burned trade off Germany as a flame burns skin off a body.'[51] This might well be an example of the unconscious of hasty language (although its appearance in the 1955 edited version might argue against mere carelessness), but in a text as figuratively overdetermined as West's, the effects of this metaphorical misprision are more than simply unfortunate. 'The war' burned trade off Germany just as it burned the skin off Jewish corpses: the difference between victim and perpetrator collapses amid a bundle of figures that appear to correlate only to one another. It is as if 'the war', or history itself, is the guilty aggressor; everyone else, like the traumatized Hess, is simply caught in its effects.

What happens when history is subsumed under trauma in this way seems to be precisely the kind of lack of moral discrimination about assigning guilt that was to trouble Arendt in the early 1960s. At issue here is also the question of what happens to judgement when it is confronted with a writing that performs its own vexed relation to historical violence. As some historians' critiques of trauma theory suggest, this question of how guilt actually gets assigned within what you could call a rhetoric of trauma is still troubling.[52] In a highly critical reading of Cathy Caruth's poetics of enigmatic survival, to give just one example from a large debate, Ruth Leys has argued that a theory which valorizes the repetitive effects of trauma risks a dangerous mystification of historical culpability. Thus in Caruth's reading of Tasso's *Tancred and Clorinda*, a text that bewitched Freud in *Beyond the Pleasure Principle*, it becomes horribly easy to forget that even though Tancred is gripped by a demonic possession that condemns him to repeated acts of violence on Clorinda, he nonetheless remains her murderer. For Caruth, Clorinda's cries articulate Tancred's traumatic dissociation; an 'enigma of [...] otherness', her voice 'witnesses a truth that Tancred himself cannot fully know'.[53] Making the voice of one, however, perform the trauma of the other ultimately makes victimhood, and hence culpability, unlocatable. If, Leys argues, 'the murderer Tancred can become the victim of the trauma and the voice of Clorinda testimony to *his* wound, then Caruth's logic would turn other perpetrators into victims too – for example it would turn the executioners of the Jews into victims and the "cries" of the Jews into testimony to the trauma suffered by the Nazis'.[54] Between the traumatized Hess and the French doctor's testimony this is almost what happens in West's writing too, as Nazi war crimes seem to sink into the generalized pathos of a situation where neither culpability nor agency has any hold. To an extent that collapse is inevitable: by definition there is no place for moral agency within the logic of psychic trauma – which is why one can feel guilty for crimes one hasn't actually committed. To try and re-establish moral agency in the unconscious is like asking someone to take responsibility for what they intend to dream. It is however a different matter when that traumatic logic reappears in a form of writing which is precisely trying to represent the act of assigning moral agency, that is, in writing about a trial (a writing that Felman has described as revealing a 'space of *slippage between law and art*'[55]).

West certainly believes in guilt, hence her commitment to the tribunal; what her writing seems to have to fight against is not so much a situation in which either victimhood or culpability *are* unlocatable within an enigmatic poetics of survival, for example, to echo Caruth's reading of *Tancred,* but in which they have *become* unlocatable within a more deadly version of performativity. Maybe what is really spooky about the grotesque cast of ventriloquists' dummies that West's writing sets up in the dock is the way that they seem to over-demonstrate a modernity which, not unlike Nazism itself, has indeed abolished all agency to a realm of mechanized forces. Rather like the marionettes in Kleist's famous short story, 'On the Marionette Theatre', the 1946 defendants are all matter without substance, all movement without purpose. Citing Paul de Man's essay on aesthetic formalization in Kleist, T.J. Clark has recast the marionette theatre as modernism's uncanny; their dance, 'unavoidable as it is deadly',[56] as de Man puts it, drives an inhuman representational machine that lurks behind modernism's more celebratory claims about the materiality of art and writing.[57] There is something of this too, I think, in the grinding together of metaphor on metaphor in the dark nightmare of the German fairy tale gone badly wrong at the heart of West's reports. In trying to give expression to this nightmare, West's writing becomes entangled in its awful mechanizations, which is partly why at moments in her reports it is as if the category of historical agency has been evacuated elsewhere, as if there is no space for it between the death's heads and the pots of cyclamens, between fairy-tale villas and villains and the inexplicable 'mysteries' or 'enigmas' of a crime without precedent.

But West, I think, knows all this, and knows it well, which is what makes her accounts of Nuremberg something more than an example of trauma writing gone awry within its own aestheticism. The marionettes and their deathly dance only encroach on her writing, they do not take it over all together. West's fury at Goering's suicide, for example (Goering cheated his captors by poisoning himself with cyanide the evening before his execution was due), was not only because Goering managed to make a myth out of himself and a fool out of international justice, but because his audacious act seemed to snatch back some agency for himself in a piece of drama made possible precisely by the way in which Nuremberg (the symbol of which, West notes at one point, was a 'giant yawn'),[58] failed to make the guilt it so plainly demonstrated culturally and morally meaningful. 'Goering should never have been given the chance to use his courage to weaken public horror at his crimes', West writes, 'to which his courage was not relevant.'[59] He should not have been allowed to cheat justice, West continues, not because he is evil, but because although the threat of the monstrous hurdy-gurdy machine is ever-present, we have the choice whether to succumb to it or not. This is West's striking definition of the status of historical agency in 1946:

> The Nazis were maniacs who plastered history with the cruelty which is a waste product of man's moral nature, as maniacs on a smaller scale plaster their bodies and their clothes with their excreta. Since sanity is to some extent a matter of choice, a surrender to certain stimuli and a rejection of others, the nature of mania should never be forgotten. It is unfair, not only to Germans, but to all the world, if the vileness of the Nazis be extenuated; and it was unfair that this Nazi of all Nazis should have been allowed to disguise his gross dementia.[60]

It is undoubtedly difficult to reconcile the idea of a 'surrender to certain stimuli and a rejection of others' in which one would be, in an extreme version of psychoanalytic materialism, purely at the mercy of a set of mechanized forces, and the thought that this might also be 'a matter of choice'. Choosing not to be mad is a frail-sounding moral category, even for 1946. Nonetheless, this perhaps is precisely where West's own writing takes us, and without that slim marker it would be as if the marionette theatre had taken over the trial itself, rendering it at best meaningless, and, at worst, a hideous prolongation of a history of deadening and horrifying materialism. What was really irksome about Nuremberg, West later wrote, was 'the perpetual confrontation with the dreary details of an ugly chapter in history which the surrounding rubble seemed to prove to have been taken out of the book and to require no further discussion: the continued enslavement by the war machine'.[61] Unlike Macaulay, West finds no redemption in the meanings cited in the rubble; only a terrifying repletion of a dull and deathly mania.

In this context choosing not to be mad emerges as an understandable defence against the more grisly logic that haunts West's writing. Where else, indeed, could West go for a description of culpability that would not melt amid her own metaphors? Later West defended Nuremberg for its services to history: for all its tedium, for all that it played out like some ghastly gothic novel, the International War Crimes Tribunal did what it set out to do and what manifestly needed to be done; it set a precedent, it established the existence of 'crimes against humanity' and it thus re-established the rule of law. What the trial struggled to do was to furnish the base political criminality at its centre with a cultural or moral significance. On the one hand, this was a proper failure: the court's job is not to make guilt resonate but to establish its absolute existence, as Arendt would later insist with reference to Eichmann. For West, however, one senses, if guilt became brittle in the places of justice in Nuremberg, it was also because the relentless click-clacking of the war machine meant that it was never really there (and never really could be there) in a culturally and psychologically adequate sense in the first place. This is not because of any failure in the law (far from it, the law absolutely demonstrated the guilt of the defendants) but because of the persistence of a dark logic in which guilt can indeed be everywhere – in 'history', in the 'war', in the 'unconscious' – and so belong to no one and everyone – which may be partly why someone like Eichmann could start pushing the meanings of guilt around so indiscriminately nearly twenty years later. (Marianna Torgovnick has pointed out that Eichmann wanted to be a 'little bit like' Goering at Nuremberg.[62])

'The trouble about Nuremberg', West wrote just before the end of the trial, 'was that it was so manifestly part of life as it is lived; the trial had not sufficiently detached itself from the oddity of the world. It was a piece with the odd things that happened on its periphery; and these were odd enough.'[63] Odd, for example, like the old crone who surprises West one evening by popping her head over a garden fence with the cry ' "I shot your King Edward" '. With her 'teeth clacking at a different rate of her speech', this grizzled aristocrat explains that she once went shooting with King Edward and then quizzes West on the fate of one of the defendants, Sauckel, for whom, she thinks, hanging would be too good. Somewhere in all this lunatic gabbling, however, it turns out that Sauckel's 'crime' is to have flooded the village with foreign labour ('scum of the earth, Russians, Balks, Balts, Slavs – Slavs, I tell you' – out of the eight and a half million slave labourers imported by Sauckel, some one million died of overwork[64]) and that although the woman, of course, thinks what Hitler did to the Jews was terrible, she is troubled that the British have appointed a Jew as their chief prosecutor ('really, really now, was that quite *gentleman*?') When it is pointed out to her that Sir David Maxwell Fyfe is not actually Jewish she ripostes with a chilling cliché: 'we Germans understand a little better about such things, and he would not dare to pretend to us that he was not a Jew'.[65] Whether inside the courtroom or out, it is as if the same grim fairy tale spins itself out.

The crone story is one of three vignettes which appear towards the end of West's reports and which recall the wonderfully adept allegorical storytelling style of West's earlier masterpiece, *Black Lamb, Grey Falcon*. The second story focuses on a figure who by turning his face against history becomes a poignant emblem for a horribly guileless complicity with Nazi crimes. The man is a swimmer, a city dweller whose thin white body, West observes, has not been starved – as it had for just about everyone else in Europe and the Far East by this point – but exercised into that state: 'he was affirming that though he had lost everything else, he still had his body, he still had that surely quite remarkable stomach muscle, he was still his unique self'.[66] This is a body which is all matter not human substance. And still the marionette theatre plays on. Only West's third character gives some sense of what it might mean to choose not to be mad. The quiet foreman's wife who West meets on the driveway up to the Schloss asks what sentence has been passed on Streicher who, it turns out, had subjected the locals to a vile tirade of 'gibbering filth about the Jews', while his SS thugs barred the doors. 'Yes', she explains to West, 'quite young boys had forced her and her husband to stay with their children in this bath of mud.' The woman stops talking: 'Again she fell silent, and her face was a solid white circle in the dusk.'[67] This is a final moment of pathos in West's writing, but unlike the mysteriously beloved pansies on the French doctor's breakfast tray, the foreman's wife is not over-figured within the text's dominant metaphorics; if anything, she is a kind of under-figure, an abstraction amid the garish kitsch of the Nuremberg marionettes. A 'solid white circle in the dusk' – what better figure for an integrity that can only be seen in direct contrast to the darkening night of post-war culture?

I do not think, however, that this is a redemptive moment. I am not sure how it could be in a context where the writing of guilt turns out to be not only the expression of a new post-war moral context, but a kind of symptom of a culture where it is no longer possible, if indeed it ever were, to make guilt meaningful *enough*, that is, as it were, to make guilt *guilty* enough. In some senses, the proliferation of guilt in a novel such as Macaulay's can be read as reaction to a situation in which guilt is both everywhere and nowhere (Jasper's 'more-than-war-guilt guiltiness'); *The World My Wilderness*'s anxious scrambling around in the metaphorical fragments of literary culture is likewise an effort to pile up meaning, not so much, it could be argued, to substitute a lack, but in the belief that adding even more to an already overdetermined context might somehow turn the literary and historical signification of guilt into something morally meaningful. Rebecca West's writing on Nuremberg reveals there to be a kind of historical truth behind this kind of fiction-making. In her work, Nuremberg represents not so much a crisis of belief (in many ways it would have been better if it had) as the persistence of a cultural modernism in which the meaning of guilt (to rephrase the title of West's other book on this subject, *The Meaning of Treason*) is overdone – in pathos, in metaphor, in the marionette theatre – and, hence, both brittle and elusive.

Taking a break from the trial, West and her then lover, Francis Biddle, the American Chief Prosecutor, journey to Prague, where they attend a British film festival. It is a supremely odd occasion. The Czechs are at best ambivalent about the British and are frankly bemused by the film that has been put on for them, *Brief Encounter*. 'Sexual renunciation on secular grounds is not a theme which Central Europe understands', West explains. The Czechs

> looked at the doctor and the suburban housewife and supposed that they would sleep together if their desire to do so was sufficiently

strong, and that they would not sleep together if their desire to do so was sufficiently weak. This reduced the element of conflict in the story to negligible proportions. They also asked themselves with some emotion whether it could really be true that in England there were no other places than railway buffets where lovers could meet. The drab and inhibited little drama seemed to unfold very slowly before this audience, which so plainly felt that if such cases of abstinence occurred in a distant country there was no need why it should have to know about them; and there was a drowsiness in the air when an American voice spoke loudly out of the darkness. A minor character had crossed the screen and at the sight this voice was saying in horror, 'My God, that man looks just like Goering.' It was one of the American lawyers from Nuremberg, who had fallen asleep and had awakened to see the screen as a palimpsest with the greater tragedy imposed on the small.[68]

On the one hand, what happens when greater tragedies are imposed upon small ones is a horrible muddle. It is tempting to think of Goering's ghoulish appearance in *Brief Encounter* in 1946 as an early correlative of a situation that, by the time Hannah Arendt was to protest against the dreamy generalizations that allowed people to think that 'all cats are gray and we are all equally guilty' in the early 1960s, no longer made any moral sense.[69] On the other hand, West's palimpsest reveals a post-war world that seems caught *between* the frames of greater and smaller tragedies. This dislocating space, like the spaces in Henry Moore's wartime sketchbooks and those revealed in the photography of the Spanish Civil War, possibly speaks less to a culture of disproportionate guilty feelings than to a culture of anxiety. The 'sense of guilt', Freud remarked famously in *Civilization and its Discontents*, 'is at bottom nothing else but a topographical variety of anxiety'.[70] Being guilty in a metaphorical sense might, in the end, be one way of fending off a situation which is considerably more anxiety-provoking – a place where the nightmares live, to paraphrase West on Hess, from where Goering can suddenly rematerialize in all his ghastly insubstantiality.

III

There were plenty of grey cats curling themselves round the shins of the delegates at the International Congress on Mental Health in London in the August of 1948 which opened with three days of papers dedicated, not without public controversy, to the theme of guilt. The conference was evangelical in its claims to make psychoanalytic sense out of recent history. 'Every paper read and every contribution to this discussion should lead us, however indirectly, towards world peace', H. Critchton-Miller reminded delegates.[71] Poul Bjerre's paper went even further: 'The second world war was the first great *common* experience of mankind, and it may be reviewed as a whole in the light of the guilt problem.'[72] But the 'guilt problem' proves by turns to be a too harsh and too dim expository light. Guilt in these papers (once again) is everywhere and nowhere. Elaborating on the crucial Kleinian distinction between depressive and persecutory guilt, H.V. Dicks goes so far as to propose a 'natural history of guilt feelings'.[73] For some delegates this natural history took too many liberties with the conference's self-declared frame of historical reference. One contributor, for example, testily reminds another that the full title of Jasper's book is the question of *German* guilt and that that specific guilt cannot and should not be generalized. Praising Margaret Mead's paper on the anthropology of guilt, and also citing the work of Horkheimer, Fromm and Elias, Frits Grewel is similarly appalled at the lack of political understanding at the conference: 'We are confronted here with a problem of collective or group guilt of the psychiatrists themselves – the guilt of not wanting to see social reality.'[74]

But in some senses it was precisely the misfit between 'social reality' and guilty feelings that was at issue in the late 1940s. Nearly all of the papers are concerned less with appropriate guilt, than with morbid guilt; the guilt that makes no sense in either judicial or historical terms, the guilt that turns historical responsibility into pathology. Such unconscious guilt, notes Ives Hedrick, doesn't exist only outside politics – it allows morbid and lethal political ideologies to flourish.[75] Because guilt, Ernest Jones reminds delegates, never quite manages to extricate itself from the 'series of vicious circles' out of which it originates ambivalently, it always has a story to tell about where it came from; which is why it can make cowards, persecutors and sinners of us all.[76] What is so fascinating about reading through the conference proceedings is the way that, while nearly all contributors have a sense of 'appropriate guilt' (the theologians suffer with Augustine to produce a better man out of guilt; Samuel Lowry advocates the anxiety-like, forward-looking pangs of conscience over the dubious pleasures of regressive guilty feelings for the past; the Kleinians rediscover morality in depressive guilt and so on), the conference's main focus is on guilt's morbid and indiscriminate power. Indeed, one way to read the conference is as an enquiry into a pathological situation in which guilt no longer has a moral or political purchase. In the pathology of guilt, it seems, we really can be both victims and perpetrators. But does this necessarily mean that psychoanalysis is feeding the kind of moral relativism, and a weakened and generalizing 'culture of guilt', that Arendt was so worried about?

I want to end with a paper, cited but not given at the 1948 conference, which sketches out some of the psychic consequences of a situation in which being guilty is the only defence against a world where your nightmares have indeed come alive. Writing in the middle of the war, W.R.D. Fairbairn proposed his own version of an object relations that would give a new dimension to Freud's libido theory. It is not pleasure that drives the psyche into its defences, denials and repressions, argued Fairbairn, but damaged object relations. In a sort of reverse reprise of the famous second chapter of *Beyond the Pleasure Principle*, Fairbairn starts with the observation of traumatized children and then moves on to a consideration of the war neuroses (Freud's chapter, recall, starts with the nightmares of the shell-shocked of World War I and ends with his famous observation of his grandson's *fort-da* cotton reel game). Daringly, Fairbairn rejects the idea that traumatized children are so reluctant to remember their abuse because of an unconscious guilt: 'To the average individual such an experience is not so much guilty as simply "bad". It is intolerable in the main, not because it gratifies repressed impulses, but for the same reason that a child often flies panic-stricken from a house [...] It is intolerable because a bad object is always intolerable.'[77] There is no original guilt then, in Fairbairn's account, but an experience of intolerable badness – or strangeness – which is then repressed. Instead guilt is a particularly pernicious and revealing form of defence against an intolerably bad situation. The guilty child, notes Fairbairn, has converted 'an original situation in which the child is surrounded by bad objects into a new situation in which his objects are good and he himself is bad'.[78] In this logic, it is 'better to be a sinner in a world ruled by God than to live in a world ruled by the Devil'.[79] Feeling guilty, then, is a way of blocking the return of an essentially traumatized subjectivity – of asserting some goodness, or moral framework for good, in a fundamentally bad world. It is an act of defence that, in wartime, proves difficult to sustain. When external situations acquire what Fairbairn describes as 'the significance of repressed situations involving relationships with bad objects', the nightmares really do start to come alive.[80] In the dreams of Fairbairn's war-ravaged patients soldiers are crushed by weights, visited by ghosts and pursued by prehistoric animals. One poor soul is haunted by 'shapeless things and staring eyes that burned right through him'.[81] Better be guilty for a crime he did not commit, better, perhaps, for us all to feel guilty, than confront a world in which our metaphors have materialized into the senseless madness of the war machine. Running, finally, Arendt and Freud together, we might say that being guilty in a metaphorical sense only is not so much immoral as the only remaining moral defence against a fundamentally intolerable situation.

+ Greene

+ Poem on Shik/
  ruins + Holocaust

+ West

+ Camino (when
  translated into
  english)

6
Hearing Them Speak: Voices in Bion, Muriel Spark and Penelope Fitzgerald

> Of course you want to hear their voices.
>
> Penelope Fitzgerald, 'Hearing Them Speak'[1]

> It would be good [...] if as Laplanche says a transference is never resolved only displaced; that the outcome of a successful analysis would be that a person would be able to bear to listen to what other people have to say. That through the experience of analysis a person might rediscover an appetite for talking and for listening and for disagreement. Which is an appetite for democracy.
>
> Adam Phillips, 'Superiorities'[2]

Visiting London just as the fires celebrating VJ day had died down in September 1945 Lacan, writing in his report, 'La psychiatre anglaise et la guerre', describes something if not precisely like an appetite for democracy, then a taste for a democratization of hierarchies which he thinks he has discovered in war-torn Britain. In flight from what he calls the 'irreality' and 'organized delirium' of collective life in Vichy France, Lacan is quick to confess that his enthusiasm for what he sees in Britain has much to do with his own desires and disappointments. This war, he notes wearily towards the end of his paper, has demonstrated how 'the dark powers of the super-ego can make alliances with the most cowardly abandonments of conscience'.[3] But if the war in France seemed to confirm Freud's bleakest prognosis about the perilous pleasures of a collective submission to tyranny, from Lacan's perspective it also provided a unique opportunity, in Britain at least, for psychoanalysis to transform collective morale in such a way as to mobilize people to work together without calling up the dark powers of tyranny.

115

The crucial text here for Lacan is a 1943 article which appeared in the *Lancet,* written by Wilfred Bion and John Rickman, describing their pioneering experimental work with groups of war-ravaged soldiers at Northfield Hospital, Birmingham. Reading this article, says Lacan, is like rediscovering the 'miracle of the Freudian approach' all over again; it is, he adds, worthy of a date of its own in psychoanalytic history. The terms in which Lacan describes Bion, the army officer, psychiatrist and analyst who in many respects is the father of group analysis, evoke a figure of enigmatic authority; an all-knowing subject (a precursor, perhaps, to Lacan's famous 'subject supposed to know'), 'like ice in his immobile mask and glasses, black commas for his moustache [. . .] you knew', Lacan writes, 'you were in the presence of an isolated but highly devoted man'.[4] What Lacan really appreciates about this icy self-contained father-figure is not only his abilities as a leader, but the way Bion leads his group of men out of its collective neurosis by, as it were, not leading them. It is what Bion does with 'the fantasy of the authoritative', in Adam Phillips's phrase, that particularly captures Lacan's imagination.[5] Bion is both the leader of this group of tired, traumatized and notoriously ill-disciplined men, and its doctor. As a doctor he follows the spirit of psychoanalysis by demonstrating to the group that the enemy they have to defeat is the enemy within – their own neuroses (this demonstration, in effect, is the basis of the 'miracle' that transforms the group into a self-critiquing work collective). However, as an officer, Bion cannot hide behind what Lacan calls the 'sham inertia' of the psychoanalyst; he cannot go too far and he certainly cannot undo the fantasy of authority to the extent that an analyst, especially perhaps a later Lacanian analyst, might attempt. Rather, says Lacan, Bion holds this fragile collectivity together by carrying it with his word – 'de tenir à portée de son verbe', he says.[6] Yet by holding the group together 'de son verbe' – with his *word* (*le verbe* in French is also *the* word, as in 'Car le mot, c'est le Verbe, et le Verbe c'est Dieu') – Bion is also speaking, like God, in a tone of unassailable authority. What kind of voice (the analyst Haydee Faimberg notes that Bion himself had a 'calm and ironic' voice)[7] holds a group together while taking its fantasies and resistances apart? How can this voice, a voice that seems to embody the very fantasy of authority that it wants to question, give way to the capacity to tolerate the voices of others?

Voices, on the one hand, carry us to the edges of intelligible life: they are, as the subtitle of the conference at which I originally presented an earlier version of this chapter, suggested, 'beyond' language.[8] Abstracted from speech, the human voice speaks to us from the limits of cultural experience. Yet, on the other hand, voices are at the heart of collective life. No one who has parented a toddler can have failed to be impressed by the brutal effectiveness of the tone of voice called 'whining'. Children have a way of making their voices heard which doesn't need speech. They 'give voice' to their needs, without telling us what those needs are, in much the same way as we still think it is important that we have a 'voice' in the way we are governed in collective, institutional and political life, even if what that voice might actually say so often remains enigmatic to us. At the beginning of the *Lancet* article, Bion describes his frustration at not being able to sit down and get on with his work without being pestered by 'importunate patients and others': I think he is being whined at.[9] One way to read what Bion was doing with the Northfield group, then, might be as an experiment that attempted to stop the voices whining at Bion and get them to try talking and listening to one another (and thus whetting what Phillips describes as an appetite for democracy). If this attempt is not wholly successful, it is perhaps only partly because the Army, appalled at the anarchy in the training wing, closed the experiment down after six weeks – it could not tolerate this sort of undoing of the fantasy of authority from its inside – but because the group could not tolerate it either. It is easier, it seems, to give in to the voice of authority, to be held by its word or even to be carried away by it, than to listen to the group. It is as though, as Phillips points out, there was something fundamentally unbearable about hearing the voices of others.

How Bion might help us think about that deafening something is the subject of the first part of this final chapter. In the second part I want to come at the same question from a different direction by exploring two fictional texts, Muriel Spark's *The Girls of Slender Means* (1963) and Penelope Fitzgerald's *Human Voices* (1980). Both novels return us, one last time (with Lacan and Bion), to the 1940s and to a moment when the question of 'group psychology' – and the anxiety that it both provoked and was threatened by – was politically and morally fraught. Looking back at the 1940s with astute psychological as well as historical hind-sight, both Spark and Fitzgerald are well placed to have something to say about the kind of collective fantasies that can attach themselves to voices. Spark worked in black propaganda in the war as part of Sefton Delmer's unit broadcasting the sham German radio station, Radio Atlantic (*Deutscher Kurzwellensender Atlantik*), an experience she later drew on for her 1973 novel, *The Hothouse by the East River*. Meanwhile, Fitzgerald was in 'white' propaganda, working as a Recorded Programmes Assistant for the BBC, the setting for *Human Voices* and the institution where Fitzgerald later said she learned to listen.[10] Both writers' fictional experiments also put their work in a fascinating parallel to Bion's work with groups. Fitzgerald later pointed out how frequently Spark clarifies the moral issues of her work by 'looking at a small community': *The Prime of Miss Jean Brodie* (1961) is set in a girls' school, *Memento Mori* (1959) in a women's geriatric ward, *The Abbess of Crewe* (1974) in a convent and *The Girls of Slender Means* itself is set in a young women's hostel.[11] Spark's last novel *The Finishing School* (2004) was also set in a school. Fitzgerald too found a particular type of fictional economy by placing her characters in institutional settings: the 'Seraglio' she finds in the group life of the BBC in *Human Voices* is one example, but she also experimented with groups in the Booker prize-winning *Offshore* (1979), which explores relations among London's houseboat community, *At Freddie's* (1982), set in a Covent Garden theatre school, and in her first novel, *The Golden Child* (1977), a mystery set in the British Museum. Most specifically, it is the question of the authority of the voice within these groups that concerns these writers as they look back to the 1940s. In any fiction we encounter the strangeness of voices; indeed in current literary theory the uncanny multi-voicedness of the novel has come to define the entire genre. In Spark's and Fitzgerald's writing, I want to suggest that strangeness is pressed up against its retrospective historical moment so tightly that the voice itself becomes an object of scrutiny. 'Of course you want to hear their voices', writes Fitzgerald at the beginning of her essay, 'Hearing Them Speak'. How we might hear those voices without becoming irrevocably subject to them is what interests me here.

I

If it is the second war that provokes Spark and Fitzgerald into thinking about voices, for Bion you could say that the voices started coming in the first. As the editors of a recent collection of essays on his work suggest, in many respects Bion's later work with groups has its origins in his experiences as a young captain in the British Army.[12] Certainly, the frequency with which the later Bion returns to the first war suggests not only a defining preoccupation, but a worry both about the voices he heard and the kind of voices with the authority to tell of or, as it were, to contain experience. In his *War Memoirs*, for example, Bion describes what it is like to be 'entirely alone with a group of mindless robots – machines devoid of humanity [...] the occasional words exchanged echoed like a conversation heard from afar'.[13] But if some voices in wartime are too far away to be human, others are much too close. It is perhaps this troubling proximity which encouraged Bion to experiment with different grammatical voices in his own various writings on the war. This, for example, is Bion in his 1958 account of the Battle of Amiens (an experience he later said he never recovered from) describing the death of a young soldier:

Bion bent his head so that his ear came as near as possible to Sweeting's mouth.

'Mother, Mother, write to mother, sir, won't you? You'll remember her address, sir, won't you? [...] Mother, Mother, Mother, Mother.'

'Oh, for Christ's sake shut up', shouted Bion, revolted and terrified.

'Write to my mother, sir, you will write to my mother, won't you?'

'Yes, for Christ's sake shut up.'

'Write to my mother, mother, mother. Why can't I cough, sir?' Gusts of steam kept billowing out from his broken side. 'Why can't I cough? You will write to her, sir?' His voice began to grow faint. 'You will write to her, Mother, Mother.' [...]

Never have I known a bombardment like this, never, never – Mother, Mother, Mother, Mother – never have I known a bombardment like this, he thought. I wish he would shut up. I wish he would die. Why can't he die?[14]

At the beginning of the passage the third-person voice works to keep the death cries of the young soldier where the repulsed young officer clearly wants them – on the outside. Bion may be physically proximate to the dying voice, but here he keeps his grammatical and his psychic distance. By the end of the passage, however, the soldier's primitive cries have come to inhabit Bion's own voice: 'Never have I known a bombardment like this, never, never – Mother, Mother, Mother –' Like Poe's raven, this is a voice that doesn't know how to keep its rhythmic distance. Whose word, we might ask, is holding whose here? Bion returns to the same scene in his later autobiography, *The Long Week-End* (1986); as though no amount of retelling will ever exorcize this ghostly inhabitation of voice by voice.[15] There are some voices, it seems, that you don't want to hear.

For psychoanalysis, we can never be rid of the voices of others, and never wholly exorcize the overwhelming guilt (for it is clearly guilt that Bion is trying to deal with in this bit of his memoirs) that comes with what you could call a type of compulsory listening. It is, most obviously, painfully difficult to turn a deaf ear to that voice of conscience that Freud recognized as the legacy of the super-ego: the voice that not only prohibits but inscribes the psychoanalytical subject as anxiously guilty from its very beginnings. Writing in 1939, Otto Isakower made an explicit and perhaps historically timely link between the capacity to hear the voices of others and their authoritarian grip on the subject. A child, he pointed out, 'is not capable by itself of constructing new words, to say nothing of a language, but […] has to build up his speech from linguistic material which is presented to him ready made. But this very fact sets in motion the process of developing an observing and criticizing institution.'[16] It is not just that a super-ego tells you what to do: merely to hear it speak, merely to listen, is to become subject to its scrutiny. Just as the ego, for Freud, is famously a body-ego, the super-ego, argues Isakower, finds its nucleus in the auditory sphere. As Mladen Dolar points out in his reading of what he calls, aptly, the object voice, it is enough just to cock an ear to the voice of the master to ensure one's obedience: 'The commanding authority of the voice is already inscribed in the very posture of listening. As soon as one listens, one has started to obey. The verb *to obey* stems from French *obeir*, which in turn stems from Latin *oboedire*, to listen. One can find the same etymological connection in German, where *Gehörsam*, obedience, comes from *hören*, to listen, and in a considerable number of other languages. *His Master's Voice* is thus a most appropriate emblem.'[17]

Whereas for Freud a large part of our canine devotion to the voice of authority comes from both our submission to and an identificatory love for the father (this is his position in *Group Psychology and the Analysis of the Ego*), for Bion, following Klein, it is not so much Oedipus as a primitive psychotic anxiety that rests at the core of both the subject and, he will later argue, of the group itself. What this means is that for Bion the voice is not only an object (such, for example, as desired by the hysteric), but a potentially pernicious part-object: loved and lost, but also cruelly attacked and hence feared. The psychotic part of the personality does not simply hear the voices that have set up residence in the auditory sphere, it can hallucinate them too. Isakower's 'linguistic material', in Bion's writing, turns out to be made of some pretty strange stuff. These voice hallucinations are still representations, they still signify, but they are not metaphors: in Bion's terms they 'attack' links between sense and meaning.[18] 'Tears come from my ears now', complains a psychotic analysand in Bion's 1953 Congress paper, 'Language and the Schizophrenic'. '[T]here was', Bion observes, 'a great deal of play with the pronunciation of tears (*teers* or *tares*) the emphasis being mostly on the inability to bring together the objects, words, or words plus pronunciation, except cruelly.'[19] In other words, the patient cannot find a voice to inhabit his words that will not rip them apart in the very act of enunciation. (That dog in *His Master's Voice,* by the way, is called 'Nipper'.) At the same time Bion also notes that his own voice, the voice of the analyst, was 'being drowned by the tears that poured from [his patient's] ears'.[20] Behind the emblem of an attentive and obedient mongrel, with Bion we find a more psychotic and certainly more surreal and disturbing image of a crying ear.

What so terrifies this patient about his analyst's words getting into his ear, is the development of what Bion calls 'verbal thought' which the analysis has provoked. By making links where before there were absences and anxiety, verbal thought is threatening to turn the patient's part objects into whole objects that he must then learn to mourn. Language is about to encroach on the hallucinatory voices that have kept him company in his struggle against depression: sometimes it is better to fill your ears with tears than with the words of others (when 'human voices' wake us, to paraphrase the last lines of Eliot's 'The Love Song of J. Alfred Prufrock', part of us, Bion would call it the psychotic part, is felt to die too). This resistance to verbal thought accounts for some of the strangeness of the language of schizophrenics: Bion describes it as a 'highly compact speech the construction of which is more akin to music'.[21] Hence the poetry of having tears in your ears. With his musical ear, the psychotic can hear the voices alright, what he cannot tolerate is hearing the echoing return of his own persecutory anxiety within them. Voices thus not only inscribe an always anxiously guilty subjectivity, for Bion, they can also return to us as persecuted and therefore, following one logic of projective identification, persecutory objects.[22] One reason why it might be so difficult to bear to listen to what other people are saying might be because they are at once too close – it is our fears and fantasies that have been projected into the other – and, for precisely the same reason, too distant; if the other is the bearer of bits of ourselves, is it not ourselves who are also speaking back to us?

If there is not much of the human (to recall Fitzgerald's title as well as Eliot's lament) in these voices it is because they frequently carry something murderous within them; something you could even call inhuman. In a familiar trope in writing about hearing voices, in Bion too the murderously inhuman is frequently connected to technology; to the radios and gramophones, for example, which also feature so noisily in writing from and about the 1930s and 1940s.[23] In his paper on hallucination Bion writes about a patient who 'is guilty of removing a life which then becomes a persecutory object, the radio that embodies electricity, sex and life itself'.[24] One more voice has turned into hallucination: in

Bion's terms it has become a 'bizarre object'. 'The nature of such objects', Bion explains, 'will depend partly on the character of the real object, say a gramophone, and partly the character of the particle of personality that engulfs it. If the piece of personality is concerned with sight, the gramophone when played is felt to be watching the patient; if with hearing, then the gramophone when played is felt to be listening to the patient.'[25] ('Chuff, chuff, chuff', goes the gramophone in the bushes in Virginia Woolf's *Between the Acts* (1941), a text almost contemporary with Bion's work at Northfield, '[c]ould they talk? Could they move? No, for the play was going on'.[26]) In this description of the psychic authority of the voice, we have to contend with the idea that the gramophone might well be listening to the nippy dog. This would not, of course, shift the direction of power; quite the contrary, in this scenario being heard implies just as much, if not more, submission to the gramophone as actually listening to it. Occupying a space anterior to symbol formation and verbal thought, these inhuman voices see your every move, listen to your every thought; they can gobble you up in their own cadences, and spit you back out. If such voices can get so close so as to potentially overwhelm us, to quite literally deafen us to experience, it is small wonder, perhaps, that for Bion, our collective life (what he would call our experience in groups) should be dominated by the effort to hear the human in the other's voice.

Bion's starting point for thinking about groups is always the profound difficulty we have in existing in such close, potentially unbearable, psychical proximity to other people: 'The adult', Bion says at the beginning of his 1955 review paper on group dynamics, 'must establish contact with the emotional life of the group in which he lives; this task would appear to be as formidable to the adult as the relationship with the breast appears to be to the infant.'[27] Yet getting to the point where a group might discover the appetite for talking and listening to one another, or getting to the point where one might want to hear what the breast has actually got to say, is invariably overshadowed by the sort of psychic deafness to the human in other voices that I have been trying to describe here. In collective life, it seems, it really is easier to cock an obedient ear to the hollow voices coming out of the gramophone in the bushes, than to listen to one another. Each of what Bion describes as the 'basic assumptions' that characterize the emotional life of the group has its own fantasy about authority. The dependent group, for example, is sustained by fantasies about its leader; the messianic-pairing group desires leadership; and the fight-flight group wants the sort of leader that it can either loathe or ignore. If our fantasies about authority are perilous for Bion, it is not just because we crave subjection but also because our leaders are as (or indeed even more) susceptible to the basic assumptions working in the group as the group itself. The ' "loss of individual distinctiveness" (characteristic of groups) applies to the leader of the group as much as to anyone else', he says, 'a fact that probably accounts for the posturing to which leading figures are prone'.[28] There is no point in loving the sound of your own voice, in other words, if you do not really believe that others love it too. If there is a misrecognition at work at the heart of collective life, it is one that is shared by the leader and it is this kind of imaginary complicity, and not say the leader's cunning, brilliance or ideology that really bothers Bion both politically as well as psychically speaking. What Lacan found so compelling and historically urgent about Bion's work with groups was, I think, the extent to which Bion was prepared to go in order to undo the fantasies that support such authoritarian posturing – which takes us back to the question of what it might mean to be held in Bion's voice.

'Dr. Bion is the only one who is ever listened to here, and he never says anything helpful' complains one of Bion's early participants in his group work.[29] Much of the humour that comes from Bion's accounts of his experiences in groups derives from his ironic refusal to inhabit the position of authority that the group wants him to occupy. Listening to Bion, one senses, is like listening to the gramophone with the sound turned down very low. You have to make an effort to catch this voice that demands not so much to be listened to as attended to. 'In so far as I am felt to be leader', he suggests in one description of his role in a group, 'and recognition of that fact is seldom absent, I [...] am invested with feelings that would be quite appropriate to the enigmatic brooding sphinx.'[30] More often than not this sphinx will be even more sphinx-like than desired. The enigmatic figure of the all-knowing analyst (who so enraptured Lacan) undercuts his authority by knowing that, in fact, he does not know (Bion's famous injunction to analysts was to learn to listen to their patients without either memory or desire).[31] Stubbornly, Bion's voice refuses to yield to the fantasies that support it, as he turns his voice into something of a recalcitrant object, persistently unavailable to the desires of others. His can perhaps be characterized as a 'withdrawing' voice: an insistent and infuriating echo that reverberates rather than commands, whispers rather than shouts. 'Only if individuals come sufficiently close to each other is it possible to give an interpretation without shouting it' he says (or perhaps whispers) at one point.[32] Working out of two world wars, Bion, it could be argued finally, wants to find a way of surviving, if not actually enjoying, our close proximity to one another without a fall into psychotic anxiety. His perhaps is a call to try and hear the human in the other's voice without one's ears filling up with tears.

Psychoanalysis, of course, makes its business out of listening. Literature too, it is often claimed, is one place where you can hear the voices of others without actually going mad: in some ways it is the consciousness of this fact that makes fiction fiction. Yet if, as many have, you want to argue that this multi-voicedness of the novel has something to do with a political history, and that hearing different voices is a kind of democratization of literary form, then there is also a point, arguably just after modernism, when fiction began to close those voices in upon themselves: where the subject became the problem of hearing the voices of others and not just their right to existence. The politics of this shift are not always subtle: Eliot's lament about being awoken by human voices is also a complaint against a culture that simply has too many clamorous babblers in it. Modernism set about the business of turning voices into artefacts, which is partly why nobody ever speaks like the characters in a Henry James novel, or has an inner voice with quite the resonance of one of Virginia Woolf's characters. By the 1930s and 1940s, however, something changes. In much fiction of this period it is as if the effort of hearing other voices has become too much. Henry Green's theory of dialogue, for example, begins with the principle that people cannot hear what others are saying to them; Elizabeth Bowen's voices do not so much communicate as silently trade secrets which remain enigmatic even to their speakers; Jean Rhys's characters are locked in dialogues of unvoiced thoughts; and Beckett of course (Bion's one-time analysand), abstracts fiction to the rattle of a single voice (without even a mouth). By the late 1950s, Oskar's voice in Gunter Grass's *The Tin Drum* (1959) can shatter the glass of Danzig at will.[33] If this closing in of voices registers a historical disenchantment with bourgeois democracy at the same time, as we have already seen with Bion, there is also a sense in which a kind of over-proximity to others is making it more and more difficult to claim that you can hear them speak. Both Muriel Spark and Penelope Fitzgerald write 'out' of the 1940s: although both started to write later (and Fitzgerald much later), their fiction not only turns thematically to the 1940s, but to this problem of how to hear the voices of others when, as it were, one's ears are already full to bursting. What is there, their fiction can be read as asking, beyond the anxious claustrophobia of a world in which others are too unbearably close and yet, by the same twist, painfully abstract phantoms of our own haunted imaginations? 'But to be really "under the skin" of others is a very big exercise', Spark remarked in a late interview: to hear them speak is just as difficult.[34] It is to this sense of difficulty I want to turn next.

II

In Muriel Spark's first novel, *The Comforters* (1957) her protagonist hears voices emanating from a typewriter. In *The Prime of Miss Jean Brodie*, the captivating voice of a girls' school teacher with a penchant for fascist spectacles carries her entranced pupils in her words. In *The Girls of Slender Means*, Joanna Childe, a rector's daughter, fair of face but disappointed in love, recites poetry in between giving elocution lessons teaching others how to do the same. Many of Spark's characters are caught by the voices of others. The schizophrenic and the poet in her writing often share an ear for the voice of the other. For some of these characters, as for their author, listening to voices is frequently a question of faith and truth. Yet although to hear in Spark's fiction might often in the end mean to obey, this is never without protest, difficulty or, importantly (and this is a characteristic she shares with Fitzgerald, another convert to Catholicism), humour. Bryan Cheyette, one of a generation of critics who have done much recently to free her work from being too rigidly defined as 'Catholic writing', has commented on how Spark has always 'played imaginatively with her own basic assumptions'.[35]

While Bion and Rickman were analysing and educating the men in Northfield's training wing on the psychic and political demands of group life (and on the shortcomings of their 'basic assumptions'), Spark was tuning her ear to the delicate intricacies of institutional living in both the women's hostel where she lodged intermittently during the war years and in her black propaganda unit, and it is this experience that she returns to nearly twenty years later in *The Girls of Slender Means*. Set in the May of Teck Club for 'the Pecuniary Convenience and Social Protection of Young Ladies of Slender Means below the age of Thirty Years', and covering the period from VE Day to the Labour Victory in 1945 (that is, roughly the same period as Lacan's visit), the novel is a study of a community on the edge of disaster. While financial poverty may unite her girls, Spark is chiefly concerned with their spiritual and moral impoverishment. Just as Bion tracked the unconscious minds of his recovering men as they went in and out of the rooms of the training wing (Bion visualized the 'projected organisation of the training wing [at Northfield] as if it were a framework enclosed with transparent walls'),[36]

Spark too gives her big Victorian house in Kensington a distinct architectural topography with which to measure her girls' means. A window at the top of the house where the older girls sleep, measuring only seven inches wide by fourteen inches long, is the parabolic aperture through which finally Spark squeezes her characters, disclosing motives and morals as they exit. Only the svelte are able to slip, sometimes with the help of a thin covering of precious rationed margarine, out of the skylight and onto the adjacent roof for sex and sunbathing. This window-game takes on a final and apocalyptic significance as a bomb buried under the flowerbeds belatedly explodes. As the house crumbles, only the girls of exceptionally slender fleshly means escape through the window: a feat which is not at all, in Spark's view, a reliable index of moral virtue. Selina, the slim beauty with fulsome sexual and worldly appetites, both survives the blast and has the audacity to return to the crumbling building in order to filch the girls' collectively-cherished Schiaparelli dress; while Joanna, spiritually well-endowed but sexually impoverished, perishes reciting psalms as the house collapses.

If the May of Teck Club is a house full of voices, it is also an institution which is confused by voices. Two of the girls, in a scenario no doubt familiar to some of Bion's patients, debate whether a wireless turned up too loud looks bad or sounds bad. 'Not a hush from anybody' says the warden, 'meaning "Not a sound"', as the girls gather to listen to Joanna record her recital of Gerard Manley Hopkins's *The Wreck of the Deutschland*.[37] Above all, it is Joanna's voice that pervades the house and the novel. Unlike Bion's patient with the tearful ear, Joanna has no inhibitions when it comes to rolling words into her voice. She plays with poetry like a cat with a bird: 'she would pounce on the stuff, play with it quivering in her mind, and when she had got it by heart, she spoke it forth with devouring relish'.[38] Joanna's is a voice of sublimated passion; the other girls compare her to Ingrid Bergman and assume she has a heroic past. '[W]ell built, fair and healthy looking, the poetic essence of tall, fair rectors' daughters who never used a scrap of make-up';[39] Joanna Childe *is* her voice, the one embodies the other, for both the girls at the club and for the novel as a whole.

Joanna's passion for Gerard Manley Hopkins's *The Wreck of the Deutschland* is particularly telling in this respect. Hopkins's ode is a conversion narrative inspired by the death of five Franciscan nuns fleeing Germany's Falck Laws, who went down with the *Deutschland* in the mouth of the Thames in the winter of 1875. The poem tells of Hopkins's own conversion and is especially enraptured by the story of the 'Tall Nun' who converted passengers and sailors with the power

of her voice as the ship sank. The poem also marks Hopkins's first experiments with his distinctive 'sprung rhythms'; a complex but extremely
subtle metre designed to spring a trap to catch converts. The poetic voice
of *The Wreck of the Deutschland* thus is crafted precisely with the aim
of carrying its listeners with its word (or *de son verbe*): it is nothing less
than a message from God.

The potential convert in *The Girls of Slender Means* is the anarchist-poet
Nicholas Farringdon who has, says Spark, been 'psychoanalysed out of the
army' (by Bion, perhaps?) Nicholas sleeps with Selina, but it is Joanna's
voice that captivates him. On the one hand, her voice is seductive because
of the impossible pleasures it seems to represent: 'Joanna needs to know
more life, thought Nicholas, as he loitered in the hall on one specific
evening, but if she knew life she would not be proclaiming these words
so sexually and matriarchally as if in the ecstatic act of suckling a divine
child.' An inaccessible mother, who can't nurture you because she is busy
feeding her words: the ecstasy here is similar to that which Lacan reads
in the face of Bernini's statue of Saint Theresa in his paper on feminine
sexuality.[40] It is also, of course, in keeping with that ambivalent venera-
tion of the maternal voice that belongs to some versions of psychoanalysis,
as well as to Catholicism. Joanna's, however, is not the only voice that
resonates through the May of Teck Club that evening.

> She continued to recite as he loitered in the hall. Everyone was
> gathered somewhere else, in the drawing-room or in the bedrooms,
> sitting round wireless sets, tuning in to some special programme.
> Then one wireless, and another, roared forth louder by far than usual
> from the upper floors; others turned in to the chorus justified in
> the din by the voice of Winston Churchill. Joanna ceased. The wire-
> lesses spoke forth their Sinaitic predictions of what fate would befall
> the freedom-loving electorate should it vote for Labour in the forth-
> coming elections. The wirelesses suddenly started to reason humbly:
> We shall have Civil Servants...
> The wirelesses changed their tones, they roared:
> No longer civil...
> Then they were sad and slow:
> No longer...
> ...*servants*.[41]

The prophetic voices from Mount Sinai put political rhetoric in the place
of spiritual ecstasy. I don't think Spark intends us simply to contrast
these two voices here, however comic the effect of bringing the two

together: more bizarrely, and bathetically, it is somehow as though the spiritual ecstasy of Joanna's voice underpins the dwindling authority (remember he is about to lose this election) of Churchill's, as the two voices merge into one in the ears of both Nicholas and the groups huddling around their wirelesses in the May of Teck Club. The other-worldliness of Joanna's voice fades into the inhuman voices from the radio (note that the emphasis is on the way the wirelesses sound, not Churchill himself): but who is really listening to them? The passage concludes:

> Nicholas imagined Joanna standing by her bed, put out of business as it were, but listening, drawing it into her bloodstream. As in a dream of his own that depicted a dream of hers, he thought of Joanna in this immovable attitude, given up to the cadences of the wireless as if it did not matter what was producing them, the politician or herself. She was a proclaiming statue in his mind.

Nicholas is listening to Joanna listening to Churchill: each is caught in the cadences of the other. Go back to the emblem of the dog and the gramophone and add a third to that picture: here one doesn't just listen to the other, but for another too. But in fact, in this scenario, no one is really listening at all. For the same reason that for Bion we can be profoundly deaf to the voice of others even as we appear to open our ears, here too a sly solipsism seems to be at work. 'As in a dream of his own that depicted a dream of hers': this is one unconscious inserting itself into another, one dream dreaming another. His mistress's voice is enclosed within so many Chinese boxes. Thus encased Joanna can only suffer the stony fate of so many female messengers from the Gods: 'She was a proclaiming statue in his mind.'

As the May of Teck Club goes down, it is Joanna's voice, coupled with evidence of Selina's evil, which converts Nicholas to the Catholic Church. But this is also a conversion, an act of absolute obedience, premised on a difficult fantasy. To reformulate my earlier point: for Spark, as for psychoanalysis, you could say we obey by turning something of a deaf ear to authority. Caught within a fantasy of a fantasy; when voices reverberate they quiver with the desires of their listeners. This is not just a point about the pleasures of subjection: I am also trying to underline how difficult it is, for fiction (and for psychoanalysis too) to account for how we actually get to listen to the voices of other people. If listening is an act of obedience, there is also something (as Freud explained about obedience in *Totem and Taboo*) truly murderous about this first act of subjection. For Freud our belated obedience to the law of the father is part of a cover-up for his murder by the herd. Here too what is human about the voices of others is put to death, or turned to salty stone, by our greedy (remember Nicholas's envy of the suckling Joanna) appropriation of the voice. In other words, when you turn a voice into an object, in one sense you cease to hear it.

There is then finally, perhaps, nothing human (or nothing worldly) about the voices in *The Girls of Slender Means*. Indeed, on the one hand, there is little reason to suppose that there should be. Spark is a writer who makes an art out of knowing that really getting under the skin of other people also means negotiating the images we carry of them (in our ears we might say here). Writing about the novel in the year of its publication, Frank Kermode noted that Spark was a poet-novelist who 'imposes patterns and the patterns are the figures of the truth'.[42] Literary authority, in many respects, means precisely that human voices are subject to the desires and designs of others (poetic 'vision', among other things, is often also a form of selective hearing). But if Spark is the kind of writer who finds solace from the ragbag of history in design, she is also acutely alert to the dangers of hearing what we think we want to hear. Nicholas is not only a convert, he is a group watcher: 'The twittering movements at other points in the room, Joanna's singular voice, beautiful aspects of poverty and charm amongst these girls in the brown-papered drawing room, Selina furled like a long soft sash, in her chair, came to Nicholas in a gratuitous flow.'[43] Nicholas, notes Spark, 'was imposing upon this society an image incomprehensible to itself': which is also what writers do and what you hope group analysts do not.[44] At the beginning of the novel we learn that Nicholas, now a missionary, has been killed ('martyred') in Haiti. With a typically Spark-like pull at the patterns she has so carefully contrived, this bit of information makes a hard little point about the connection between the imagination and authority. There are some human voices, some groups of people, who object to not being listened to, and some bits of history that cannot be redeemed though figures of truth.

III

' "Sam, are you human?" ' Jeffrey Haggard, the laconic Director of Programme Planning in a besieged wartime BBC, asks his friend, Sam Brooks, in Fitzgerald's *Human Voices*. ' "If I'm not" ', Sam replies, ' "I can't see who is." '[45] Sam isn't and he can't. His department, known as a Seraglio to his colleagues, is a mini-authoritarian state within the

BBC, and is premised on the absolute power of a leader who, like one of Bion's narcissistic despots, exists only by hearing echoes of himself within others. 'It's only a matter of listening', one of his juniors explains to a new employee. 'He sounds like a selfish shit to me', Lise replies.[46] In its own way, it is an effective sort of authority. Sam lures his juniors 'into the circle' of his 'words';[47] thus trapped, like converts to a cause, they feel ready to do anything for him; caught in a voice that can hear only itself. This kind of authoritarian posturing (albeit from a man who is positively Prufrockian in his self-pitying helplessness), is ill-suited to an institution that absolutely believes in the benign power of the human voice. A thorn in the side of the Ministry of Defence, the BBC ('a cross between a civil service, a powerful moral force, and an amateur theatrical company') is an 'institution that cannot tell a lie'.[48] One reading of the novel would be to view it as a defence of the political necessity of hearing the voices speak – of the dissemination of truth in politically compromised times. At the same time, however, Fitzgerald is also acutely sensitive to the ways in which voices furl themselves into objects of fantasy that resist the very democratic ideal they are said to support.

As in much of Spark's fiction, when the motives of Fitzgerald's characters often seem obscure it is usually because they are caught up in parabolic or allegoric pattern-making. Fitzgerald too believes that fiction can provide an order where history fails. The epigraph to her last novel, *The Blue Flower* (1995) cites its hero, Friedrich von Hardenberg, later better known as Novalis: 'Novels arise out of the shortcomings of history.' No less than Spark, however, Fitzgerald also understands that fiction does not so much redeem history, as echo back its failings. On one level, then, Fitzgerald wants to tell a story, which is also a political allegory, about how Sam finally awakens to the human in the voices of others. But this is a story that stops well short of redemption. Where Spark looked to Hopkins, it is the melancholy irony of Heinrich Heine which echoes through Fitzgerald's text. In Heine's 'Der Asra' the power of the human voice turns out to be self-defeating. 'I wish to know your name, your home, your kin!', the Sultan's beautiful daughter demands of the visibly love-sick slave who she meets by the fountain every evening. 'I am called Mohamet, I come from the Yemen, and my tribe are the Asras who die when they love.'[49] Having an appetite for conversation is not always good for human happiness.

For Eliot this cruel irony is grist to the mill of modernity's tawdry hopes: the human voices that awaken us are not only melancholy, but menacing too. Fitzgerald is more equivocal – and funnier. In *Human Voices*, it is Annie Asra, the piano-tuner's child with a finely-trained ear, who breaks through the 'fairy tale atmosphere' of Sam's walls of silence to minister love's first words. With her musical ear and devotion to love, it is Annie who points out that Sam is in fact tone deaf. ' "It was flat, Mr Brooks" ', she says, as he plays her one of his precious recordings: ' "I'm very glad to learn about quality and balance [...], but the singer was flat." '[50] Like an analyst, Annie can hear things that Sam doesn't want her to. 'She chose to set up her sense of hearing against mine', he complains.[51] When Annie declares her love for Sam he, like a patient in the grip of the transference, bathes his wounded narcissism with the belief that he has now at least found the perfect listener. As they hurry off to toast their newly found communion in a Greek café called, appropriately, Demos, it might even look as though the lovers have achieved that kind of open-ended transference that whets the appetite for 'talking and for listening and for disagreement' which is also, Adam Phillips suggested in the quote with which I opened this chapter, 'an appetite for democracy'.

Not everyone, however, shares this appetite. ' "That's what I've rung up to tell you." ' twitters an over-excited Sam to his friend Jeff. ' "I want you to come to the Demos Café, the Greek place in Margaret Street, D-E-M-O-S, Demos." "I'm familiar with the word," said Jeff. "I just don't want to go there." '[52] In Heine's poem, hearing the human in the voice of the other ends with a miserable irony. Fitzgerald does not so much turn romantic agony into a happy ever after (significantly, we are never offered a resolving image of the lovers' communion) as displace that despair onto a more pronounced political and historical register. It is the cynical and worn-out Jeffrey Haggard, not Annie, who dies, and who, like many of the writers I have been discussing in this book, has every good reason not to have an appetite for what is served up at the Café Demos. All respond to a time that not only saw authoritarianism pitted against democracy, but when democracy, or so it was claimed, had to be defended by authoritarian means. This is why Jeff, for example, has to pull the plug when the newly evacuated General Pinard begins to berate the British population for its failure to come to France's aid and urges capitulation. This is great comedy, but the scene also acts as a dark counterpoint to the novel's commitment to 'an institution that could not tell a lie'.[53] It is not only that there are some voices you cannot hear, or don't want to hear, but also some voices that must not be heard. When Bion tried to get the voices in the training wing to stop whining at him and start talking to one another, he also knew that the internal limits to his project, our psychic deafness to the human in the other's voice, would be buttressed by an institution which insisted on the absolute authority of the object voice. When Spark runs the voice of Joanna Childe into Churchill's, she too is making a point, albeit a comic one, about the political infrangibility of the voice. If an earlier response to an authoritarian imposition of the voice was to call for more voices, more disagreements, more talking, this option no longer seems so readily digestible. Bion's desperate turning away from the dying voice of the young soldier in Amiens, his inability to hear a voice that is lodged too firmly in his ear, in this respect, turns out to be a prescient figure for an anxious culture that can no longer bear to hear the human in the voice of the other.

As the V1 rockets start to fall the newsreaders at the BBC discover they have a problem with pronouncing the word 'aerial'. ' "Ayeerial torpedoes... airial torpedoes... ayereeal torpedoes..." murmured Director (Talks), Director (Public Relations) and Director (Home).'[54] Something gets stuck on the tongue here; as with Bion's patient with the tearful ear, there is a problem with bringing words and pronunciation together. In Fitzgerald's text, this problem has to do with the voice itself: for it is not just bombs that whizz through the air in wartime Europe, but voices too; messengers from the gods with dubious claims to authority. As he looks up at Eric Gill's famous carvings of Prospero and his messenger, Ariel, that sit on the brow of Broadcasting House, Jeffrey Haggard thinks to himself:

> But who, after all, was Ariel? All he ever asked was to be released from his duties. And when this favoured spirit had flown off, to suck where the bee sucks, and Prospero had returned with all his followers to Italy, the island must have reverted to Caliban. It had been his, after all, in the first place. When all was said and done, oughtn't he to preside over the BBC? Ariel, it was true, had produced music, but it was Caliban who listened to it, even in his dreams. And Caliban, who wished Prospero might be stricken with the red plague for teaching him to speak correct English, never told anything but the truth, presumably not knowing how to. Ariel, on the other hand, was a liar, pretending that someone's father was drowned full fathom five, when in point of fact he was safe and well. All this was so that virtue should prevail. The old excuse.[55]

Shortly after this scene, Jeffrey is killed when he mistakes a parachute bomb for a taxi. 'His voice in particular', writes the Assistant Deputy Director General in his obituary, 'will be much missed.'[56]

What if, and this is perhaps the lesson of psychoanalysis as well, we follow Fitzgerald and replace the image of the obedient mongrel in *His Master's Voice* with that of the more petulantly currish Caliban? Like the whining child, and possibly like the inhabitants of Haiti in Spark's novel, Caliban's rage rests not only on not being listened to but with being given a voice that has no power. Nothing in today's political culture perhaps dampens the appetite for democracy quite so much as the promise of being listened to. The ubiquitous 'we hear what you're saying' is not so much a lie (or not only a lie) as testimony to the airy weightlessness of the 'consultation exercises' that pervade political, cultural and institutional life. We are at best disenchanted, and, at worst, deeply suspicious of the power of our own voices. Addressing the Medical Section of the British Psychological Society in 1947, Bion described a culture of 'the emotionally under-developed but mimetically well equipped'. Our affective lives, he notes, have been atrophied: 'Stimuli are removed but return as provocations of another level [...] We follow the fortunes of our favourite football team but cannot even help by giving up smoking.' Psychically 'disinherited', we lack the scope, says Bion, for the development of our 'political appetite'.[57] What is required, urges Bion in terms which pick up some of the themes of Lacan's paper of the same year, is a 'creative leadership'; one that knows how to lead by not leading, one that relinquishes power by holding onto it: a voice that holds by withdrawing. Lacan himself was later to embody the difficulties of this intense and paradoxical type of authority in his part in the notorious history of the l'école freudienne.[58] If the promise that enthused Lacan in September 1945 has turned out to be unfulfilled, what we are left with now is not (or at least not only) the necessity of hearing them speak, but also an imperative for a more articulate kind of whining.

∗ ∗ ∗

The psychoanalysts I discuss in this book, like some of the writers, can perhaps be fairly described as pretty marginal figures in the cultural and literary history of twentieth-century British culture. Winnicott and Bion, like Rose Macaulay and Henry Green, don't lend themselves to the kind of criticism that can make representative statements about either the human psyche or the state of a national literary culture. They are tricksy figures; exhilarating to read and hard to categorize. Read together, as I have argued here, these second-generation psychoanalysts and modernists share a concern with the sheer difficulty of trying to imagine some kind of agency in wartime in ways which are essentially to do with thinking about how history is represented in the mind.[59]

Although I had not set out to write a book about the significance of World War Two at the turn of the new century, it would be disingenuous to suggest that much of it was not written with a view to the present. The first chapter was begun in the wake of the fiftieth anniversary of VE day in Britain and New Labour's rise to power. As the culture of wartime memory – and indeed the culture of memory itself – acquired a new affective and political legitimacy, discovering a somewhat darker psychopathology to Britain's wartime imaginary felt (churlishly perhaps) appropriate. I'm ending this book on the sixtieth anniversary of the Nuremberg Trials, at a moment at which international lawlessness has seemingly acquired a new political legitimacy, and at which, to cite Freud from 1915 one last time, we are once again 'ourselves waylaid by the significance of the impressions that overwhelm us and by the values of the judgements which we form'.

Notes

Introduction: 'dreading forward': the writing of anxiety at mid-century

1. Sigmund Freud, 'Thoughts for the Times on War and Death' (1915), Penguin Freud Library (PFL), vol. 12 (Harmondsworth: Penguin, 1985), p. 72. The translation here is Samuel Weber's, 'Wartime', *Violence, Identity and Self-Determination*, ed. Hent de Vries and Samuel Weber (Stanford: Stanford University Press, 1997), p. 90.
2. Elizabeth Bowen, citing 'a friend', Postscript to *The Demon Lover* (1945), reprinted in *The Mulberry Tree: Writings of Elizabeth Bowen*, ed. Hermione Lee (London: Vintage, 1999), p. 96.
3. Paul Fussell, *The Great War and Modern Memory* (Oxford: Oxford University Press, 1975); Trudi Tate, *Modernism, History and the First World War* (Manchester: Manchester University Press, 1998); J.M. Winter, *Sites of Memory, Sites of Mourning: the Great War in European Cultural History* (Cambridge: Cambridge University Press, 1995) – to name but three important, and very different, studies of the First World War and cultural modernism. For an excellent exposition and critical analysis of the association between shock, trauma and modernism, see Tim Armstrong, 'Two Types of Shock in Modernity', *Critical Quarterly*, 42(1) (2001): 60–73.
4. Marina MacKay has demonstrated the extent to which late modernist writers redefined modernism within the context of the Second World War. See Marina MacKay, *Modernism and World War II* (Cambridge: Cambridge University Press, 2007).
5. For a cultural history of fear and anxiety, see Joanna Bourke's extremely useful *Fear: a Cultural History* (London: Virago, 2005). Bourke opens each chapter with a quote from W.H. Auden's *The Age of Anxiety*. Auden's 1948 baroque eclogue confirms not only the anxiety (and the drunken hysteria of the moment) but also his age's historical self-understanding. But just as the poem is undoubtedly of its time, it often feels as though there is also an ostentatious over-naming of anxiety in its writing – it is, after all, baroque. Not only in Auden's poem, but elsewhere too it is as if the 'age of anxiety' seems to have a kind of anachronism built into its historical phrasing, so that by the time a culture recognizes itself as anxious, to an extent it has ceased to be so but, rather, has become self-consciously fearful about its anxieties, which is something different. When, only two years after Auden's play for voices appeared, Rollo May published his widely influential *The Meaning of Anxiety* (1950), a blend of cultural and historical analysis with a compelling existential period flavour, it became clear (particularly in the US) that anxiety had firmly established itself as the affect proper to mid-century historical malaise. Perhaps it is more accurate to say as proper to mid-century historical recoil, for anxiety about the human condition, at

135

least by the 1950s, had begun to displace a possibly more troubled set of
anxieties about the psychic and political consequences of the Second World
War and its aftermath. By contrast, this book tries to capture a moment
before, so to speak, anxiety went cultural and existentially transcendent. See
W.H. Auden, *The Age of Anxiety: a Baroque Eclogue* (London: Faber and Faber,
1948) and Rollo May, *The Meaning of Anxiety* [1950] (New York and London:
Norton, 1996). For an excellent cultural history of anxiety and architecture
see Anthony Vidler, *Warped Space: Art, Architecture and Anxiety in Modern
Culture* (Cambridge, MA: MIT Press, 2000).

6. Elizabeth Bowen, Postscript to *The Demon Lover*, p. 96. See Jacqueline Rose,
'Bizarre Objects: Mary Butts and Elizabeth Bowen', *Critical Quarterly*, 42(1)
(2000): 75–85, for an important argument about the relation between history
and hallucination in Bowen's *The Heat of the Day*. See also Maud Ellmann's
superb reading of this novel and of Bowen's wartime short stories, especially 'The Happy Autumn Fields' which beautifully exemplifies what Bowen
meant by the compensations of hallucination in wartime: Maud Ellmann,
Elizabeth Bowen: the Shadow across the Page (Edinburgh: Edinburgh University
Press, 2003), pp. 128–75.

7. Walter Benjamin, 'On Some Motifs in Baudelaire', in *Illuminations*, ed. Hannah
Arendt, trans. Harry Zhon (New York: Schocken Books, 1985), p. 158.

8. Baudelaire, writes Benjamin: 'envisioned blank spaces which he filled with
his poems. His work cannot merely be categorized as historical, like anyone
else's, but intended it to be so and understood itself as such.' Ibid., p. 162.

9. For the most influential proponents of trauma theory, see Cathy Caruth,
Unclaimed Experience: Trauma, Narrative and History (Baltimore: Johns
Hopkins University Press, 1996) and Shoshana Felman and Dori Laub, *Testimony: Crisis of Witnessing in Literature, Psychoanalysis and History* (New York
and London: Routledge, 1992). For a history of trauma and a critique of
the underlying assumptions behind much trauma theory, see Ruth Leys,
Trauma: a Genealogy (Chicago and London: Chicago University Press, 2000).

10. Sigmund Freud, *Beyond the Pleasure Principle* (1920), PFL 11, *On Metapsychology* (Harmondsworth: Penguin, 1984), p. 292.

11. Ibid., p. 304.

12. Walter Benjamin, 'Some Motifs in Baudelaire', pp. 161–2.

13. Virginia Woolf, 'A Sketch of the Past', *Moments of Being: Autobiographical
Writings* [1976], ed. Jeanne Schulkind (London: Pimlico, 2002), p. 85.

14. Ibid., pp. 109, 116, 122, 130.

15. Ibid., p. 79.

16. Ibid., p. 109.

17. H.D. quoted in Norman Holmes Pearson, 'Foreword', *Tribute to Freud*
(Manchester: Carcanet, 1985), p. v.

18. Existential psychoanalysis flourished after the war, particularly in the US.
See in particular, Paul Tillich, *Systematic Theology I–III* (Chicago: Chicago
University Press, 1964).

19. Sigmund Freud, *Analysis of a Phobia in a Five-Year-Old Boy* (1909), PFL 9.

20. Samuel Weber, 'Wartime', pp. 96–105. Marianna Torgovnick has extended
this insight into a study of what she calls the 'war complex'. See Marianna
Torgovnick, *The War Complex: World War II in Our Time* (Chicago and
London: Chicago University Press, 2005).

21. Jean Paul Sartre, *Sketch for a Theory of the Emotions* [first published as *Esquisse d'une theorie des emotions* in 1939], trans. Philip Mairet (London and New York: Routledge, 2002), pp. 34–64. For Sartre's critique of how psycho-analysis fails to account for how affect signifies to consciousness see especially pp. 28–34.

22. Jean Paul Sartre, *Existentialism and Humanism* [1948], trans. Philip Mairet (London: Methuen, 1963), pp. 35–9. 'You are free', says Sartre to his student, 'therefore choose – that is to say, invent', p. 38.

23. Sigmund Freud, *Civilization and Its Discontents, The Standard Edition of the Complete Psychological Works of Sigmund Freud (SE)* 21, p. 135.

1. Anxiety at a time of crisis: psychoanalysis and wartime

1. See in particular, Adam Piette's excellent study, *Imagination at War: British Fiction and Poetry 1939–1945* (London: Macmillan, 1995). See also the essays collected in Rod Mengham and N.H Reeve (eds), *The Fiction of the 1940s: Stories of Survival* (Basingstoke: Palgrave, 2001), and in Marina MacKay and Lyndsey Stonebridge (eds), *British Fiction After Modernism: the Novel at Mid-Century* (Basingstoke: Palgrave, 2007).

2. Macdonald's account of this patient and of the manifest and latent content of Mass Observers' anxiety dreams can be found in his handwritten report to Tom Harrisson dated September 1939, Mass Observation Archive, University of Sussex, M-OA: TC - DREAMS Box 1/D. Harrisson had persuaded the Ministry of Information to commission Mass Observation to report on the state of civilian morale. At that time, R.A. Macdonald is listed as a guest member of the British Psycho-Analytic Society (and as the Society's acting librarian). He became a full member in 1942. For later Mass Observation work on civilian morale, see Tom Harrisson and Charles Madge (eds), *War Begins at Home* (London: Chatto and Windus, 1940).

3. This description of the work of the 1938 Committee is drawn from Edward Glover's 'Notes on the Psychological Effects of War Conditions on the Civilian Population (1)', *International Journal of Psycho-Analysis*, 22 (1941): 132–46 (hereafter cited as *IJPA*). See also the collection of essays by medical officers, Army psychiatrists and members of the Tavistock Clinic, *The Neuroses in War*, ed. Emmanuel Miller (London: Macmillan, 1940). The collection includes extracts from the famous 'Report of the War Office Committee on Enquiry on Shell-Shock' (1922) which was one of the key documents for considering the risks of a comparable outbreak of civilian shock in the coming war. As Glover points out, the Committee was mainly comprised of psychologists who had worked with the 1918 armies or with the Ministry of Pensions. As a result their recommendations tended to treat the civilian population as though it were an army division 'strung out in battle-formation' (see 'Description of the Treatment Facilities for Civilian Psycho-neurotic Casualties provided by the Emergency Medical Service' (1940), reprinted in *Neuroses in War*). In the event, the Ministry of Health proposed its own plan. Glover notes 'Reverting to the ideologies of the last war but one, the Minister decided [...] to put the organization of the emergency mental services in the hands of a neurologist assisted by a psychiatrist. And

that was the end of a sorry story, which threatened to set back the development of clinical psychology by twenty years and did in fact shut the door on any prospect of systematic research on the psychology of a people at war' (p. 133). Glover is being somewhat disingenuous here. Many thought that it was Glover's own adherence to a particularly orthodox version of psychoanalysis that kept the British Society out of the war.

4. Edward Glover, 'Notes on the Psychological Effects of War Conditions on the Civilian Population (1)', p. 133.

5. Other analysts in this group included Marjorie Brierley, W.R.D. Fairbairn (who reported from Scotland), Kate Friedlander (who came to London from Vienna in 1933 with Paula Heimann), Willi Hoffer (who fled to London in 1938 with Sigmund and Anna Freud), Karin Stephen (a long-standing member of the British Psycho-Analytical Society and sister-in-law to Virginia Woolf) and William Gillespie (who joined the Emergency Medical Service and worked in the relocated Maudsley Hospital at Mill Hill). What is particularly interesting about this group formation is the extent to which it brought together analysts from different strands of psychoanalytic thought that were current in the British Psycho-Analytic Society. Far from being a homogeneous and companionable group the Society was bitterly divided in the 1940s. Melanie Klein arrived in Britain, at Ernest Jones's invitation, in 1926 and quickly established a reputation and a following. Edward Glover and Klein's daughter, Melitta Schmideberg, had begun to oppose her work in the mid-1930s. With the arrival of the Freuds and other exiles in 1938 the Society began to fracture. The result of these tensions culminated in the intensely acrimonious 'Controversial Discussions' held during the war (see note 20, below). At the same time as this group of analytic observers were sharing their work, the British Society was engaged in a bitter power struggle about the running of the Society (partly prompted by the outbreak of war).

6. Edward Glover, 'Notes on the Psychological Effects of War Conditions on the Civilian Population (III. The "Blitz" – 1940–1)', *IJPA*, 23 (1942): 29–30 and 36–7.

7. Sigmund Freud, *Inhibitions, Symptoms and Anxiety* (1926 [1925]), *SE* 20, p. 166.

8. Theodor Reik, 'Aggression from Anxiety' [1937], *IJPA*, 22 (1941): 8.

9. Sigmund Freud, *Inhibitions, Symptoms and Anxiety*, p. 165.

10. Edward Glover, *The Psychology of Fear and Courage* (Harmondsworth: Penguin, 1940), pp. 21–2.

11. See, for example, Freud's 'Draft E. "How Anxiety Originates" ' (1894), *The Origins of Psychoanalysis: Letters to Wilhelm Fliess, drafts and notes*, eds Marie Bonaparte, Anna Freud and Ernst Kris (London and New York: Imago Publishing, 1954), and 'On the Grounds for Detaching a Particular Syndrome from Neurasthenia under the Description "Anxiety Neurosis" ' (1895), *SE* 3.

12. Sigmund Freud, *Inhibitions, Symptoms and Anxiety*, p. 138.

13. Samuel Weber, 'The Witch's Letter', *Return to Freud: Jacques Lacan's Dislocation of Psychoanalysis* (Cambridge: Cambridge University Press, 1991), p. 152.

14. Sigmund Freud, *Inhibitions, Symptoms and Anxiety*, p. 138.

15. As I discuss in Chapter 4, see pp. 54–64.

16. As James Strachey points out in his editor's introduction to *Inhibitions, Symptoms and Anxiety*, Freud's final theory of anxiety corresponds partic-

ularly with his new work on female sexuality. 'The Dissolution of the Oedipus Complex', for example was published in 1924 and 'Some Psychical Consequences of the Anatomical Distinction between the Sexes' was published in 1925, that is, the same year in which Freud was writing *Inhibitions* (p. 138). Both essays can be found in *SE* 19. In *Inhibitions, Symptoms and Anxiety* itself Freud returns to the case of 'Little Hans' (the first child analysis in psychoanalytic history), and rehearses his new theories of female sexuality (little girls have castration complexes but they can't, logically, have castration anxiety as they've nothing to lose: they do, however, suffer from separation anxiety).

17. For Lacan, it is not the ego which is the 'seat' of anxiety, rather anxiety relates to the desire of the other. 'From the start I have indicated that the anxiety-provoking function of the desire of the other was tied to the fact that I do not know what *objet a* I am for this desire', Jacques Lacan, *Le seminaire livre X: l'angoisse, 1962–1963*, unpublished, seminar 3.7.63., pp. 364–5. I compare Klein and Lacan on anxiety at more length in 'Anxiety in Klein: the Missing Witch's Letter', *Reading Melanie Klein*, eds John Phillips and Lyndsey Stonebridge (London: Routledge, 1998), pp. 190–202.

18. See *Inhibitions, Symptoms and Anxiety*, pp. 129–30. See also Freud's 'Introduction to Psycho-Analysis and the War Neuroses', *SE* 17.

19. Anna Freud in collaboration with Dorothy Burlingham, *Infants without Families and Reports on the Hampstead War Nurseries 1939–1945* (New York: International Universities Press, 1974). The full quote reads: 'We often say half-jokingly, that there is a continual war raging in the nursery. We mean by this that at this time of life the destructive and aggressive impulses are still at work in children in a manner in which they rear in adults only when they are let loose for the purposes of war' (p. 162). See also Denise Riley's *The War in the Nursery: Theories of the Child and Mother* (London: Virago, 1983).

20. The 'Controversial Discussions' refer to the ten scientific meetings set up to debate and clarify the differences between Kleinian psychoanalysis and 'Freudian' psychoanalysis (1943–44), although in fact debate began earlier in 1942 in a series of Extraordinary Business Meetings called in response both to anxieties about Klein's influence and the running of the Society. These discussions are published in full in Pearl King and Riccardo Steiner (eds), *The Freud-Klein Controversies: 1941–45*, New Library of Psychoanalysis, vol. 11, (London: Tavistock/Routledge, 1991). For accounts of the controversies see Phyllis Grosskurth, *Melanie Klein: Her World and Work* (New York: Knopf, 1986); Teresa Brennan, 'Controversial Discussions and Feminist Debate' and Pearl King, 'Early Divergences between the Psycho-Analytic Societies in London and Vienna', both in *Freud in Exile, Psychoanalysis and its Vicissitudes*, eds Edward Timms and Naomi Segal (New Haven: Yale University Press, 1988); and Jacqueline Rose, 'Negativity in Melanie Klein' and 'War in the Nursery' in *Why War? Psychoanalysis, Politics and the Return to Melanie Klein* (Oxford: Blackwell, 1993).

21. Melanie Klein, *The Psychoanalysis of Children* [1932], (London, Virago, 1989).

22. Melanie Klein notes (KLE/P.33). These are in the Melanie Klein Archives held in the Contemporary Medical Archives Centre at the Wellcome Institute of the History of Medicine and reproduced here by the kind permission of the Melanie Klein Trust.

23. Anna Freud, *The Ego and the Mechanisms of Defence* [first translation 1937], (London: Hogarth, 1966), p. 70.
24. Melanie Klein, 'Symbol Formation in Ego Development', in *Love, Guilt and Reparation and Other Works, 1921–1945* (London: Virago, 1988), p. 221. The relation between anxiety and symbol formation is more fully explored in Hanna Segal, 'Notes on Symbol Formation', in *Delusion and Artistic Creativity and Other Psycho-Analytic Essays: the Work of Hanna Segal* (London: Free Association Books, 1986), pp. 49–65. For Lacan's famous criticism of Klein's 'brutal' symbolization see his two 1954 seminars, 'Discourse Analysis and Ego Analysis' and 'The Topic of the Imaginary', in *The Seminar of Jacques Lacan: Book 1*, ed. Jacques-Alain Miller, trans. John Forrester (Cambridge, Cambridge University Press, 1988), pp. 62–88. Shoshana Felman gives an extremely helpful reading of Lacan's take on the case history in *Jacques Lacan and the Adventure of Insight* (Cambridge, MA: Harvard University Press, 1987), p. 116. For a reading that reads the case history through not only Lacan, but Julia Kristeva, see Mary Jacobus, ' "Tea Daddy": Poor Mrs. Klein and the Pencil Shavings', *First Things: the Maternal Imaginary in Literature, Art, and Psychoanalysis* (London/New York: Routledge, 1995), pp. 129–52.
25. Melanie Klein, 'Symbol Formation in Ego Development', p. 225.
26. The nurseries were funded by the Foster Parents' Plan for War Children, Inc., New York. For an account of this work see Elizabeth Young-Bruehl, *Anna Freud: a Biography* (New York: Summit Books, 1988).
27. Anna Freud and Dorothy Burlingham, *Infants without Families and Reports on the Hampstead War Nurseries 1939–1945*, p. 27.
28. Ibid., p. 166.
29. Joan Riviere letter to Melanie Klein dated 3 June 1940, in the Melanie Klein Archives (PP/KLE/C.96).
30. Melanie Klein, 'What Does Death Represent to the Individual?', in the Melanie Klein Archives (PP/KLE/C.95), p. 2.
31. Jacques Lacan, *Ecrits*, trans. Alan Sheridan (London: Tavistock/Routledge, 1989), pp. 20–2.
32. John Berger, 'Francis Bacon and Walt Disney', *About Looking* (London: Writers and Readers Publishing Cooperative, 1980), pp. 111–18.
33. Melanie Klein, *Narrative of a Child Analysis: the Conduct of the Psycho-Analysis of Children seen in the Treatment of a Ten-Year-Old Boy* [1961] (London: Virago, 1989), p. 214. I am indebted here to Mary Jacobus's fascinating reading of the *Narrative* in 'Portrait of the Artist as a Young Dog', *The Maternal Imaginary*, pp. 173–204. Jacobus is particularly astute on how the cartographies of Richard's phantasies are also those of war. 'War', she writes, 'gives Richard a language for destructiveness that, for Klein, in any case characterizes the young child's inner world – reminding us that our access to the "reality" of contemporary events is mediated by something that is never simply attributable to either the sociopolitical or the death instinct. The terrible meaning of Hitler is neither ahistorical nor apolitical, but (qua meaning) freighted from the outset with this cargo of infantile anxiety' (p. 181).
34. I discuss Macaulay's ruin poetics in Chapter 5.
35. Melanie Klein, *Narrative of a Child Analysis*, pp. 214–15.
36. Ibid., p. 217.

37. Jacobus describes two drawings depicting Richard and 'Mrs. K' riding to London in an aeroplane as 'wonderfully achieved rhythmic drawings – somewhere between a Picasso and a Henry Moore' ('Portrait of the Artist as a Young Dog', p. 186); while Donald Meltzer has compared the similarities between Richard's realistic work and his more abstract efforts to similar equivalents in 'different periods in Picasso's work' (quoted in Jacobus, 'Portrait', p. 193).

38. M. Merleau-Ponty, 'Cézanne's Doubt' [1945], in *Sense and Non-Sense*, ed. H.L. Dreyfus and P. Allen Dreyfus (Evanston, IL: Northwestern University Press, 1964), p. 25. I discuss this essay at greater length in ' "In saying yes he says farewell": T.J. Clark's Freud', *Critical Quarterly*, 44(2) (Summer 2002): 30–41.

39. Letter to the Boulangers, Klein (KLE/C3) 11/9/52, Melanie Klein Archives. Unfortunately, I have been unable able to trace these lectures.

40. Anna Freud in collaboration with Sophie Dann, 'An Experiment in Group Upbringing' [1951], *Indications for Child Analysis and Other Papers, 1945–1956* (London: Hogarth Press and the Institute of Psycho-Analysis, 1969), p. 196.

41. Ibid., p. 219.

42. Ibid.

43. See Richard M. Titmuss, *Problems of Social Policy* (London, HMSO, 1950) p. 22, and Tom Harrisson, *Living through the Blitz* (London: Collins, 1976) pp. 17–28 and 38–40.

44. Tom Harrisson, *Living through the Blitz*, pp. 39 and 77.

2. The childhood of anxiety

1. Gertrude Stein, *Wars I have Seen* [1945] (New York: Brilliance Books, 1984), p. 7.

2. Stevie Smith, 'The Wanderer', *The Collected Poems of Stevie Smith*, ed. James MacGibbon (Harmondsworth: Penguin, 1979).

3. Jean MacGibbon, *I Meant to Marry Him: a Personal Memoir* (London: Victor Gollancz, 1984), p. 151. Jean MacGibbon's (*née* Howard) (1913–2001) short stories were published in John Lehmann's *Penguin New Writing* and *Orion* in the 1940s. Her first full-length novel, *When the Weather's Changing*, describing the politics of village life during the war, was published in 1945. An accomplished reviewer and critic, her insightful review of Henry Green's *Concluding* (published in *Horizon*) was greeted enthusiastically by Green himself. She also reviewed for the *Spectator, The Times Literary Supplement* and the *Observer*. She began writing for children in the 1960s (*A Special Providence*, 1964; *Liz*, 1965; *Hal*, 1975; and *Three's Company*, 1978). In 1997, she published a fascinating biography of her former lover, the psychoanalyst, Adrian Stephen, *There's the Lighthouse: a Biography of Adrian Stephen* (London: James and James, 1997).

4. Jean MacGibbon, *I Meant to Marry Him*, p. 134.

5. Caroline Brothers, *War and Photography* (London and New York: Routledge, 1997), p. 175.

6. Quoted in Caroline Brothers, *War and Photography*, p. 176.

7. Ibid., p. 176.

8. Ibid., p. 176.

9. Virginia Woolf, *Three Guineas* (1938), reprinted in *A Room of One's Own and Three Guineas*, ed. Morag Shiach (Oxford, Oxford University Press, 1992), p. 164.
10. Elena Gualtieri, '*Three Guineas* and the Photograph: the Art of Propaganda', in *Women Writers of the 1930s: Gender, Politics and History*, ed. Maroula Jounnou (Edinburgh: Edinburgh University Press, 1999), pp. 165–78.
11. Virginia Woolf, *Three Guineas*, p. 164.
12. Sigmund Freud, *Beyond the Pleasure Principle*, pp. 296–7. While Woolf might appear to be anticipating what would later become a well-established connection between trauma and photography, within the terms of her essay the anxiety provoked by the Madrid photographs turns out, in fact, to be very much part of the argument she is trying to make:

    > When we look at the photographs some fusion takes place within us; however different the education, the traditions behind us, our sensations are the same; and they are violent. You, Sir, call them 'horror and disgust'. We also call them horror and disgust. And the same words rise to our lips. War, you say, is an abomination; a barbarity; war must be stopped. For now at last we are looking at the same picture; we are seeing with you the same dead bodies, the same ruined houses. (p. 164)

    Where the violence of the Madrid photographs made MacGibbon feel politically and psychologically helpless, for Woolf, the anxiety they generate forges a point of consensus with her interlocutor, the man who wrote her a letter asking her how we might prevent war and to whom *Three Guineas* is written as a belated response. Just as the 'crude statement of fact' seems in an unmediated and perhaps unprecedented way literally to get into our systems (in a flash), just as there is something like an incursion of the outside into the inside, the excoriating pain associated with looking at the dead children of Getafe, seems to fade under the gaze of shared spectatorship. 'For now at last we are looking at the same picture', says Woolf. Looking at a picture and sharing its meanings are a lot less anxiety-provoking than having it turn you inside out, or having it 'break' in on you, to go back to MacGibbon's metaphor. It is as if the violent sensations Woolf says the photographs incite ('our emotions are the same; and they are violent') are not just shared, but sublimated and, indeed, pacified as they are harnessed into the rhetoric of consensus.
13. Susan Sontag, *Regarding the Pain of Others* (London: Hamish Hamilton, 2003), p. 7. Sontag is critical of the way that Woolf uses the photographs to make generalizations about war. What actually happens when the photographs become part of Woolf's rhetorical currency, she argues, is less a confirmation of the photographs' political power, than a stripping away of history and politics. 'To read in the pictures, as Woolf does, only what confirms a general abhorrence of war is to stand back from an engagement with Spain as a country with a history', Sontag writes: 'It is to dismiss politics' (p. 8).
14. Caroline Brothers, *War and Photography*, p. 178.
15. Whereas for Brothers, we disavow the reality of the image because of its horror, for Christian Metz we routinely disavow the absence of the object

proclaimed by the photograph, which is why, for Metz, photography is also a kind of fetish. As in the construction of the fetish, we know that the object in the photograph is missing, yet all the same we stubbornly treat it as though it were there. What is at stake in both accounts is the status of belief; of how looking is also a kind of unbelieving. See Metz, 'Photography and Fetish' [1984], reprinted in *The Photography Reader*, ed. Liz Wells (London and New York: Routledge, 2003), pp. 138–45.

16. Susan Sontag, *Regarding the Pain of Others*, p. 9.
17. See Anne Higonnet, *Pictures of Innocence: the History and Crisis of Ideal Childhood* (New York and London: Thames and Hudson, 1998), p. 116.
18. Ibid., p. 117.
19. As Higonnet notes: 'The most challenging pictures of children have been produced by a combined faith in the child's innocence and the camera's neutrality: photographs which force us, as viewers, to see what our ideals deny, just as they expressed what their own makers could not admit' (ibid., p. 10).
20. Roland Barthes, *Camera Lucida* [1980], trans. Richard Howard (London: Vintage, 2000), p. 27.
21. For a fascinating account of the history of how the child came to figure a sense of subjective interiority for modernity, see Carolyn Steedman's *Strange Dislocations: Childhood and the Idea of Human Interiority, 1780–1930* (London: Virago, 1995).
22. Susan Sontag, *Regarding the Pain of Others*, pp. 26–7.
23. The two images come together in the wartime work of Henry Moore, as I discuss in Chapter 4.
24. Clive Scott, *The Spoken Image* (London: Reaktion Books, 1999), p. 66.
25. For Lacan, the skull in Holbein's painting was a trap for the observer. As 'subjects, we are literally called in the picture, and represented here as caught [...] it reflects our own nothingness, in the figure of the death's head'. In other words, it is ourselves who are put into question by the painting. See Jacques Lacan, *The Four Fundamental Concepts of Psycho-Analysis* [1973], trans. Alan Sheridan (Harmondsworth: Penguin, 1987), p. 92.
26. Anna Freud and Dorothy Burlingham, *Infants without Families and Reports on the Hampstead War Nurseries*, p. 209.
27. Samuel Weber, 'Wartime', p. 90.
28. Carolyn Steedman, *Strange Dislocations: Childhood and the Idea of Human Interiority, 1780–1930*, p. 4.
29. Amber Blanco White, *The New Propaganda*, Left Book Club Edition (London: Victor Gollancz Ltd, 1939), p. 34. Amber Blanco White (née Reeves) (1887–1981) is probably remembered today for her affair with H.G. Wells, and as the more than likely model for Wells's *Ann Veronica*. In the early part of the century she published four novels, *The Reward of Virtue* (1911), *A Lady and Her Husband* (1914) (her most interesting novel), *Helen in Love* (1916) and *Give and Take: a Novel of Intrigue* (1923). She taught adult education classes at Morley College in London. Her non-fiction work demonstrates Blanco White's impressive interdisciplinary imaginativeness and political verve. After *The New Propaganda* she published the wonderfully entitled, *Worry in Women* (1941), another work of popular psycho-politics. The book begins with White observing women shopping in a department store: 'They

looked worried, damped down, purposeless, flat, often discouraged, and again, worried, worried, worried', *Worry in Women* (London: Gollancz, 1941), p. 10. *Ethics for Unbelievers*, a post-war, post-Freudian take on the problem of guilt, appeared in 1948 (London: Routledge and Kegan Paul, 1948).

30. Amber Blanco White, *The New Propaganda*, p. 140.
31. See *On the Bringing up of Children*, ed. John Rickman (London: Kegan Paul, Trench, Trubner and Co. Ltd., 1936), pp. 42–5.
32. Melanie Klein, 'On the Theory of Anxiety and Guilt' (1948), in *Envy and Gratitude and Other Works 1946–1963* (London: Virago, 1988), p. 39.
33. Renata Salecl, 'Anxiety at Times of War', in *On Anxiety* (London and New York: Routledge, Taylor and Francis, 2004), p. 24. The difference from the 1940s is that today the objects that terrified Klein's patients into manic denial and that probably sent Klein's future analysand, Jean MacGibbon, crazy have become what Salecl describes as the subject of a knowing kind of anti-anxious art. Today the wartime atrocity photograph is now part of a culture in which the dead are no longer un-presentable, but over-present and over-exposed (pp. 40–8).
34. Jean MacGibbon, *I Meant to Marry Him*, p. 157.
35. Susan Isaacs, 'The Nursery as a Community', in *On the Bringing up of Children*, p. 208, Isaacs refers explicitly to a contemporary court case concerning an escaped monkey who had attacked a child in its pram. This monkey did, Isaacs argues against the evidence of the doctor called by the defence, actually *traumatize* the child. In a recent rape case in Britain, it was also argued that as the infant victim was so young, the traumatic effects of the rape would be negligible.
36. Katherine M. Wolf, 'Evacuation of Children in Wartime', *Psychoanalytic Study of the Child*, 1 (1945): 389. Wolf writes: 'History has here made a cruel psychological experiment on a large scale' (p. 398). In 1940 a Fabian Society report similarly described the evacuation as 'a laboratory experiment in state control upon which the student of politics can ponder and ratiocinate', *Evacuation Survey: a Report to the Fabian Society*, eds Richard Padley and Margaret Cole (London: Routledge, 1940), p. 3.
37. John Bowlby, Emanuel Miller and D.W. Winnicott, 'Letter to the *British Medical Journal*', 16 December, 1939, reprinted in D.W. Winnicott, *Deprivation and Deliquency*, ed. Clare Winnicott, Ray Shepherd and Madeline Davis (London and New York: Routledge, 1990), p. 14.
38. D.W. Winnicott, 'Review of *The Cambridge Evacuation Survey: a Wartime Study in Social Welfare and Education*, ed. Susan Isaacs, 1941', reprinted in *Deprivation and Deliquency*, p. 22.
39. Anna Freud and Dorothy Burlingham, *Infants without Families*, p. 159.
40. D.W. Winnicott, 'Children and their Mothers', originally published in *The New Era in Home and School* (1940), reprinted in *Deprivation and Deliquency*, p. 15.
41. Anna Freud, *Infants without Families*, p. 184.
42. D.W. Winnicott, 'Home Again' (1945), reprinted in *Deprivation and Delinquency*, p. 51.
43. D.W. Winnicott, 'Hate in the Countertransference' (1947), reprinted in *Through Paediatrics to Psycho-Analysis: Collected Papers* [1958] (New York: Brunner/Mazel, 1992), p. 199.

44. Ibid., p. 199.
45. Ibid., p. 200.
46. N.H. Reeve, 'The Girl on a Swing: Childhood and Writing in the 1940s', in *British Fiction After Modernism: the Novel at Mid-Century*, eds Marina MacKay and Lyndsey Stonebridge (Basingstoke: Palgrave, 2007), pp. 92–3.
47. Elizabeth Taylor, 'A Sad Garden', in *Hester Lilly and Other Stories* (London: Virago, 1990), p. 131.
48. Ibid., p. 133.
49. Ibid., pp. 134–5.
50. N.H. Reeve, 'The Girl on a Swing: Childhood and Writing in the 1940s', p. 97.
51. Elizabeth Taylor, 'Plenty Good Fiesta', in *Hester Lilly and Other Stories*, p. 186.
52. Ibid., pp. 190–1.
53. Many thanks to Rod Mengham for directing me to this scene in *Hue and Cry*.
54. Sigmund Freud, *Beyond the Pleasure Principle*, p. 285.

3. Bombs and roses: the writing of anxiety in Henry Green's *Caught*

1. Henry Green, *Caught* [1943] (London: Hogarth, 1950), pp. 76-7. All future quotations from the novel will be taken from this edition. Page numbers will be given in parenthesis in the main body of the text. I'm indirectly indebted throughout this chapter to Rod Mengham's still unsurpassed study of Green, *The Idiom of the Time: the Writings of Henry Green* (Cambridge: Cambridge University Press, 1982). For more on Green's life in wartime, see Jeremy Treglown's indispensable, *Romancing: the Life and Work of Henry Green* (London: Faber, 2000), pp. 124–77.
2. 'And the fire and rose are one', intones T.S. Eliot famously at the end of 'Little Gidding', one of *The Four Quartets*, his exhausted plea for some still point of time outside of the rubble of war. For a strikingly different twist on the same comparison, see Elizabeth Bowen's short story 'Look at all those Roses' (1941), in *The Collected Stories of Elizabeth Bowen*, ed. Angus Wilson (Harmondsworth: Penguin, 1983).
3. 'In the war people in our walk of life entertained all sorts and conditions of men, with a view to self-preservation, to keep the privileges we set such store [...] after those to whom we were kind enough to win the war for us', Henry Green, *Pack My Bag* [1940] (London: Hogarth, 1979), p. 68.
4. See Cathy Caruth, *Unclaimed Experience: Trauma, Narrative and History* (Baltimore: Johns Hopkins University Press, 1996).
5. For a rigorous argument as to why the historical and the psychic cannot and should not be thought of analogically, see Joan Copjec, *Read My Desire: Lacan against the Historicists* (Cambridge, MA: MIT Press, 1994).
6. Slavoj Žižek, *The Plague of Fantasies* (London and New York: Routledge, 1997), pp. 216–17.
7. See Walter Benjamin, 'The Storyteller: Reflections on the Works of Nikolai Leskov', in *Illuminations*, trans. Harry Zohn (London: Jonathan Cape, 1970).
8. The two besides *Caught* are *Loving* (1945) and *Back* (1946). Green saw the war as presenting new stylistic opportunities for writing. In a spirited defence of

C.M. Doughty, he notes: 'Now that we are at war, is not the advantage for writers, and for those who read them, that they will be forced, by the need they have to fight, to go out into territories, it may well be home, which they would never otherwise have visited, and they will be forced, by way of their own selves, towards a style which, by the impact of a life strange to them and by their honest acceptance of this, will be as pure as Doughty's was, so that they will reach each one his own style that shall be his monument?', 'Apologia', originally published in *Folios*, 4 (1941), reprinted in *Surviving: the Uncollected Works of Henry Green*, ed. Matthew Yorke (London: Chatto and Windus, 1992), p. 96.

9. Other writers who belong in this handful might include Elizabeth Bowen, Patrick Hamilton, Inez Holden (*Night Shift*, 1941); William Sansom (*Fireman Flower and Other Stories*, 1944), Malcolm Lowrie, Julian Maclaren-Ross, James Hanley and Arthur Gywnn-Browne, to name just a few. See the essays collected in Rod Mengham and N.H. Reeve, *The Fiction of the 1940s: Stories of Survival* (Basingstoke: Palgrave, 2001), for readings of this work, and Adam Piette's *Imagination at War: British Fiction and Poetry 1939–1945* (London: Macmillan, 1995).

10. Henry Green, *Pack My Bag* [1940] (London: Hogarth, 1979), p. 54. The search for 'things remembered' had, of course, become formulaic by the time Green and other second-generation modernists were writing. Compare William Sansom's narrator in *Fireman Flower*: 'One wishes to envisage the future; one cannot; one casts around for a substitute; one substitutes the picture of the past, sufficiently alien from the present, a vision – yet one that can be controlled,' *Fireman Flower and Other Stories* (London: Hogarth, 1944), p. 150. By contrast, from the first generation of modernists, Virginia Woolf despairs at the way the turbulence of the present war prevents the easy interpenetration of past into the present: 'But to feel the present sliding over the past, peace is necessary. The present must be smooth, habitual', 'Sketch of the Past', in *Moments of Being*, ed. Jean Schulkind (London: Grafton, 1982), p. 114.

11. Maurice Blanchot, *The Writing of Disaster*, trans. Ann Smock (Lincoln and London: University of Nebraska Press, 1995), p. 36.

12. See Walter Benjamin, 'Some Motifs in Baudelaire' and 'The Image in Proust' in *Illuminations*.

13. Compare Cathy Caruth, *Unclaimed Experience: Trauma, Narrative and History*, pp. 10–11.

14. Henry Green is the *nom de plume* of Henry Yorke. Rod Mengham notes how Yorke settled for Green only after toying with Browne, *The Idiom of the Time*, pp. 10 and 62.

15. Sigmund Freud, 'The Dissection of the Psychical Personality', in *New Introductory Lectures on Psychoanalysis* (1933 [1932]), PFL 12, p. 112.

16. Howard Caygill, *Walter Benjamin: the Colour of Experience* (London and New York: Routledge, 1998), pp. 9–13, 82–6.

17. Cathy Caruth, *Unclaimed Experience: Trauma, Narrative and History*, p. 11.

18. 'Dreading forward' is a phrase Green uses in his unfinished factual account of fire-fighting, *London and Fire 1940*. Extracts from this work were published under the title 'Before the Great Fire' in *The London Magazine*, 7 (1960) and in the *Texas Quarterly* (titled 'Firefighting') (1960). Reprinted in *Surviving:*

the Uncollected Works of Henry Green, p. 261. See also Green's short-story of interminable waiting 'The Lull', originally published in *New Writing and Daylight*, Summer 1943, also reprinted in *Surviving*.

19. The woman was the indomitable and beautiful Mary Keene, and the rivalry was amicable. After Smith's 1944 show at the Redfern Gallery, Green writes to him: 'Why we must all be grateful to you all our lives is that you have put into women everything that goes to make up our loves and have made a glory out of what is glorious [...] I came away feeling as though my self had been restated', quoted in Alice Keene, *The Two Mr Smiths: the Life and Work of Sir Matthew Smith 1879–1959* (London: Lund Humphries Publishers, 1995), p. 68. Note how putting into women re-states the self: it is this kind of gendering as self-engendering that I am also tracing here.

20. Elaine Scarry has argued that 'perceptual mimesis' is the common property of literary vegetation. It is much easier, Scarry notes, to recall a flower to mind than a face. 'Imagining Flowers: Perceptual Mimesis (Particularly Delphinium)', *Representations*, 57 (Winter 1997): 90–115. By comparison, Green's writing blocks such perceptual mimesis both through the profusion of the flowers themselves and by a stylistic imitation – or by literary rather than a perceptual mimesis – of similar passages in the work of the key progenitors of the flowery funereal tradition in literary modernism, Baudelaire, Proust and Lawrence.

21. Compare Rod Mengham, *The Idiom of the Time*, p. 85. See Claude Levi-Strauss's *The Elementary Structures of Kinship*, trans. John Doe (Boston: Beacon Press, 1969) for the classic structural anthropological account of incest and exchange, and Jacques Lacan for the equally classic structural psychoanalytical account. Gayle Rubin was the first to reveal the feminist implications of the structure of exchange for anthropology ('The Traffic in Women: Notes towards a Political Economy', in Rayna Reiter (ed.), *Towards an Anthropology of Women*, New York: Monthly Review Press, 1975). See Elaine Scarry's *The Body in Pain: the Making and Unmaking of the World* (Oxford: Oxford University Press, 1987), pp. 60–75 for a thorough analysis of the referential instability of war within symbolic exchange systems.

22. Melitta Schmideberg, 'Some Observations on Individual Reactions to Air Raids', *IJPA*, 23 (1942): 155.

23. See for example Edward Glover's BBC radio broadcasts reprinted in *The Psychology of Fear and Courage* (Harmondsworth: Penguin, 1940).

24. Anna Freud, 'Comments on Trauma', in *Psychic Trauma*, ed. Sidney S. Furst (New York: Basic Books, 1967), p. 238. However, she goes on to caution against over-hasty judgements about the status of historical trauma. 'This', she notes 'happened during the war when Americans, from the greater safety of their home scene, thought of their British friends under bombing as exposed to continuous traumatization, or as "heroic", while in Britain, at this time stimulus barriers had been raised to include the danger as a familiar, nontraumatic item' (p. 239). For a chilling account of how Americans might be educated to see the threat of nuclear war as a 'familiar nontraumatic item', see I.L. Janis, *Air War and Emotional Stress: Psychological Studies of Bombing and Civilian Defense* (New York: The Rand Corporation, McGraw Books, 1951). Janis's study is based on accounts of the civilian bombing of Europe and Japan in World War II.

25. Jacques Lacan, 'La Psychiatre anglaise et la guerre', *Travaux et Interventions* (Paris: 1947): 294.
26. Sigmund Freud, *Inhibitions, Symptoms and Anxiety* (1926 [1925]), *SE* 20, p. 166.
27. André Green, 'Conceptions of Affect', in *On Private Madness* (Madison, CT: International Universities Press, 1986), p. 206.
28. The argument about anxiety refusing to fit into the oppositional structures that are established to contain it is Samuel Weber's. See his 'The Witch's Letter', *Return to Freud: Jacques Lacan's Dislocation of Psychoanalysis*, trans. Michael Levine (Cambridge: Cambridge University Press, 1991), p. 157.
29. Sigmund Freud, 'Fetishism' (1927), in *On Sexuality*, PF 7, p. 352. Melanie Klein, by contrast, *did* believe that there was an unconscious representation of death.
30. Freud, *Inhibitions, Symptoms and Anxiety*, p. 138.
31. Freud, 'Introduction', *Psycho-Analysis and the War Neuroses*, Proceedings of the Symposium held at the Fifth International Psycho-Analytical Congress at Budapest, September 1918, S. Ferenczi et al. (Vienna, London, New York: The International Psychoanalytic Press, 1921), pp. 1–4. See also *SE* 17.
32. Compare Samuel Weber's reading of this logic in 'Wartime', in *Violence, Identity and Self-Determination*. Writing on Freud's 'Thoughts for the Times on War and Death', Weber notes: 'The paradox [...] resides in that to think of death as one normally thinks of other things, namely, by representing it, is to transform it into a spectacle and ourselves into the spectators and thereby miss precisely what is at stake in death: the cessation of our being in the world. Imagining death thus becomes the opposite of what it seems: a way of ostensibly overcoming the threat of nonbeing, of no longer being there, in the world' (p. 97).
33. Sigmund Freud, *Inhibitions, Symptoms and Anxiety*, p. 138.
34. Sigmund Freud, 'Fetishism' (1927), in *On Sexuality*, PF 7, p. 352.
35. Sigmund Freud, *Inhibitions, Symptoms and Anxiety*, p. 170.
36. Samuel Weber, *Return to Freud*, p. 155.
37. As Laplanche puts it: 'Anxiety [...] is the impact of destructuration produced on the ego and its objects by the drive attack: it is the irreconcilable ego-dystonic residue of sexual desire', 'A Metapsychology Put to the Test of Anxiety', *IJPA*, 62 (1981): 89.
38. Sigmund Freud, 'Fetishism', p. 353.
39. Walter Benjamin, *The Rainbow: a Dialogue on Phantasie*, quoted and translated by Howard Caygill, *Walter Benjamin: the Colour of Experience* (London and New York: Routledge, 1998), p. 11.
40. For responses to the evacuation see Tom Harrisson and Charles Madge (eds), *War Begins at Home* (London: Chatto and Winclus, 1940). John Furse, the painter, recalls the experience of evacuation: 'I was evacuated: I looked up the meaning of the word and it seemed to fit. The word means, so it said – evacuate v.t (uable) empty (stomach, etc): (esp. of troops) withdrawal from (place); discharge (excrement, etc) evacuation, n. (vacuum). It all fits, the withdrawing, the emptiness, the troops, the vacuum – above all the vacuum. I was evacuated. I won't comment on the excrement', quoted in Ruth Inglis, *The Children's War: Evacuation, 1939–1945* (London: Collins, 1989), p. 158.

41. It has become conventional to think of the relation between the image and the ego through Lacan's famous experiment with the inverted vase and the bouquet of flowers. What Lacan demonstrates in 'The Topic of the Imaginary' is how the ego is not in cognitive control of its images, but is the *effect* of the structure of the imaginary. It is not the gaze of the 'I' that puts the bouquet into the vase, it is the optical trick of light by which the flowers appear to be arranged in the vase that produces the illusion of the 'I'. Jacques Lacan, 'The Topic of the Imaginary', *The Seminar of Jacques Lacan: Book I*, ed. Jacques-Alain Miller, trans. John Forrester (Cambridge: Cambridge University Press, 1988), pp. 77–8. In answer to Wittengstein's problem: 'I don't *see* that the colours of bodies reflects light into my eye', one could respond: 'because if you could see that, you would also see that it is the logic of optics that is a condition of your seeing in the first place; the experience of vision is an effect, not a cause of a logic that lies not in consciousness, but beyond the subject.' Wittengstein, *Remarks on Colour*, ed. G.E.M. Anscombe, trans. Linda L McAlister and Margarete Schattle (Berkeley and Los Angeles: University of California Press, 1977), p. 16e. Similarly, to Freud's thesis in *Inhibitions* it is possible to add the qualification that the anxious ego which starts to make images in response to the trauma of perceptual loss can only do so by labouring under the misperception that it is the master of this imaginary domain. Another way to understand what Green is doing with images in *Caught*, is to think of him as arranging Lacan's bouquet; a cluster of red roses dappled with white in the centre, hyacinths to give height at the back, at the front a border of yellow magnolias to give the illusion of depth, all framed and held in place by greenery: then to think of him knocking it over.
42. Mark Cousins. 'The Traumatic Image: *Vertigo*', paper presented at the Society for Humanities, Cornell University, April 1998.
43. Wilfred Bion, 'On Hallucination', *Second Thoughts* (New Jersey and London: Jason Aronson, 1993), p. 75.
44. Jean Laplanche, p. 86. Or as Henry Green himself remarked: 'Any work of art if it is alive, carries the germs of its death, like any other living thing, around with it', 'An Unfinished Novel', *Surviving*, p. 254.
45. Sigmund Freud, *Beyond the Pleasure Principle*, PF 11, p. 338.
46. Henry Green, *Back* [1946] (New York: New Directions, 1981), p. 4.
47. Ibid., p. 3. In an uncanny act of identification – or appropriation – it was in fact Green's lover, Mary Keene, who had a prosthetic leg.
48. Ibid., pp. 63–4.
49. Ibid., p. 39.
50. Ibid., p. 7.
51. Ibid., p. 188.

4. Bombs, birth and trauma: Henry Moore and D.W. Winnicott

1. Inez Holden, *It Was Different at the Time* (London: John Lane, The Bodley Head, 1943), p. 69.
2. Samuel Weber, *Return to Freud: Jacques Lacan's Dislocation of Psychoanalysis*, trans. Michael Levine (Cambridge: Cambridge University Press, 1991), p. 167.

3. *London Bulletin*, nos 18–20 (June) 1940, quoted in Alexander Robertson et al., *Surrealism in Britain in the Thirties* (Leeds: Leeds City Art Galleries, 1986), p. 84.
4. See Freud's *Three Essays on Sexuality*, PF 7, p. 91. Adorno noted, in relation to Max Ernst, that what surrealism and psychoanalysis shared was the way that each 'blasted' our childhood into the present, and so forced our 'pre' into our history. In 'Looking Back at Surrealism', Adorno noted: 'One must therefore trace the affinity of surrealistic technique for psychoanalysis, not to a symbolism of the unconscious, but to the attempt to uncover childhood experiences by blasting them out.' Quoted in Rosalind Krauss, *The Optical Unconscious* (Cambridge, MA: MIT Press, 1994), p. 34.
5. Bryher, *The Days of Mars: a Memoir, 1940–1946* (London: Calder and Boyars, 1972), p. 150
6. Andrew Causey, 'Henry Moore and the Uncanny', in *Henry Moore: Critical Essays*, eds Jane Beckett and Fiona Russell (Aldershot: Ashgate, 2003), pp. 81–106.
7. Adam Phillips, *Winnicott* (Cambridge, MA: Harvard University Press, 1998), pp. 14–15. Carroll is frequently cited as the forerunner of British Surrealism. For Pompey, English woman turned spy turned soldier and the heroine of Stevie Smith's grimly entertaining 1938 novel *Over the Frontier*, a surrealist pre-war dreamtime turns into a militaristic nightmare.
8. It was not only indifference, but also an initial lack of adequate home defence strategies that drove people into underground stations, warehouses and other communal places in the early weeks of the first Blitz. For an account of this chapter of the war in Britain see Tom Harrisson's *Living Through the Blitz* (London: Collins, 1976).
9. Alan Wilkinson, *The Drawings of Henry Moore* (London: Tate Gallery Publications, 1977), p. 36.
10. John Russell, *Henry Moore* (London: Pelican, 1973), p. 117.
11. Quoted in Alan Wilkinson, *The Drawings of Henry Moore*, p. 29.
12. John Russell, *Henry Moore*, p. 112.
13. Frances Carey identifies the reviewer as Keith Vaughan. See Frances Carey, 'Commentary', *Henry Moore: a Shelter Sketchbook* (London: British Museum Publications, 1988), pp. 18–19.
14. Erich Neumann, *The Archetypal World of Henry Moore* (London: Routledge, Kegan and Paul, 1959), p. 60.
15. For a full and fascinating discussion of motherhood in Moore's work, see Anne Wagner, 'Henry Moore's Mother', *Representations*, 65 (Winter 1999): 93–110. See also Julian Stallabrass, 'The Mother and Child Theme in the Work of Henry Moore', in *Henry Moore: Mutter und Kind/Mother and Child* (Much Hadham: Henry Moore Publications, 1992), pp. 13–39.
16. David Sylvester, *About Modern Art: Critical Essays 1948–96* (London: Chatto and Windus, 1996), p. 189.
17. Peter Fuller, *Henry Moore: an Interpretation*, ed. Anthony O'Hear (London: Methuen, 1993), p. 41.
18. Appropriately a cast of one such figure, *Large Figure in a Shelter* (1985–86), now stands on a hill overlooking the park and municipal buildings in Guernica. Moore had seen the beginnings of Picasso's *Guernica* in Paris in the latter's studio in 1937. At the time Moore, along with Auden, Spender

and others, was trying to get to Spain to aid the war effort, but was prevented from going at the last moment (Alan Wilkinson, *The Drawings of Henry Moore*, pp. 129–30).

19. Roger Berthoud, *The Life of Henry Moore* (London: Faber and Faber, 1987), p. 181.
20. What I am casting as anxiety here could be read equally well in terms of desire (anxiety's finer side). It is very tempting to re-title the drawing with Lacan's famous remark about the need to take desire literally: 'the signifier of the phallus plays a central role beneath a transparent veil'. Lacan, 'The Direction of Treatment and the Principles of its Power', *Ecrits: a Selection*, trans. Alan Sheridan (London and New York: Tavistock/Routledge, 1977), p. 251.
21. Quoted in Alan Wilkinson, *The Drawings of Henry Moore*, p. 36.
22. Ibid., p. 33.
23. I discuss this debate in more detail in Chapter 1.
24. See Adam Phillips, 'Bombs Away', *History Workshop Journal*, 45 (Spring 1998): 183–98; and Maria Torok et al., 'Melanie Mell By Herself', trans. Ian Patterson, in *Reading Melanie Klein*, eds Lyndsey Stonebridge and John Phillips (London and New York: Routledge, 1998), pp. 51–80.
25. Adam Phillips, 'Bombs Away', p. 194.
26. D.W. Winnicott, 'Primitive Emotional Development' [1945], in *Through Paediatrics to Psycho-Analysis: Collected Papers* [1958] (New York: Brunner/Mazel, 1992), p. 145.
27. Otto Rank, *The Trauma of Birth* [1924] (London: Kegan, Paul, Trench, Trubner & Co Ltd, 1929), p. 81.
28. D.W. Winnicott, 'Birth Memories, Birth Trauma and Anxiety' [1949], in *Through Paediatrics to Psycho-Analysis*, p. 179.
29. Ibid.
30. Letter to the *British Medical Journal* (16 December 1939), quoted in D.W. Winnicott, *Deprivation and Delinquency*, eds Clare Winnicott, Ray Shepherd and Madeline Davis (London and New York: Routledge, 1990), p. 14.
31. D.W. Winnicott, 'Birth Memories', p. 185.
32. Ibid., p. 184.
33. D.W. Winnicott, 'Anxiety Associated with Insecurity', in *Through Paediatrics to Psycho-Analysis*, p. 99.
34. D.W. Winnicott, 'Birth Trauma', pp. 185–6. Writing just after the First World War, it was Freud who first suggested the connection between being buried alive and birth phantasies. 'To some people the idea of being buried alive by mistake is the most uncanny thing of all. And yet psychoanalysis has taught us that this terrifying phantasy is only a transformation of another phantasy which originally had nothing terrifying about it at all, but was qualified by a certain lasciviousness – the phantasy, I mean, of intra-uterine existence.' 'The Uncanny' [1919], PF 14, pp. 366–7.
35. D.W. Winnicott, 'Birth Trauma' p. 185. This intolerable situation is also Winnicott's way of describing trauma. The argument is developed in his classic 1956 paper, 'Primary Maternal Preoccupation'. 'Maternal failures produce phases of reaction to impingement and these reactions interrupt the "going on being" of the infant. An excess of this reaction produces not frustration but a threat of annihilation. This in my view is a very real

primitive anxiety, long antedating any anxiety that includes the word death in its description', *Through Paediatrics to Psycho-Analysis*, p. 303.
36. Freud, *Inhibitions, Symptoms and Anxiety, SE* 20, p. 251.
37. Melitta Schmideberg, 'Some Observations on Individual Reactions to Air Raids', *International Journal of Psychoanalysis*, 23(1942): p. 152.
38. Melanie Klein, 'Notes on Some Schizoid Mechanisms [1946], in *Envy and Gratitude and Other Works 1946–1963* (London: Virago, 1988), p. 4.
39. D.W. Winnicott, 'Birth Trauma', p. 181.
40. Roger Berthoud, *The Life of Henry Moore*, pp. 162–3.
41. Alan Wilkinson, *The Drawings of Henry Moore*, p. 31.
42. Rosalind Krauss, *The Optical Unconscious* (Cambridge, MA: MIT Press, 1994), pp. 33–93.
43. Compare Weber's discussion of frames and fields of vision in Peter Greenaway's *Draughtsman's Contract* in *Return to Freud*, pp. 166–7: 'For the spectator, to be sure, it is precisely the presence of those curious objects that don't "fit in," that raise the issue of the frame by pointing elsewhere, to another place, to the "space between knowing and seeing" within which the "intelligent man" feels increasingly "confined." ' Weber's analysis draws from Lacan's discussion of the anxiety provoked by the window in the Wolfman's dream and the curtain at the theatre in his seminar on anxiety: both fall out of a cognitive frame of reference, hence the anxiety. See Lacan, *L'angoisse: tome 2*, 6.26. (1963).
44. Elizabeth Bowen, *The Heat of the Day* [1948] (Harmondsworth: Penguin, 1962), p. 92.

5. The writing of post-war guilt: Rose Macaulay and Rebecca West

1. Graham Greene, *The Ministry of Fear: an Entertainment* [1943], (Harmondsworth: Penguin, 1973), p. 195.
2. Sigmund Freud, 'Dostoevsky and Parricide' (1928 [1927]), *SE* 21, p. 189
3. Hannah Arendt, *Eichmann in Jerusalem: a Report on the Banality of Evil* [1963] (London: Penguin, 1994), p. 298. For a reading of the significance of the Eichmann trial, particularly for its American audience, see Marianna Torgovnick, 'Eichmann's Ghost', in *The War Complex: World War II in Our Time* (Chicago: Chicago University Press, 2005), pp. 45–70.
4. Hannah Arendt, *Eichmann in Jerusalem*, p. 242.
5. Ibid., pp. 3–35.
6. Ibid., p. 286.
7. Sigmund Freud, 'Psychoanalysis and the Establishment of Facts in Legal Proceedings' (1906), *SE* 9, p. 113.
8. See Freud's 'Criminals from a Sense of Guilt', the third essay in his 'Some Character-Types Met with in Psycho-Analytic Work' (1916), *SE* 14, p. 332.
9. Sigmund Freud, 'The Expert Opinion in the Halsmann Case' (1931 [1930]), *SE* 21, p. 252.
10. Writing about the Eichmann trial, Shoshana Felman reads Arendt's commitment to a strictly legal reading of the trial as an example of an ultimately 'conservative jurisprudential argument', at odds with a more radical historiography that Arendt elsewhere advocates for understanding the holocaust.

See Shoshana Felman, ' "Theaters of Justice": Arendt in Jerusalem, the Eichmann Trial, and the Redefinition of Legal Meaning in the Wake of the Holocaust', *Critical Inquiry*, 27(2) (Winter 2001): 201–38.

11. Karl Jaspers, *The Question of German Guilt* [1947], trans. E.B. Ashton (New York: Fordham University Press, 2000), p. 42. As well as meaning you are criminally, morally or political guilty, in Jasper's terms 'you are guilty' can also mean that you are metaphysically guilty: this is the guilt of the innocent, the guilt of the co-responsibility which, Jaspers argues, comes from human solidarity. See especially the chapter 'Scheme of Distinctions'.

12. Ibid., p. 15.

13. For a fascinating account of the problem of guilt after Freud, see Roberto Speziale-Bagliacca, *Guilt: Revenge, Remorse and Responsibility after Freud*, trans. Ian Harvey (Hove and New York: Brunner-Routledge, 2004).

14. William Empson, 'Introduction', *Coleridge's Verse: a Selection*, ed. William Empson and David Pirlie (London: Faber and Faber, 1972), pp. 13–100.

15. T.S. Eliot, 'Hamlet' [1919], in *The Selected Prose of T.S. Eliot*, ed. Frank Kermode (London: Faber and Faber, 1975), p. 49.

16. Shoshana Felman, 'Education and Crisis', in *Testimony: Crises of Witnessing in Literature, Psychoanalysis, and History*, Shoshana Felman and Dori Laub (London and New York: Routledge, 1992), p. 5.

17. Penelope Fitzgerald, 'Introduction' to Rose Macaulay, *The World My Wilderness* [1950] (London: Virago, 2000), p. ix.

18. Ibid., p. 58.

19. Ibid., p. 166.

20. Leo Mellor, 'Words from the Bombsites: Debris, Modernism and Literary Salvage', *Critical Quarterly*, 46(4) (2004): 77–90.

21. Ibid., p. 71.

22. Rose Macaulay, *The Pleasure of Ruins* (London: Thames and Hudson, 1953), p. 453.

23. Rose Macaulay, *The World My Wilderness*, p. 193.

24. Ibid., p. 93.

25. Ibid., p. 91.

26. Ibid., p. 7.

27. Ibid., p. 29.

28. D.W. Winnicott, 'Some Psychological Aspects of Juvenile Delinquency (an Address to Magistrates' [1946], in *Deprivation and Deliquency*, eds Clare Winnicott, Ray Shepherd and Madeline Davis (London and New York: Routledge, 1990), pp. 113–19.

29. Rose Macaulay, *The World My Wilderness*, p. 252.

30. Paul Tillich, *Systematic Theology: 1–111* (Chicago: Chicago University Press, 1964).

31. See Denis Hollier's account of French wartime writing, *Absent without Leave: French Literature under Threat of War*, trans. Catherine Porter (Cambridge, MA and London: Harvard University Press, 1997).

32. Nevil Shute, *Requiem for a Wren* [1955] (London: Heinemann and Heron Books, n.d.), p. 202.

33. Ibid., p. 246.

34. By the time Greene writes *The End of the Affair* (1951), the novel that turns the erotics of adultery into the pornography of Christian sacrifice, it is as

though the war itself – here in the form of the blast that compels Bendrix's lover, Sarah, into her perverse pact with God – has become the pitiless correlative for original sin (Harmondsworth: Penguin, 1975).

35. Marghanita Laski, *Little Boy Lost* [1949] (London: Persephone Books, 2001).
36. Rebecca West, 'The Revolutionary', in *The Meaning of Treason* [1949] (London: Penguin, 1965), p. 14.
37. Rebecca West, 'A Reporter at Large: Extraordinary Exile', *New Yorker*, 22, (7 September 1946): 40. Rebecca West, 'Greenhouse with Cyclamens I', *A Train of Powder: Six Reports on the Problem of Guilt and Punishment in Our Time* (Chicago: Ivan R. Dee, 1955), p. 18. Unless otherwise stated, all quotations are from the 1955 version.
38. Rebecca West, 'Greenhouse with Cyclamens I, *A Train of Powder*, p. 25.
39. Ibid., p. 24.
40. Ibid., p. 26.
41. Ibid., pp. 5–6.
42. Ibid., p. 5.
43. Ibid., p. 7.
44. Ibid., p. 5.
45. See Sigmund Freud, *Beyond The Pleasure Principle* (1920), PF 1, pp. 298–301.
46. Rebecca West, 'Greenhouse with Cyclamens III', *A Train of Powder*, p. 246.
47. Rebecca West, 'Greenhouse with Cyclamens I', p. 21.
48. Sybille Bedford, 'The Worst that Ever Happened', *Saturday Evening Post*, (October, 1963): 29–100.
49. Rebecca West, 'Greenhouse with Cyclamens I', p. 21.
50. Ibid., p. 21.
51. Ibid., p. 27.
52. From within history see the debate between Hayden White and Martin Jay on the question of modernism and the historical representation of the Holocaust. Hayden White, 'Historical Emplotment and the Problem of Truth', and Martin Jay, 'Of Plots, Witnesses and Judgments', in *Probing the Limits of Representation: Nazism and the Final Solution*, ed. Saul Friedlander (Cambridge, MA and London: Harvard University Press, 1992), pp. 37–53 and pp. 91–107. Dominick LaCapra has criticized the valorizing tendencies of trauma theory. See especially 'Lanzmann's *Shoah*: Here There is no Why', *Critical Inquiry*, 23 (Winter, 1997): 231–69, and the introduction to *History and Memory after Auschwitz* (Ithaca and London: Cornell University Press, 1998). For a thorough critique of the way trauma theory 'passes' issues of culpability, see Debarati Sanyal, 'A Soccer Match in Auschwitz: Passing Culpability in Holocaust Criticism', *Representations*, 79 (Summer 2002): 1–27.
53. Quoted in Ruth Leys, 'The Pathos of the Literal: Trauma and the Crisis of Representation', in *Trauma: a Genealogy*, p. 295.
54. Ruth Leys, 'The Pathos of the Literal', p. 297.
55. Shoshana Felman, ' "Theaters of Justice": Arendt in Jerusalem, the Eichmann Trial, and the Redefinition of Legal Meaning in the Wake of the Holocaust', p. 202.
56. Paul de Man, 'Aesthetic Formalization: Kleist's *Uber das Marionettentheater*', in *The Rhetoric of Romanticism* (New York: Columbia University Press, 1984), p. 288.

57. T.J. Clark, *Farewell to an Idea: Episodes from a History of Modernism* (New Haven and London: Yale University Press, 1999), pp. 166–7. See also Christopher Prendergast, 'Modernism's Nightmare? Art, Matter and Mechanism', *New Left Review*, 10 (July/August 2001): 42, for a reading of Clark's insight in relation to modernism.

58. Rebecca West, 'Greenhouse with Cyclamens I', p. 10.

59. Ibid., p. 69.

60. Ibid.

61. Ibid., p. 8. West's original version of these lines extends the mechanization-as-death-drive metaphor that runs through both the original and later reports: 'A machine is running down, a great machine, the greatest machine that has ever been created – the war machine, by which mankind, in spite of its infirmity of purpose and its frequent desire for death, has defended its life. It was a hard machine to operate; its processes were unlovely. It is the natural desire of all those who served it [...] that it should become scrap. There is another machine, which is warming up – the peace machine, by which mankind means to live its life.' 'A Reporter at Large: Extraordinary Exile', *New Yorker*, 22 (7 September 1946): 36.

62. Marianna Torgovnick, 'Eichmann's Ghost', in *The War Complex: World War II in Our Time*.

63. Rebecca West, 'Greenhouse with Cyclamens I', p. 51.

64. See Janet Flanner's reporting of the case against Sauckel in her 'Letter from Nuremberg', 27 February 1946, also originally published in *The New Yorker*, reprinted in *Janet Flanner's World: Uncollected Writings 1932–1975*, ed. Irving Drutman (New York and London: Harcourt Brace Jovanovich, 1979), pp. 107–8.

65. Rebecca West, 'Greenhouse with Cyclamens I', p. 53.

66. Ibid., p. 54.

67. Ibid., p. 55.

68. Ibid., p. 65.

69. Hannah Arendt, *Eichmann in Jerusalem*, p. 297.

70. Sigmund Freud, *Civilization and its Discontents*, SE 21, p. 135.

71. *Vol III: Proceedings of the International Conference on Medical Psychotherapy, 11–14th August, International Congress on Mental Health, London, 1948*, ed. J.C. Flugel (London and New York: H.K. Lewis and Columbia University Press, 1948), p. 47.

72. Ibid., p. 77.

73. Ibid., p. 84.

74. Ibid., p. 91.

75. Ibid., p. 27.

76. Ibid., p. 34.

77. W.R.D. Fairbairn, 'The Repression and Return of Bad Objects (with special reference to the "War Neuroses")' [1943], originally published in the *British Journal of Medical Psychology*, 19, (3–4), republished in *Psychoanalytic Studies of the Personality* (London and Boston: Routledge & Kegan Paul, 1984), p. 63.

78. Ibid., p. 68.

79. Ibid., p. 67.

80. Ibid., p. 67.

81. Ibid., p. 77.

6. Hearing them speak: voices in Bion, Muriel Spark and Penelope Fitzgerald

1. Penelope Fitzgerald, 'Hearing them Speak' (1993), reprinted in *The Afterlife*, ed. Terence Dooley, with Christopher Carduff and Mandy Kirkby (New York: Counterpoint, 2003), p. 361.
2. Adam Phillips, 'Superiorities', in *Equalities* (London: Faber and Faber, 2002), p. 12.
3. Jacques Lacan, 'La psychiatre anglaise et la guerre', *Travaux et interventions* (1947): 312.
4. Ibid., p. 290.
5. Phillips, *Equalities*, p. 4.
6. Lacan, 'La psychiatre anglaise et la guerre', p. 301.
7. Haydee Faimberg, 'Whom was Bion addressing? "Negative capability" and "listening to listening"', in *W.R. Bion: Between Past and Future*, ed. Parthenope Bion Talamo, Franco Borgogno and Silvio A. Merciai (London and New York: Karnac Books, 2000), p. 81.
8. A version of this chapter was first delivered at the conference, 'Life Beyond Language: the Psychoanalytical Voice', at the Tavistock Clinic, organized by Therip and the Freud Museum in March 2005.
9. W.R. Bion and John Rickman, 'Intra-Group Tensions in Therapy: Their Study as the Task of the Group' [1943], reprinted in *Experiences in Groups and other Papers* (London and New York: Routledge, 1994), p. 12.
10. Penelope Fitzgerald, 'Curriculum Vitae' [1989], reprinted in *The Afterlife*, p. 342.
11. Penelope Fitzgerald, 'A Character in One of God's Dreams: *Reality and Dreams* by Muriel Spark' [1997], Ibid., p. 279.
12. 'Introduction', *Bion's Legacy to Groups*, eds Parthenope Bion Talamo, Franco Borgogno and Silvio A. Merciai (London: Karnac Books, 1998), p. 7.
13. Wilfred Bion, 'Commentary' [1972], *War Memoirs 1917–19*, ed. Francesca Bion (London: Karnac Books, 1997), p. 204.
14. Wilfred Bion, 'Amiens' [1958], *War Memoirs 1917–19*, pp. 256–7.
15. Wilfred Bion, *The Long Week-End 1897–1919* (London: Free Association Books, 1986), pp. 248–9.
16. Otto Isakower, 'On the Exceptional Position of the Auditory Sphere', *IJPA*, 20 (1939): 345. For a fascinating account of the trials of inner speech in history and theory see Denise Riley, ' "A voice without a mouth": Inner Speech', *Qui Parle*, 14(2) (2004): 57–104.
17. Mladen Dolar, 'The Object Voice', in *Gaze and Voice as Love Objects*, ed. Renata Salecl and Slavoj Žižek (Durham and London: Duke University Press, 1996), p. 28.
18. See Wilfred Bion, 'Attacks on Linking' (1959), in *Second Thoughts: Selected Papers on Psycho-Analysis* (New Jersey and London: Jason Aronson, 1993), pp. 93–109.
19. Wilfred Bion, 'Language and the Schizophrenic' [1953], in *New Directions in Psycho-Analysis: the Significance of Infant Conflict in the Pattern of Adult Behaviour*, eds Melanie Klein, Paula Heimann and R.E. Money-Kyrle (London: Karnac, 1985), pp. 231–2.
20. Ibid., p. 231.

21. Wilfred Bion, 'Development of Schizophrenic Thought' [1956], *Second Thoughts*, p. 41.
22. As Robert Hinshelwood points out it was Bion who first categorized projective identification into two types. 'The difference', notes Hinshelwood, 'depends on the degree of violence in the execution of the mechanism. There are two alternative aims of projective identification: (i) one is to evacuate violently a painful state of mind leading to forcibly entering an object, in phantasy, for immediate relief and often with the aim of an intimidating control of the object; and (ii) the other is to introduce into the object a state of mind, as a means of communicating with it about this mental state.' Robert Hinshelwood, *A Dictionary of Kleinian Thought* (London: Free Association Books, 1991), p. 182. The precarious fault-line between intimidating control and communication runs right through the voices I am trying to describe here.
23. More than a few of Bion's patients carry an echo of George Harvey Bone, the anti-hero in Patrick Hamilton's *Hangover Square* (1941). In the final scenes of that novel, George, persecuted by voices, creates a net around his murder victims while Chamberlain delivers his infamous 1939 declaration of war broadcast. Bion was also Samuel Beckett's analyst for a period in the 1930s. Quite how Beckett's voice interacts with Bion's (particularly the later autobiographical Bion of works such as *A Memoir of the Future*, 1991) is an engrossing topic. See Didier Anzieu, *Beckett et le psychanalyste* (Paris: Editions Mentha: 1992) for a fascinating treatment of this theme. Beckett, of course, also frequently wrote his voices for radio.
24. Wilfred Bion, 'On Hallucination' [1958], *Second Thoughts*, p. 82.
25. Ibid. pp. 47–8.
26. Virginia Woolf, *Between the Acts* [1941] (Harmondsworth: Penguin, 1992), p. 51.
27. Wilfred Bion, 'Group Dynamics: a Re-view' (1955), *Experiences in Groups*, p. 141.
28. Ibid. p. 177.
29. Wilfred Bion, 'Experiences in Groups', *Experiences in Groups*, p. 41.
30. Wilfred Bion, 'Group Dynamics: a Re-view', p. 456.
31. See Wilfred Bion, 'Notes on Memory and Desire' (1967), in *Melanie Klein Today, Vol.2: Mainly Practice* (London: Routledge, 1988), pp. 17–21.
32. Wilfred Bion, 'Group Dynamics: a Re-View', p. 461.
33. Thanks to Richard Robinson for pointing out the shocking power of Oskar's voice in Grass's novel, and to Tony Gash for discussions about the ends of heteroglossia. The classic text for thinking about voice and the novel is M.M. Bakhtin's *The Dialogic Imagination: Four Essays*, trans. M. Holquist and C. Emerson (Austin: University of Texas Press, 1981). See also Julia Kristeva, 'Word, Dialogue and Novel', in *The Kristeva Reader*, ed. Toril Moi (Oxford: Blackwell, 1986), pp. 34–61.
34. ' "The Same Informed Air": An interview with Muriel Spark', Martin McQuillan, in *Theorizing Muriel Spark: Gender, Race, Deconstruction*, ed. Martin McQuillan (Basingstoke: Palgrave, 2002), p. 218.
35. Bryan Cheyette, *Muriel Spark* (Tavistock: Northcote House in association with the British Council, 2000), p. 10. See also the essays collected in Martin McQuillan (ed.), *Theorizing Muriel Spark*.

36. W.R. Bion and John Rickman, 'Intra-Group Tensions in Therapy: Their Study as the Task of the Group', p. 14.
37. Muriel Spark, *The Girls of Slender Means* (Harmondsworth: Penguin, 1966), p. 106.
38. Ibid., p. 11.
39. Ibid., p. 21.
40. See Jacques Lacan, 'God and the Jouissance of The Woman', in *Feminine Sexuality: Jacques Lacan and l'école freudienne*, ed. Juliet Mitchell and Jacqueline Rose, trans. Jacqueline Rose (London: Macmillan, 1982), p. 142.
41. Muriel Spark, *The Girls of Slender Means*, pp. 86–7.
42. Frank Kermode, 'Muriel Spark', in *Modern Essays* (London: Fontana, 1971), p. 272.
43. Muriel Spark, *The Girls of Slender Means*, p. 61.
44. Ibid., p.71.
45. Penelope Fitzgerald, *Human Voices* [1980] (London: Flamingo, 1997), p. 122.
46. Ibid., p. 8.
47. Ibid., p. 96.
48. Ibid., p. 77.
49. Heinrich Heine, 'Der Asra', in *Selected Verse* [1968], ed. and trans. Peter Branscombe (London: Penguin, 1986), p. 182.
50. Penelope Fitzgerald, *Human Voices*, pp. 81–2.
51. Ibid., p. 84.
52. Ibid., p. 142.
53. Ibid., p.77.
54. Ibid., p. 135.
55. Ibid., p. 141.
56. Ibid., p. 144.
57. Wilfred Bion, 'Psychiatry at a Time of Crisis', *British Journal of Medical Psychiatry*, 21 (1948): 84–5.
58. See Moustapha Safouan, *Jacques Lacan and the Question of Psychoanalytic Training*, trans. and intro. Jacqueline Rose (London: Macmillan, 2000).
59. A full cultural history of how it is that Britain continues to enshrine its memory of the war while remaining astonishingly indifferent – if recently a little embarrassedly so – about the consequence of its own actions, is still much needed. Despite the impact of studies such as Angus Calder's hugely influential *Myth of the Blitz*, British literary history and theory has been slow to come to grips with its version of what Marianna Torgovnick has described as the 'war complex' (*The War Complex: World War II in Our Time*, pp. 1–21). Torgovnick's study reveals how it was that American cultural memory valorized some events from World War II, but left others to linger, neither exactly invisible nor entirely present.

Select Bibliography

Archive sources

Mass Observation Archive, University of Sussex.
Melanie Klein Archives, Contemporary Medical Archives Centre at the Wellcome Institute of the History of Medicine.

Books and journals

Anon ('Art Critic'), 'War Artists and the War', *The Penguin New Writing*, 4(3) (January–March 1943): 108–17.

Anzieu, Didier, *Beckett et le psychanalyste* (Paris: Editions Mentha, 1992).

Arendt, Hannah, *Eichmann in Jerusalem: a Report on the Banality of Evil* [1963] (London: Penguin, 1994).

Armstrong, Tim, 'Two Types of Shock in Modernity,' *Critical Quarterly*, 42(1) (2001): 60–73.

Auden, W.H., *The Age of Anxiety: a Baroque Eclogue* (London: Faber and Faber, 1948).

Bakhtin, M.M., *The Dialogic Imagination: Four Essays*, trans. M. Holquist and C. Emerson (Austin: University of Texas Press, 1981).

Barthes, Roland, *Camera Lucida* [1980], trans. Richard Howard (London: Vintage, 2000).

Bedford, Sybille, 'The Worst that Ever Happened', *Saturday Evening Post* (October, 1963): 29–100.

Benjamin, Walter, *Illuminations*, trans. Harry Zohn (London: Jonathan Cape, 1970).

Berger, John, *About Looking* (London: Writers and Readers Publishing Cooperative, 1980).

Bersani, Leo, *The Culture of Redemption* (Cambridge, MA: Harvard University Press, 1990).

Berthoud, Roger, *The Life of Henry Moore* (London: Faber and Faber, 1987).

Bion, Wilfred. 'Psychiatry at a Time of Crisis', *British Journal of Medical Psychiatry*, 21 (1948): 81–9.

——. 'Language and the Schizophrenic' [1953], in *New Directions in Psycho-Analysis: the Significance of Infant Conflict in the Pattern of Adult Behaviour*, ed. Melanie Klein, Paula Heimann and R.E. Money-Kyrle (London: Karnac, 1985), pp. 220–39.

——. 'Notes on Memory and Desire' [1967], in *Melanie Klein Today, Vol. 2: Mainly Practice*, ed. Elizabeth Bott-Spillius (London: Routledge, 1988).

——. *The Long Week-End 1897–1919* (London: Free Association Books, 1986).

——. *Second Thoughts* (New Jersey and London: Jason Aronson, 1993).

——. *Experiences in Groups and Other Papers* (London and New York: Routledge, 1994).

———. *War Memoirs 1917–19*, ed. Francesca Bion (London: Karnac Books, 1997).

Bion Talamo, Parthenope, Franco Borgogno and Silvio A. Merciai (eds), *Bion's Legacy to Groups* (London: Karnac Books, 1998).

Blanchot, Maurice, *The Writing of the Disaster*, trans. Ann Smock (Lincoln and London: University of Nebraska Press, 1995).

Blanco White, Amber, *The New Propaganda* (Left Book Club Edition) (London: Victor Gollancz Ltd, 1939).

———. *Worry in Women* (London: Victor Gollancz Ltd, 1941).

———. *Ethics for Unbelievers* (London: Routledge and Kegan Paul, 1948).

Bourke, Joanna, *Fear: a Cultural History* (London: Virago, 2005).

Bowen, Elizabeth, *The Heat of the Day* [1948] (Harmondsworth: Penguin, 1962).

———. *The Collected Stories of Elizabeth Bowen*, ed. Angus Wilson (Harmondsworth: Penguin, 1983).

———. *The Mulberry Tree: Writings of Elizabeth Bowen*, ed. Hermione Lee (London: Vintage, 1999)

Brothers, Caroline, *War and Photography* (London and New York: Routledge, 1997).

Bryher, *The Days of Mars: a Memoir, 1940–1946* (London: Calder and Boyars, 1972).

Calder, Angus, *The Myth of the Blitz* (London: Cape, 1991).

Canetti, Elias, *Party in the Blitz*, trans. Michael Hofmann (London: The Harvill Press, 2005).

Caruth, Cathy, *Unclaimed Experience: Trauma, Narrative and History* (Baltimore: Johns Hopkins University Press, 1996).

Causey, Andrew, 'Henry Moore and the Uncanny', in *Henry Moore: Critical Essays*, eds Jane Beckett and Fiona Russell (Aldershot: Ashgate, 2003).

Caygill, Howard, *Walter Benjamin: the Colour of Experience* (London and New York: Routledge, 1998).

Cheyette, Bryran, *Muriel Spark* (Tavistock: Northcote House in association with the British Council, 2000).

Clark, T.J., *Farewell to an Idea: Episodes from a History of Modernism* (New Haven and London: Yale University Press, 1999).

Copjec, Joan, *Read My Desire: Lacan against the Historicists* (Cambridge, MA: MIT Press, 1994).

Cousins, Mark, 'The Traumatic Image: Vertigo', unpublished paper presented at the Society for Humanities, Cornell University, April 1998.

de Man, Paul, *The Rhetoric of Romanticism* (New York: Columbia University Press, 1984).

Dolar, Mladen, 'The Object Voice', in *Gaze and Voice as Love Objects*, eds Renata Salecl and Slavoj Žižek (Durham and London: Duke University Press, 1996), pp. 7–31.

Doolittle, Hilda (H.D.), *Tribute to Freud* (Manchester: Carcanet, 1985).

Eliot, T.S., *The Four Quartets* (London: Faber and Faber, 1979).

———. 'Hamlet' [1919], in *The Selected Prose of T.S. Eliot*, ed. Frank Kermode (London: Faber and Faber, 1975).

Ellmann, Maud, *Elizabeth Bowen: the Shadow across the Page* (Edinburgh: Edinburgh University Press, 2003).

Empson, William, 'Introduction', *Coleridge's Verse: a Selection*, ed. William Empson and David Pirlie (London: Faber and Faber, 1972).

Faimberg, Haydee, 'Whom was Bion Addressing? "Negative capability" and "listening to listening" ', in *W.R. Bion: Between Past and Future*, ed. Parthenope Bion Talamo, Franco Borgogno and Silvio A. Merciai (London and New York: Karnac Books, 2000), p. 81.

Fairbairn, W.R.D., *Psychoanalytic Studies of the Personality* (London and Boston: Routledge & Kegan Paul, 1984),

Felman, Shoshana, *Jacques Lacan and the Adventure of Insight* (Cambridge, MA: Harvard University Press, 1987).

——. 'Education and Crisis, or the Vicissitudes of Teaching', in *Trauma: Explorations in Memory*, ed. Cathy Caruth (Baltimore: Johns Hopkins University Press, 1995), pp. 13–60.

——. ' "Theaters of Justice": Arendt in Jerusalem, the Eichmann Trial, and the Redefinition of Legal Meaning in the Wake of the Holocaust', *Critical Inquiry*, 27(2) (Winter, 2001): 201–38.

—— and Dori Laub *Testimony: Crisis of Witnessing in Literature, Psychoanalysis and History* (New York and London: Routledge, 1992).

Fitzgerald, Penelope, *Human Voices* [1980] (London: Flamingo, 1997).

——. *The Afterlife*, ed. Terence Dooley, with Christopher Carduff and Mandy Kirkby (New York: Counterpoint, 2003).

Flanner, Janet, *Janet Flanner's World: Uncollected Writings 1932–1975*, ed. Irving Drutman (New York and London: Harcourt Brace Jovanovich, 1979).

Flugel, J.C. (ed.), *Vol III: Proceedings of the International Conference on Medical Psychotherapy, 11–14th August, International Congress on Mental Health, London, 1948* (London and New York: H.K. Lewis and Columbia University Press, 1948).

Freud, Anna, *The Ego and the Mechanisms of Defence* [first translation 1937], (London: Hogarth,1966).

——. 'Comments on Trauma', in *Psychic Trauma*, ed. Sidney S. Furst (New York: Basic Books, 1967), pp. 235–45.

—— in collaboration with Sophie Dann, 'An Experiment in Group Upbringing' [1951], *Indications for Child Analysis and Other Papers, 1945–1956* (London: Hogarth Press and the Institute of Psycho-Analysis, 1969), pp. 163–229.

—— in collaboration with Dorothy, Burlingham, *Infants without Families and Reports on the Hampstead War Nurseries 1939–1945* (New York: International Universities Press, 1974).

Freud, Sigmund, 'Draft E. "How Anxiety Originates" ' [1894], in *The Origins of Psychoanalysis Letters to Wilhelm Fliess, drafts and notes*, eds Marie Bonaparte, Anna Freud and Ernst Kris (London and New York: Imago Publishing, 1954).

——. 'Psychoanalysis and the Establishment of Facts in Legal Proceedings' [1906], *Standard Edition of the Complete Works of Sigmund Freud* (SE) 9.

——. 'On the Grounds for Detaching a Particular Syndrome from Neurasthenia under the Description "Anxiety Neurosis" ' [1895], *SE* 3.

——. *Analysis of a Phobia in a Five-Year-Old Boy* [1909], Penguin Freud Library (PF) 9

——. 'Thoughts for the Times on War and Death' (1915), PF 12.

——. 'Some Character-Types Met with in Psycho-Analytic Work' [1916], *SE* 14.

——. 'The Uncanny' [1919], PF 14.

——. *Beyond the Pleasure Principle* [1920], PF 11.

——. 'Introduction', *Psycho-Analysis and the War Neuroses*, Proceedings of the Symposium held at the Fifth International Psycho-Analytical Congress at Budapest, September 1918, ed. S. Ferenczi et al. (Vienna, London, New York: The International Psychoanalytic Press, 1921) (also in *SE* 17).

——. *Inhibitions, Symptoms and Anxiety* (1926 [1925]), *SE* 20 (also PF 10).

——. 'Fetishism' (1927), *On Sexuality*, PF 7.

——. 'Dostoevsky and Parricide' (1928 [1927]), *SE* 21.

——. 'The Expert Opinion in the Halsmann Case' (1931 [1930]), *SE* 21.

——. 'The Dissection of the Psychical Personality', *New Introductory Lectures on Psychoanalysis* (1933 [1932]), PF 12.

——. *Civilization and its Discontents* (1930 [1929]) *SE* 21.

Fuller, Peter, *Henry Moore: an Interpretation*, ed. Anthony O'Hear (London: Methuen, 1993).

Fussell, Paul, *The Great War and Modern Memory* (Oxford: Oxford University Press, 1975).

Glover, Edward, *The Psychology of Fear and Courage* (Harmondsworth: Penguin, 1940).

——. 'Notes on the Psychological Effects of War Conditions on the Civilian Population (1)', *International Journal of Psychoanalysis*, 22 (1941): 132–46.

——. 'Notes on the Psychological Effects of War Conditions on the Civilian Population (III. The 'Blitz' – 1940–1)', *International Journal of Psychoanalysis*, 23 (1942): 29–30 and 36–7.

Green, André, *On Private Madness* (Madison, CT: International Universities Press, 1986).

Green, Henry, *Pack My Bag* [1940] (London: Hogarth, 1979).

——. *Caught* [1943] (London: Hogarth, 1950).

——. *Back* [1946] (New York: New Directions, 1981).

——. *Surviving: the Uncollected Works of Henry Green*, ed. Matthew Yorke (London: Chatto and Windus, 1992).

Greene, Graham, *The End of the Affair* [1951] (Harmondsworth: Penguin, 1975).

——. *The Ministry of Fear: an Entertainment* [1943] (Harmondsworth: Penguin, 1973).

Grosskurth, Phyllis, *Melanie Klein: Her World and Work* (New York: Knopf, 1986).

Gualtieri, Elena, 'Three Guineas and the Photograph: the Art of Propaganda', in *Women Writers of the 1930s: Gender, Politics and History*, ed. Maroula Joannou (Edinburgh: Edinburgh University Press, 1999).

——. Harrisson, Tom, *Living Through the Blitz* (London: Collins, 1976).

——. and Charles Madge (eds), *War Begins at Home* (London: Chatto and Windus, 1940).

Hartley, Jenny, *Millions Like Us: British Women's Fiction of the Second World War* (London: Virago, 1997).

Heine, Heinrich, *Selected Verse* (1968), ed. and trans. Peter Branscombe (London: Penguin, 1986).

Higonnet, Anne, *Pictures of Innocence: the History and Crisis of Ideal Childhood* (New York and London: Thames and Hudson, 1998).

Hinshelwood, Robert, *A Dictionary of Kleinian Thought* (London: Free Association Books, 1991).

Holden, Inez, *It Was Different at the Time* (London: John Lane, The Bodley Head, 1943).

Hollier, Denis, *Absent without Leave: French Literature under Threat of War*, trans. Catherine Porter (Cambridge, MA and London: Harvard University Press, 1997).

Inglis, Ruth, *The Children's War: Evacuation 1939–1945* (London: Collins, 1989).

Isakower, Otto, 'On the Exceptional Position of the Auditory Sphere', *International Journal of Psychoanalysis*, 20 (1939): 340–8.

Jacobus, Mary, *First Things: the Maternal Imaginary in Literature, Art and Psychoanalysis* (London/New York: Routledge, 1995).

Janis, I.L., *Air War and Emotional Stress: Psychological Studies of Bombing and Civilian Defense* (New York: The Rand Corporation, McGraw Books, 1951).

Jaspers, Karl, *The Question of German Guilt* [1947], trans. E.B. Ashton (New York, Fordham University Press, 2000).

Jay, Martin, 'Of Plots, Witnesses and Judgments', in *Probing the Limits of Representation: Nazism and the Final Solution*, ed. Saul Friedlander (Cambridge, MA and London: Harvard University Press, 1992), pp. 97–107.

Keene, Alice, *The Two Mr Smiths: the Life and Work of Sir Matthew Smith 1879–1959* (London: Lund Humphries Publishers, 1995).

Kermode, Frank, *Modern Essays* (London: Fontana, 1971).

King, Pearl and Riccardo Steiner (eds), *The Freud-Klein Controversies: 1941–45*, New Library of Psychoanalysis, vol. 11 (London: Tavistock/Routledge, 1991).

Klein, Melanie, *The Psychoanalysis of Children* [1932] (London: Virago, 1989).

——. *Narrative of a Child Analysis: the Conduct of the Psycho-Analysis of Children Seen in the Treatment of a Ten-Year-Old Boy* [1961] (London: Virago,1975).

——. *Love, Guilt and Reparation, and Other Works 1921–1945* (London: Virago, 1988)

——. *Envy and Gratitude and Other Works 1946–1963* (London: Virago, 1988).

Koestler, Arthur, *The Yogi and the Commissar and Other Essays* (London, Jonathan Cape, 1945).

Krauss, Rosalind, *The Optical Unconscious* (Cambridge, MA: MIT Press, 1994).

Kristeva, Julia, 'Word, Dialogue and Novel', in *The Kristeva Reader*, ed. Toril Moi (Oxford: Blackwell, 1986).

Lacan, Jacques, 'La Psychiatre anglaise et la guerre', *Travaux et Interventions* (Paris) (1947): 293–318.

——. *L'angoisse: tome 2* 6:26 (1963).

——. *Ecrits: a Selection*, trans. Alan Sheridan (London and New York: Tavistock/Routledge, 1977).

——. *The Four Fundamental Concepts of Psycho-Analysis* [1973], trans. Alan Sheridan (London: Penguin, 1987).

——. *The Seminar of Jacques Lacan: Book 1*, ed. Jacques-Alain Miller, trans. John Forrester (Cambridge: Cambridge University Press, 1988).

——. 'God and the Jouissance of ~~The~~ Woman', in *Feminine Sexuality: Jacques Lacan and l'école freudienne*, ed. Juliet Mitchell and Jacqueline Rose, trans. Jacqueline Rose (London: Macmillan, 1982).

LaCapra, Dominick, 'Lanzmann's *Shoah*: Here There is no Why', *Critical Inquiry*, 23 (Winter 1997): 231–69.

——. *History and Memory after Auschwitz* (Ithaca and London: Cornell University Press, 1998).

Laplanche, Jean, 'A Metapsychology Put to the Test of Anxiety', *International Journal of Psychoanalysis*, 62 (1981): 81–9.

Laski, Marghanita, *Little Boy Lost* [1949] (London: Persephone Books, 2001).

Lévi-Strauss, Claude, *The Elementary Structures of Kinship*, trans. John Doe (Boston: Beacon Press, 1969).

Leys, Ruth, *Trauma: a Genealogy* (Chicago and London: Chicago University Press, 2000).

MacGibbon, Jean (as Jean Howard), 'The Picnic', *Orion*, vol. 3, ed. C.D. Lewis, D. Kilham Roberts and Rosamond Lehmann (London: Nicholson and Watson, 1946), pp. 32–46.

——. *I Meant to Marry Him: a Personal Memoir* (London: Victor Gollancz, 1984).

——. *There's the Lighthouse: a Biography of Adrian Stephen* (London: James and James, 1997).

——. 'Childhood's Analyst', *Guardian* (16 May 1960).

Macaulay, Rose, *The World My Wilderness* [1950] (London: Virago, 2000).

——. *The Pleasure of Ruins* (London: Thames and Hudson, 1953).

MacKay, Marina, *Modernism and World War II* (Cambridge: Cambridge University Press, 2007).

—— and Lyndsey Stonebridge (eds), *British Fiction After Modernism: the Novel at Mid-Century* (Basingstoke: Palgrave, 2007).

May, Rollo, *The Meaning of Anxiety* [1950] (New York and London: Norton, 1996).

McQuillan, Martin (ed.), *Theorizing Muriel Spark: Gender, Race, Deconstruction* (Basingstoke: Palgrave, 2002).

Mellor, Leo, 'Words from the Bombsites: Debris, Modernism and Literary Salvage', *Critical Quarterly*, 46(4) (2004): 77–90.

Mengham, Rod, *The Idiom of the Time: the Writings of Henry Green* (Cambridge: Cambridge University Press, 1982).

—— and N.H. Reeve (eds), *The Fiction of the 1940s: Stories of Survival* (Basingstoke: Palgrave, 2001).

Merleau-Ponty, M., *Sense and Non-Sense*, eds H.L. Dreyfus and P. Allen Dreyfus (Evanston, IL: Northwestern University Press, 1964).

Miller, Emmanuel (ed.), *The Neuroses in War* (London: Macmillan, 1940).

Neumann, Erich, *The Archetypal World of Henry Moore* (London: Routledge, Kegan and Paul, 1959).

Padley, Richard and Margaret Cole (eds), *Evacuation Survey: a Report to the Fabian Society* (London: Routledge, 1940).

Phillips, Adam, *Winnicott* (Cambridge, MA: Harvard University Press, 1988).

———. *Equalities* (London: Faber and Faber, 2002).

———. 'Bombs Away', *History Workshop Journal*, 45 (Spring 1998): 183–98.

Piette, Adam, *Imagination at War: British Fiction and Poetry 1939–1945* (London: Macmillan, 1995).

Plain, Gill, *Women's Fiction of the Second World War: Gender, Power and Resistance* (Edinburgh: Edinburgh University Press, 1996).

Prendergast, Christopher, 'Modernism's Nightmare? Art, Matter and Mechanism', *New Left Review*, 10 (July/August 2001): 141–56.

Rank, Otto, *The Trauma of Birth* [1924] (London: Kegan, Paul, Trench, Trubner & Co. Ltd, 1929).

Rawlinson, Mark, *British Writing of the Second World War* (Oxford: Oxford University Press, 2000).

Reeve, N.H., 'The Girl on a Swing: Childhood and Writing in the 1940s', in *British Fiction after Modernism: the Novel at Mid-Century*, eds Marina MacKay and Lyndsey Stonebridge (Basingstoke: Palgrave, 2007).

Reik, Theodor, 'Aggression from Anxiety' [1937], *International Journal of Psycho-analysis*, 22 (1941): 7–16.

Rickman, John (ed.), *On the Bringing up of Children* (London: Kegan, Paul, Trench, Trubner & Co. Ltd, 1936).

Riley, Denise, *The War in the Nursery: Theories of the Child and Mother* (London: Virago, 1983).

———. ' "A voice without a mouth": Inner Speech', *Qui Parle*, 14(2) (2004): 57–104.

Robertson, Alexander et al. (eds), *Surrealism in Britain in the Thirties* (Leeds: Leeds City Art Galleries, 1986).

Rose, Jacqueline, 'Bizarre Objects: Mary Butts and Elizabeth Bowen', *Critical Quarterly*, 42(1) (2000): 75–85.

———. *Why War? Psychoanalysis, Politics and the Return to Melanie Klein* (Oxford: Blackwell, 1993).

Rubin, Gayle, 'The Traffic in Women: Notes towards a Political Economy', in *Towards an Anthropology of Women*, ed. Rayna Reiter (New York: Monthly Review Press, 1975).

Russell, John, *Henry Moore* (London: Pelican, 1973).

Safouan, Moustapha, *Jacques Lacan and the Question of Psychoanalytic Training*, trans. and intro. Jacqueline Rose (London: Macmillan, 2000).

Salecl, Renata, *On Anxiety* (London and New York: Routledge, Taylor and Francis, 2004).

Samson, William, *Fireman Flower and Other Stories* (London: Hogarth, 1944).

Sanyal, Debarati, 'A Soccer Match in Auschwitz: Passing Culpability in Holocaust Criticism', *Representations*, 79 (Summer 2002): 1–27.

Sartre, Jean-Paul, *Existential and Humanism* [1948], trans. Philip Mairet (London: Methuen, 1963).

——. *Sketch for a Theory of the Emotions* [first published as *Esquisse d'une theorie des emotions* in 1939], trans. Philip Mairet (London and New York: Routledge, 2002).

Scarry, Elaine, *The Body in Pain: the Making and Unmaking of the World* (Oxford: Oxford University Press, 1987).

——. 'Imagining Flowers: Perceptual Mimesis (Particularly Delphinium)', *Representations*, 57 (Winter 1997): 90–115.

Schmideberg, Melitta, 'Some Observations on Individual Reactions to Air Raids', *International Journal of Psychoanalysis*, 23 (1942): 146–76.

Scott, Clive, *The Spoken Image* (London: Reaktion Books, 1999).

Shute, Nevil, *Requiem for a Wren* [1955] (London: Heinemann and Heron Books, n.d.).

Sontag, Susan, *Regarding the Pain of Others* (London: Hamish Hamilton, 2003).

Spark, Muriel, *The Girls of Slender Means* (Harmondsworth: Penguin, 1966).

Speziale-Bagliacca, Roberto, *Guilt: Revenge, Remorse and Responsibility after Freud*, trans. Ian Harvey (Hove and New York: Brunner-Routledge, 2004).

Steedman, Carolyn, *Strange Dislocations: Childhood and the Idea of Human Interiority, 1780–1930* (London: Virago, 1995).

Stein, Gertrude, *Wars I have Seen* (New York: Brilliance Books, 1984).

Stonebridge, Lyndsey, ' "In saying yes he says farewell": T.J. Clark's Freud', *Critical Quarterly*, 44(2) (Summer 2002): 30–40.

Strachey, J.S.L., *Borrowed Children: a Popular Account of Some Evacuation Problems and their Remedies* (New York: The Commonwealth Fund, 1940).

Strachey, Julia, 'Fragment of a Diary', *The Penguin New Writing*, ed. John Lehmann, no.14 (July–September 1942).

Sylvester, David, *About Modern Art: Critical Essays 1948–96* (London: Chatto and Windus, 1996).

Tate, Trudi, *Modernism, History and the First World War* (Manchester: Manchester University Press, 1998).

Taylor, Elizabeth, *Hester Lilly and Other Stories* (London: Virago, 1990).

Tillich, Paul, *Systematic Theology I–III* (Chicago: Chicago University Press, 1964).

Timms, Edward and Naomi Segal (eds), *Freud in Exile, Psychoanalysis and its Vicissitudes* (New Haven: Yale University Press, 1988).

Titmuss, Richard M., *Problems of Social Policy* (London: HMSO, 1950).

Torgovnick, Marianna, *The War Complex: World War II in Our Time* (Chicago and London: Chicago University Press, 2005).

Torok, Maria et al., 'Melanie Mell by Herself', trans. Ian Patterson, in *Reading Melanie Klein*, eds Lyndsey Stonebridge and John Phillips (London and New York: Routledge, 1998).

Treglown, Jeremy, *Romancing: the Life and Work of Henry Green* (London: Faber, 2000).

Trustees of the British Museum, *Henry Moore: a Shelter Sketchbook* (London: British Museum Publications, 1988).

Vidler, Anthony, *Warped Space: Art, Architecture and Anxiety in Modern Culture* (Cambridge MA: MIT Press, 2000).

Wagner, Anne, 'Henry Moore's Mother', *Representations*, 65 (Winter 1999): 93–110.

Weber, Samuel, *The Legend of Freud* (Minneapolis: University of Minnesota Press, 1982).

——. *Return to Freud: Jacques Lacan's Dislocation of Psychoanalysis*, trans. Michael Levine (Cambridge: Cambridge University Press, 1991).

——. 'Wartime', in *Violence, Identity and Self-Determination*, eds Hent de Vries and Samuel Weber (Stanford, CA: Stanford University Press, 1997), pp. 80–105.

Wells, Liz (ed.), *The Photography Reader* (London and New York: Routledge, 2003).

West, Rebecca, *The Meaning of Treason* [1949] (London: Penguin, 1965).

——. 'A Reporter at Large: Extraordinary Exile', *New Yorker*, 22 (7 September 1946).

——. *A Train of Powder: Six Reports on the Problem of Guilt and Punishment in Our Time* (Chicago: Ivan R. Dee, 1955).

White, Hayden, 'Historical Emplotment and the Problem of Truth', in *Probing the Limits of Representation: Nazism and the Final Solution*, ed. Saul Friedlander (Cambridge, MA and London: Harvard University Press, 1992).

Wilkinson, Alan, *The Drawings of Henry Moore* (London: Tate Gallery Publications, 1977).

Winnicott, D.W., *Deprivation and Deliquency*, eds Clare Winnicott, Ray Shepherd and Madeline Davis (London and New York: Routledge, 1990).

——. *Through Paediatrics to Psycho-Analysis: Collected Papers* [1958] (New York: Brunner/Mazel, 1992).

Winter, J.M., *Sites of Memory, Sites of Mourning: the Great War in European Cultural History* (Cambridge: Cambridge University Press, 1995).

Wittengstein, Ludwig, *Remarks on Colour*, ed. G.E.M Anscombe, trans. Linda L. McAlister and Margarete Schattle (Berkeley and Los Angeles: University of California Press, 1977).

Wolf, Katherine M., 'Evacuation of Children in Wartime', in *Psychoanalytic Study of the Child*, 1 (New York: International Universities Press, 1945), pp. 389–404.

Woolf, Virginia, *Moments of Being: Autobiographical Writings* [1976], ed. Jeanne Schulkind (London: Pimlico, 2002).

——. *Three Guineas* [1938], reprinted in *A Room of One's Own and Three Guineas*, ed. Morag Shiach (Oxford: Oxford University Press, 1992).

——. *Between the Acts* [1941] (Harmondsworth: Penguin, 1992).

Worringer, Wilhem, *Abstraction and Empathy: a Contribution to the Psychology of Style* [1908], trans. Michael Bullock (London: Routledge & Kegan Paul, 1967).

Young-Bruehl, Elizabeth, *Anna Freud: a Biography* (New York: Summit Books, 1988).

Žižek, Slavoj, *The Plague of Fantasies* (London/New York: Routledge, 1997).

Index